A Trusting Heart by Carrie Turansky
Swedish immigrant Annika Bergstrom travels to Wyoming as a mail-order bride, but when her prospective groom, Chase Simms, disappears, she finds herself falling in love with his brother Daniel. Will she take hold of her chance for love, or wait for the man she has promised to marry?

The Prodigal Groom by Vickie McDonough
Jolie Addams is orphaned and hired to work for a lecherous benefactor. She chooses instead to become a mail-order bride, but on the way to Nevada, her stage is robbed. She and a wounded passenger are stranded. They are rescued the next day, but Jolie's intended refuses to marry her after she spent the night alone with Clay Jackson. She and Clay are forced to marry. Can a relationship and love grow from such an awful beginning?

Hidden Hearts by Therese Stenzel
After facing a series of tragic events, Elisabeth Lariby agrees to become a mail-order bride. Hoping to build a new life in Nebraska, she is determined to hide her grief-stricken heart from her new husband. Driven to be a success, Zane Michaels quietly obtains a wife through a mail-order bride society, but feels he must hide his past and his recent wealth from his new wife. When their secrets are revealed, will their fledgling marriage survive?

Mrs. Mayberry Meets Her Match by Susan Page Davis
Amelia Mayberry's rewarding career as a matchmaker is winding down. She'd like to close shop and spend her sunset years in peace. There's only one unfinished piece of business—an unsatisfied customer for whom she needs to set things right. The question is: Will Lennox Bailey allow her to make amends?

CHRISTMAS
MAIL-ORDER BRIDES

FOUR-IN-ONE COLLECTION

TRAVEL THE TRANSCONTINENTAL RAILROAD
IN SEARCH OF LOVE

SUSAN PAGE DAVIS
VICKIE MCDONOUGH
CARRIE TURANSKY
THERESE STENZEL

BARBOUR
PUBLISHING

This book is a work of fiction. Names, characters, places, and incidents are either products of the author's imagination or used fictitiously. Any similarity to actual people, organizations, and/or events is purely coincidental.

All scripture quotations are taken from the King James Version of the Bible.

Cover design: Kirk DouPonce, DogEared Design

Published by Barbour Publishing, Inc., P.O. Box 719, Uhrichsville, OH 44683, www.barbourbooks.com

Our mission is to publish and distribute inspirational products offering exceptional value and biblical encouragement to the masses.

Member of the
Evangelical Christian
Publishers Association

Printed in the United States of America.

A TRUSTING HEART

by Carrie Turansky

Dedication

To my twin daughters, Megan and Elizabeth,
who are a treasure and blessing.

Trust in the Lord with all thine heart;
and lean not unto thine own understanding.
In all thy ways acknowledge him,
and he shall direct thy paths.
PROVERBS 3:5–6

Chapter 1

*An intelligent widower of twenty-eight years from a fine
family wishes to correspond with an honorable maiden
or widow eighteen to twenty-five years with a loving
disposition who is interested in matrimony and would
like a good husband and a life of plenty in Wyoming.*

October, 1880

The shrieking blast of the train whistle shook the platform of the Chicago Central Train Station. Annika Bergstrom clutched her twin sister, Sophia, and swallowed her tears. She must be strong for Sophia's sake.

"I don't know how I shall ever get along without you." Tears ran down her sister's cheeks. She reached up and brushed them away with her gloved hand.

Sophia's new husband, Lars, stepped forward and tenderly

placed his arm around his wife's shoulder. "We'll pray for you, Annika, every day."

"Thank you, Lars." Annika studied the man who had won her sister's heart. He would take care of Sophia. They were a good match and had a wonderful future ahead, serving the Lord at a small, rural church in northern Illinois.

Would her future husband treat her with such love and tenderness? Annika forced a smile. "I promise to pray for you both as well. I'm sure God will keep us safe in His loving care." She truly believed that, but she said it aloud to reassure herself as well as her sister and Lars.

"And you must write to us often," Sophia said. "I'll be waiting for your letters."

Annika's hands trembled, and she grabbed her sister once more. "I will. I promise. And you must do the same. I want to hear all about your new church as soon as you're settled."

Annika stepped back and gazed at her sister, memorizing the curve of her cheek and the look of devotion in her blue eyes. If she didn't love Sophia so much, she could never leave her like this. Since the day they were born, and even those nine months before, they had never been parted. How would she survive without Sophia?

The huge, black locomotive hissed. Puffs of steam and smoke filled the air. All around her travelers said their last good-byes, gathered up their belongings, and moved to board the train.

The conductor, dressed in a black uniform and cap, walked toward them. "All aboard," he called.

A shot of panic raced through Annika. Was it too late

to change her mind? But if she did, how would she support herself? For the last five years, since their parents' deaths, she and Sophia had worked as maids at the Hillman School for Girls. Even when they combined their meager salaries, they barely made enough to scrape by. She could never afford to live on her own now that Sophia was leaving Chicago.

No. Her decision was made. She had accepted Charles Simms's proposal of marriage, and she was a woman of her word. She would travel to Wyoming as his mail-order bride and make a new life for herself. But more importantly, she would free Sophia to make a new life with Lars.

"It's time, Annika." Lars nodded to the conductor as he approached.

"Are you headed to Omaha, miss?" the gray-haired conductor asked.

Annika gripped the handle of her bag. "Yes, sir, and then on to Laramie, Wyoming."

"My goodness, all the way to Wyoming?" He chuckled and turned to Lars. "Don't worry. I'll keep an eye on her this first leg of the trip." He took Annika's bag and walked toward the train.

Sophia kissed her cheek. "Good-bye, dear heart. I love you."

Annika was afraid her reply would come out as a sob, so she kissed her sister, then followed the conductor to the train.

He checked her ticket and directed her to the second-class coach.

She lifted her skirts and mounted the steps. Making

her way down the aisle, she looked for an open seat by the window so she could catch one last glimpse of her sister and Lars. How long would it be until she saw them again? Six months? A year? Five years? Would her sister be holding a baby in her arms the next time they met? Would Annika? She gulped and pushed that thought away. The possibility of having a baby with a man she had never met was too much to consider at the moment.

The train creaked and groaned as the engine built up steam. The car lurched forward and rolled away.

She waved to Sophia, then pressed her face against the cool, dirty glass, watching her sister grow smaller and disappear from sight as the train rounded a curve. She let her tears fall, but only a few. This was the right decision. Her parents' loving and selfless example had taught her to put Sophia's needs above her own.

Sophia had initially refused Lars's proposal because she didn't want to leave Annika alone in Chicago. It was only after Annika found a suitable groom through Mrs. Mayberry's Matrimonial Society for Christians of Moral Character that Sophia had finally agreed to move ahead with her wedding plans.

Annika took a handkerchief from her bag and wiped her nose and cheeks. Perhaps if she read the letters again it would calm her heart and strengthen her for the journey.

She pulled the small packet from her bag. A pale blue ribbon tied the five envelopes together, one from Mrs. Amelia Mayberry and four from Charles Simms. She scanned Charles's first letter dated June 18, although she had read it so many times during the last four months she had almost memorized it.

A man's penmanship told a great deal about him, and Charles's writing was neat and precise. Even though he had been raised in the West, he was obviously an intelligent, educated man with a caring heart.

His description of the family's large cattle ranch intrigued her. She'd lived on a small farm in Sweden until her family immigrated to America when she was twelve. Living in the country again after spending the last ten years in Chicago sounded wonderful. The Simms's ranch was only six miles from Laramie, a small town on the Pacific Railway Line about halfway between Omaha and San Francisco. Life would be different in Wyoming, but she was strong, she knew how to work hard, and she was willing to learn how to be a rancher's wife.

She looked down at the letters again, and her gaze rested on the last paragraph where Charles mentioned his prayers for a loving wife for himself and a kind and caring mother for his seven-year-old daughter, Mariah. Annika had prayed for a thoughtful and understanding husband. His willingness to allow them a month to get acquainted before the wedding convinced her she had made the right choice. And Mrs. Mayberry had assured her she only referred responsible Christian men who provided good references for their character and position.

So many nights she had prayed for God's direction. Finally, everything had fallen into place. This had to be His answer. Her parents' marriage had been arranged by their families, and it had been a loving union. Surely she could build a new life with Charles Simms. She might not love him at first the way Sophia loved Lars, but in time love would grow. She clasped her hands and stared out the window.

Dear Lord, let it be true.

The aroma of fresh-brewed coffee, ham, and eggs greeted Daniel Simms at the back door. He stomped the mud off his boots and hustled into the kitchen. Warmth radiated from the cast-iron stove, drawing him closer. He rubbed his hands together and held them out toward the heat. "Breakfast almost ready?"

Song Li, their Chinese cook, looked up and scowled at Daniel. "You come in too soon. Breakfast not ready."

Daniel held back a grin. Song Li might work for them, but he owned the kitchen. "I'll just get a cup of coffee while you finish up."

Song Li muttered in his native tongue, then returned to flipping ham slices with a vengeance, while his long, black braid swung across his back.

"Uncle Daniel, look what I made." Mariah hurried over, carrying a tin plate of puffy, golden biscuits.

"Mmm, those sure look good." He smiled at her and ran his hand over the top of her head, smoothing down her wild hair. "Why don't you run up and get a brush, and we'll see if we can tame these curls."

Her face puckered into a frown. "My hair don't need

brushin'." She placed the biscuits next to her plate and pushed her hair back with floury hands. "'Sides, Song Li needs my help."

"You done now," Song Li said. "Obey Uncle Daniel. Go get brush."

She huffed. "Why does everyone fuss about my hair!" She stomped off toward the stairs.

Daniel shook his head. That girl was too smart for her own good and cute enough to get away with it. She needed a firm hand, or she was going to turn out as ornery as a wild mustang.

Charles Simms Sr. strode into the kitchen.

"Morning, Pa. Why are you dressed up?"

"I'm going into town after breakfast."

"How come?" It wasn't Sunday, and his father hadn't mentioned a meeting of the cattlemen's association.

His father frowned, ignoring the question, and glanced around the room. "Where's Chase?"

Daniel shrugged. The last time he'd seen his older brother he'd been sound asleep, snoring like a grizzly bear. But he didn't want to set his father off with a report like that, especially when he already seemed bothered about something.

His father huffed. "That boy will be the death of me yet. Where's Mariah?"

"She went up to get a hairbrush."

"Well, at least someone's getting ready for the day." His father turned toward the stairs. "Chase, get yourself down here!"

13

Daniel stifled a groan. His father shouldn't treat Chase like a kid, but the way he'd been acting lately, staying out late and carousing around with a wild bunch of cowboys, he almost deserved it.

"Grampa, I can't find my hairbrush," Mariah called.

His father growled and pounded up the stairs.

Daniel hustled after him, ready to protect his niece from the older man's temper. Charles Simms loved his grand-daughter, but he had a short fuse, and the fact that Chase did little to care for his daughter infuriated him.

"I'll help her, Pa," Daniel said as he reached the top of the stairs.

His father ignored him and banged on Chase's door. "Time to get up!"

A low groan issued from the bedroom. "Go away."

Daniel shook his head, knowing exactly what was coming.

His father shoved the door open with a bang and marched into the room. "Charles Joseph Simms, get out of that bed!" He yanked back the covers and snatched the pillow off his son's head.

Daniel watched from the doorway, praying for a quick end to the confrontation.

Chase blinked and lifted his head. "Pa, what are you doing?"

"You need to get up and get dressed. We're going to town."

"What?" Chase squinted toward the window, then moaned and flopped back on the pillow. "I can't go anywhere. My head's killing me."

"You'd feel a whole lot better this morning if you hadn't been drinking so much last night."

"Don't lecture me, Pa. I'm a grown man."

"You're still living under my roof, so you'll do as I say. Now get out of bed."

Mariah grabbed Daniel's leg and looked up at him with a trembling chin.

Daniel patted her shoulder. "It'll be all right." Whenever his father and Chase raised their voices, she sought refuge with him. He didn't blame her; all their hollering made him wish he could head to the barn, but he wouldn't desert Mariah.

His father picked up a wrinkled shirt and a dusty pair of pants off the floor and tossed them toward Chase. "Put those on and be downstairs in five minutes."

Chase groaned. "Ah, Pa, what's the hurry?"

"We're meeting the eleven o'clock train." His father straightened. "You're future wife is on board, and you need to be there to meet her."

Chase's mouth gaped open. "My what?"

"You heard me. Your bride arrives at eleven. We need to leave right away."

"What? Are you crazy?" Chase grabbed his shirt and stuffed his arms in the sleeves.

"No, but I'm tired of watching you waste your life."

"My life is just fine."

"No it's not. You need to get married again and settle down, so I found you a wife."

"You *are* crazy!" Chase jumped into his pants, grabbed

his hat, boots, and jacket, and charged out of the bedroom door.

"Papa, wait. Where are you going?" Mariah reached for Chase as he flew past, but he didn't even slow down.

Daniel blew out a disgusted breath and shook his head. His father had really done it this time. He hustled down the stairs after them with Mariah close behind.

Chase dropped his boots on the kitchen floor and shoved his feet into them. "You can't run my life, Pa." Glaring at his father, he jammed his hat on his head. "I'm not going to town, and I'm not marrying some woman I never met!" He stormed out the door and slammed it behind him.

His father jerked open the door. "Come back in here, young man!"

Chase marched straight for the barn.

His father spun around, his face flushed and his gray moustache twitching. "Go after him, Daniel. Talk some sense into him."

"Me?" Daniel huffed. "What am I supposed to say?"

His father pulled a photo from his jacket and held it out. "Show him her picture. Tell him she's a decent woman who'd make a good wife and mother, and he ought to think about someone besides himself for a change." He glanced down at Mariah, and his angry expression softened a bit.

Daniel examined the photo. A fair-haired young woman with large, pale eyes and a shy smile looked back at him. "Who is she?"

"Her name's Annika Bergstrom. She's from Sweden by way of Chicago. She speaks English and writes a fine hand,

and she has good references from her minister and head of the school where she worked."

Daniel rubbed his chin. "She looks mighty young."

"She's twenty-two and never been married. She can sew, tend a garden, clean, and cook."

Song Li gasped, banged a lid on the frying pan, and began ranting in Chinese.

His father spun around. "What's the matter with you?" he boomed.

Song Li waved a wooden spoon and shouted back in Chinese, then switched to English. "Song Li cook! Song Li clean! Song Li take care of family!"

Mariah burst into tears and clutched Daniel's leg.

Daniel laid his hand on Mariah's shoulder and closed his eyes.

Lord, help us!

Chapter 2

The conductor tapped Annika on the shoulder. "We'll arrive in Laramie in a few minutes, miss."

"Oh, thank you." She rose from her seat and hurried down the aisle to the curtained area referred to as "The Necessary." She combed her hair and secured it with a ribbon. Frowning, she tried to brush the dust and cinders from her skirt. The stench from the toilet combined with the swirling cloud of dust set her coughing.

She sagged against the wall of the swaying coach and closed her eyes. Four days of smoke, baking sun, cold nights, unpredictable meals, and little sleep had taken a toll on her. Her head pounded from the noise and smells. Her back and neck ached from the cramped conditions, and her stomach twisted from nervousness and lack of food.

"Next stop, Laramie," the conductor called. "Larrrramie, Wyyyyyoming!"

Annika gasped and hurried back to her seat. Looking

out the window, she scanned the rolling hills dotted with scraggly pine trees. Then they passed a few scattered homes, a small church, a blacksmith, a livery, a general store, a hotel, and a saloon. The train screeched and slowed.

She reached up and wrestled her bag from the overhead rack. Gripping the handle, she stared out at the dozen or so people waiting on the platform. Off to the side, two men and a young girl stood together. The older man looked about sixty and had a bushy silver moustache. The girl with brown curly hair and an impish smile wore a faded blue dress and scuffed brown leather boots. The younger man was tall with broad shoulders and long sturdy legs. His wide-brimmed, wheat-colored hat shaded his tanned face, dark hair, and eyes. He was clean-shaven and handsome in a rugged sort of way.

Her heartbeat picked up. That had to be Charles.

Oh, why did she have to meet him looking so travel-worn? Well, it couldn't be helped. Her mother had always said a pleasant smile and warm greeting made anyone look becoming. She hoped it was true because that was all she could offer today.

The conductor took her bag and set it on the platform, then offered his hand to help her down the stairs.

Mr. Simms walked toward her, followed by his son and granddaughter. He swooped his hat off, revealing a thick head of silver hair. "Miss Bergstrom?"

She smiled and nodded. "Yes, I'm Annika Bergstrom, and you must be Mr. Simms."

"That's right. And this—"

The girl rushed forward and tried to tug the bag from her hand. "I can carry your bag for you. I'm real strong."

"Hold on, sweetie." The other man reached to help the girl. "You better let me get it." He nodded to Annika, but his expression seemed cool.

Her stomach clenched. Was he not pleased with her? Did she look that bad?

"This is my granddaughter, Mariah." Mr. Simms patted the girl on the shoulder. Then his expression faltered. "And this is my son. . .Daniel."

The name jolted her to a stop, and she blinked. This wasn't Charles? She glanced around the platform, searching for her future groom.

Daniel frowned and looked away. "Do you have any other bags?"

"Yes." She pointed to the baggage car, where a man unloaded her dark brown leather trunk. "That's mine as well."

"I'll load them in the wagon." Daniel strode off down the platform, Mariah at his heels, lugging the smaller bag.

Mr. Simms's moustache twitched, and he turned his hat in his hands. "I suppose you're wondering about Charles."

"Yes. . .I thought he'd be here to meet me."

Mr. Simms nodded and glanced down the platform. "We had some trouble at the ranch this morning, and Chase, that's what he goes by since we're both named Charles, needed to take care of it. But you'll meet him later at the ranch."

"Oh, I see." Although she really didn't understand why

Chase would send his family to meet her, rather than coming himself.

Mr. Simms escorted her to their wagon. Daniel joined them and helped the stationmaster lift the heavy trunk into the back. Mr. Simms invited her to sit up front with him, but Mariah begged her to sit in back. Annika settled in with Mariah on a pile of folded blankets behind the bench seat. Daniel sat next to his father.

As they rolled out of town, Mariah chatted away, telling Annika about all the things she wanted to show her at the ranch, including her doll and her horse, Buttercup. "Let's lay down and look at the clouds." She tugged on Annika's arm.

Annika joined her on the soft quilts and gazed up at the puffy clouds drifting by.

"My Uncle Daniel taught me to find things in the clouds. See that one." She pointed to a cloud on the left. "It looks like our cat, Precious. My momma named her that. She's mostly black, but she has a white tummy and paws." She was quiet for a moment. "That one over there looks like a milk bucket."

Annika nodded and yawned, trying to take in everything Mariah said, but soon her eyes drifted closed, and she floated off to sleep, dreaming of a dark-eyed cowboy with a wheat-colored hat.

Daniel glanced over his shoulder as the wagon rounded the curve and rolled toward the house. Both Mariah and Annika had fallen asleep only a few minutes into the hour-long ride back to the ranch. They lay side-by-side now, nestled in the blankets.

He studied the young woman and frowned slightly, concern tightening his stomach. She looked much younger than twenty-two and didn't appear to weigh more than an armful of firewood. How would she handle the hardships of ranch life? He'd hate to see her get sick and waste away like Mariah's momma, Eliza. Her death had hit them all hard, especially Chase. His brother hadn't been the same since.

Daniel sighed and shook his head. He, Pa, and Mariah adjusted over time, but Chase continued to run wild since losing his wife. And the fact Mariah looked more like her mother every day didn't help.

Was that why Chase spent so little time at home? When he was there, he rarely gave his daughter the affection and attention she longed for. It wasn't right. He'd tried talking to Chase about it, but that hadn't helped. Maybe this young woman would give Chase a reason to stay home and spend time with his daughter again, but that seemed like an awful burden to place on her, especially with the way Chase had been acting lately.

Would he treat her kindly or break her heart? That was what really worried him. He didn't like the idea of his father springing a bride on Chase. It wasn't fair to either of them. But he could understand why he'd done it. Somehow, he'd have to get Chase to give the girl a chance.

"Whoa now." Pa reined in the horses, and the wagon rolled to a stop.

Daniel scanned the barnyard and corral looking for

Chase, but he didn't see him or his bay gelding, Sundancer.

"Time to rise and shine," Pa boomed to the girls.

Annika sat up quickly and looked around; then she gently brushed the hair from the sleeping girl's face. His father helped Annika climb down.

"I'll take Mariah in." Daniel lifted his niece into his arms and glanced at Annika. Uncertainty creased her pale brows as she looked at the ranch house.

He turned and took in the view as a newcomer might. The large, two-story log house looked sturdy with a fine rock chimney and wide front porch. A small stream wove through the rich grasslands beyond the barnyard, and granite hills rose in the distance. His family had lived on the property for almost twelve years, since the Pacific Railroad came through and brought them here. He and Chase had been fourteen and sixteen at the time. Their mother had died two years later. It wasn't an easy life, especially for women.

He climbed the porch steps and called Song Li. The cook pushed open the door but scowled when he saw Annika. As soon as Daniel and Mariah passed through, Song Li let the door bang closed.

Pa yanked it open. "Come in, Miss Bergstrom."

"Please, call me Annika."

He nodded and set her bag on the floor. "Daniel, you and Song Li get Miss Bergstrom's trunk. I'll take Mariah upstairs."

Daniel nodded and passed him the sleeping girl, then headed out the door. Song Li trailed behind him, muttering in Chinese.

Daniel and Song Li hauled the heavy trunk upstairs. When Daniel reached the top, he stopped and glanced back at Annika. "I suppose you can stay with Mariah for now."

Her cheeks bloomed pink. "Yes, thank you. That will be fine."

They set her trunk down, and she stepped in the room, taking a wide path around him. The poor girl looked scared as a fawn separated from her mother.

He took off his hat and wiped his damp forehead. "Why don't you get yourself settled and then come downstairs? I'm sure Song Li will have supper ready soon."

Song Li glowered at Daniel then hurried out the door.

Annika watched the cook with an anxious expression.

"Don't mind him. He's just worried you're going to send him packing."

Her eyes widened. "Why would he think that?"

"Song Li has been our cook for the last three years since Eliza passed away."

"Eliza?"

"Chase's wife."

Her face flushed. "Oh yes, of course."

"He doesn't like change or anyone telling him how to do his job. But he'll settle down and accept you by-and-by."

She sank down on the edge of the bed where Mariah slept. "Thank you." Her voice came out in a hoarse whisper, and tears collected in her blue eyes.

Daniel nodded and backed toward the door, uncertain what he'd do if her tears overflowed. "Take your time. There's no hurry," he said and ducked out the door.

Chapter 3

Sunbeams slanted through the window the next morning, waking Annika. The other side of the bed was empty, and the angle of the sun told her it was already mid-morning. She flipped back the covers and hopped out of bed. The cool wood floor sent shivers racing up her legs. She washed and dressed quickly, hoping Chase and his family wouldn't think she was a lazy woman intent on sleeping the day away.

Buttoning her dress up the back without her sister's help was a challenge, but she managed it with a bit of wiggling and tugging. With a final glance in the mirror, she smoothed back her hair, ready to face the day and hopefully meet her future husband.

Her stomach fluttered. Would he be as handsome as his brother? What a silly thought. A man's character was more important than his outward appearance. Chase had shown who he was through his letters. That was enough for her. But if he did resemble his brother, she certainly wouldn't mind.

Energy hummed through her as she opened her trunk, took out her apron, and slipped it on over her dress. Today she would begin her new life on the ranch and make a place for herself in the family.

As she descended the stairs to the kitchen, the aroma of coffee and bacon rose to greet her. Her mouth watered.

The only person in the kitchen was the Chinese cook, Song Li. He stood at the counter kneading dough.

"Good morning." She greeted him with a smile.

He glanced her way and continued kneading. "You late for breakfast."

"Oh, I'm sorry." Her face flamed. "I don't usually over-sleep. I'm used to rising early. I suppose it was the long trip and the wonderful feather bed."

His somber expression didn't change.

A plate covered with a pie tin sat on the back of the stove. Had they saved her some breakfast? Should she ask about cooking her own?

Straightening her shoulders, she faced Song Li. She was going to be mistress of this house when she married Chase. He ought to show her more respect or at least common courtesy.

But memories of the rude way she had been treated by some of the wealthy students at the Hillman School came flooding back. Looking down on him or treating him unkindly simply because he worked for her would not be wise. Kindness and teamwork would more likely win him over. "Something smells wonderful. What are you making?"

"I cook meat for dinner."

"You certainly are an accomplished cook. The chicken

you prepared yesterday was very tender, and the dumplings were delicious, the best I've ever had."

Song Li gave her a curt nod.

She heard voices and the sound of footsteps on the back porch. "You look busy. Shall I cook myself some breakfast?"

Song Li gasped, and his dark eyes flashed. "You no cook in my kitchen! Song Li cook! Song Li clean! Song Li take care of family!"

Mr. Simms, Daniel, and Mariah walked in during Song Li's outburst.

"I understand. I simply asked if I could make myself some breakfast."

"Your food on stove!" Song Li slammed the bread dough down and wrestled with it as if it was alive.

Daniel hustled over and snatched the plate off the back of the stove. "Morning, Annika." He set it on the table and lifted the lid, revealing a stack of pancakes, scrambled eggs, and several slices of bacon. "Would you like some coffee?"

"Yes, please." Her voice trembled slightly.

"Song Li, I want to speak to you outside." Mr. Simms motioned the cook to follow him.

Song Li slapped the dough down and stalked out of the room. The front door slammed.

Bowing her head, she prayed and asked God to give her peace in the midst of this unexpected storm. After a whispered, "Amen," she lifted her head.

"How'd you sleep?" Daniel asked as he passed her a cup of coffee and took a seat across from her. His gentle tone and smile soothed her.

"Fine, thank you. The bed was very comfortable."

"You didn't mind sharing with me?" Mariah asked, climbing into a chair next to her uncle.

"Not at all. I'm used to sharing with my twin sister, Sophia, so it was a comfort to have you there." She smiled at Mariah, pleased to see the girl's eyes sparkle.

But then, Mariah's warm expression melted away. "I don't have any sisters or brothers, and my momma is in heaven."

Annika's heart clenched. She looked at Daniel.

He didn't seem bothered by the turn in the conversation. His warm gaze rested on Mariah. "Your momma is probably looking down right now proud as can be to see the way you're growing up." He laid his hand on Mariah's shoulder and winked at her.

Her smile resurfaced, and she turned to Annika. "You gonna eat all those pancakes yourself?"

Annika held back a grin. "I believe there are too many for me. Would you like some?"

"I sure would. I been cleaning stalls with Uncle Daniel, and I'm real hungry." She hopped up and got a plate and fork from the stack of clean dishes on the counter.

Annika slid two large pancakes onto Mariah's plate, and the girl sat down again to eat.

Song Li marched back in the kitchen, followed by Mr. Simms. The cook bowed to Annika, his expression grim. "I sorry for bad words. You most welcome in this house." He almost choked on his apology, and Annika suspected he only spoke under threat of losing his job.

"Thank you, Song Li." Annika turned to Mr. Simms.

"Has Chase returned yet?"

Mr. Simms exchanged an uneasy glance with Daniel. "Not yet. I think I'll ride out with a few men and see if we can find him."

Annika's stomach tensed. "Do you think something's happened to him?"

Mr. Simms rubbed his chin. "Well now, I wouldn't worry. He's probably fine, just taking his time to settle some things before he comes back."

What did that mean? She glanced at Daniel, hoping he might explain.

But he got up from the table and turned away. "I'll go with you, Pa."

"No, you stay here, show Annika around, and keep an eye on Mariah."

The muscles in Daniel's jaw tightened, but he didn't argue with his father.

Mariah stuffed the last piece of pancake in her mouth. "I don't need no one to watch me. I'm big 'nuff to take care of myself." Then she jumped up from the chair and grabbed her uncle's arm. "Could you take me and Annika for a ride? Please, Uncle Daniel, please."

Annika froze, her gaze riveted on Daniel. She'd welcome a tour of the ranch, but getting on a horse was the last thing she intended to do.

Daniel grabbed his hat and strode out the door. Some days he'd like to tell his father exactly what he thought of his harebrained ideas. He didn't mind staying behind or keeping an eye on Mariah, but he disliked keeping the truth about the situation with Chase from Annika.

The struggle between his controlling father and freedom-loving brother was a longstanding battle. He usually tried to stay out of it or work behind the scenes to help them forge a temporary truce. But bringing Annika here added more fuel to the flames, and he wasn't sure he could stop the smoldering argument from turning into a raging wildfire this time.

He could see why Chase was upset, but running off and leaving them to deal with his unexpected bride wasn't right either. And shoot, it wasn't Annika's fault. What was going to happen to her?

He glanced over his shoulder. Mariah and Annika walked side-by-side a few paces behind him.

"That's the smokehouse where we put all the ham and bacon after we butcher the hogs," Mariah said. "And that's the chicken coop. I feed them every morning and collect the eggs. Over there is the springhouse. That's where we keep all the milk and butter."

Annika smiled. "My family used to have a dairy farm back in Sweden. I helped my parents make butter and cheese."

"Song Li lets me help make butter, but we never made cheese before."

"Well, maybe I can teach you how."

Mariah grinned and took Annika's hand. "That sounds good."

Daniel slowed so they could catch up. It was nice to see

Mariah happy for a change. Having Annika around would be good for her, and it would be good for Chase, too, if he'd get himself back here and take some time to get to know her. She had a real pleasing way about her, and those blue eyes of hers looked like the sky on a summer day. Chase would have to hunt a long time to find another bride as fine as Annika.

Well, there was nothing he could do about his brother right now. He might as well help Annika find her way around the ranch. "Over there's the bunkhouse." Daniel pointed past the corral to a long, low building off to the left. "We have about a dozen hired hands. They have their own cook and eat their meals out there, so you won't see too much of them. They're all hard workers, but they can be a little rough around the edges."

Annika's golden brows dipped, and she bit her lower lip.

"They shouldn't give you any trouble. If they do, just let me know. I'll take care of it."

Her expression eased, and she nodded. "Thank you."

"That's the old barn next to the bunkhouse," he added. "We store hay there and use the stalls during calving season. And this is our new barn." He lifted the latch on the big double door and pulled it open. "We mainly use this for the horses."

Annika hesitated in the doorway then she hurried in, staying close to Daniel. The sweet smell of hay mixed with the pungent aroma of horseflesh floated out to meet them.

"That's Buttercup." Mariah dragged a stool over to the second stall. She stood on top and reached up to rub her horse's nose. "Isn't she pretty? Come pet her."

31

Annika shook her head, her face pale.

"It's all right. She's real gentle. She won't hurt you." Mariah's voice was soft and coaxing, but Annika stayed by Daniel's side.

He tipped his hat up and studied her. "Have you ever ridden a horse?"

"Yes, I used to ride when I was younger. But a horse bucked me off. I broke my arm and ankle and had to stay in bed for weeks. A few months after that, we left Sweden and came to Chicago. I've never ridden since."

Daniel rubbed his chin. "That could be a real problem."

She looked up at him, her blue eyes wide. "What do you mean?"

"That's how we get around out here."

"But you have a wagon and carriage." She pointed to the carriage parked at the other end of the barn.

"They're made for the road. If you're going anywhere else on the ranch, you have to ride. . .or I suppose you could walk, but it would take a mighty long time to cover sixteen hundred acres."

Annika's eyes widened again. "Sixteen hundred?"

"That's right." Daniel nodded. "We raise more than three hundred head of cattle, plus all our own grain for feed. Riding is a necessity out here."

Annika bit her lip and stared at the horses, looking like that was the worst news she'd heard since she'd arrived.

Annika sat on the porch steps with Mariah seated in front of her, brushing out the girl's hair. It was so tangled she could only do one small section at a time.

"Owww!" Mariah reached up and clamped her hand over the brush.

"Just a little more and we'll be done," Annika said gently.

Mariah sighed and let go. "All right, but my head feels like it's gonna come off."

"I'm sure you'll be fine. And once we get these tangles out, we can braid it. That'll keep it nice and neat."

"Can we just stop for a minute?"

"All right." Annika leaned back and scanned the rocky peaks and grassy, rolling hills beyond the barn. There was no sign of Mr. Simms and the other men who were still out searching for Chase.

Late-afternoon sunshine slanted across the Ponderosa pines, giving them a golden glow. Even in late October, this was a beautiful spot, so different than the busy streets of Chicago or quiet country lanes in Sweden. Even the sky looked different here, so broad and clear and somehow closer, as though she could reach right up and touch it.

"You think they're gonna find my papa?" Mariah asked, gazing toward the hills.

Annika tensed. "Of course they will." She began brushing Mariah's hair again.

"My grampa says my papa misses my momma, and that's why he's always running off."

Annika's hand stilled. "What do you mean, running off?"

"Sometimes he leaves and doesn't come back for a while."

Annika frowned. "How long is he gone?"

"Two or three days, sometimes longer. I get real worried, but he always comes back."

Chase had told her he was a widower, but he'd said nothing about feeling so distraught over his wife's death that he left home for days at a time. In his letters he sounded strong and steady and eager to marry again. Perhaps Mariah misunderstood her grandfather, or she was talking about something she had heard months or years ago.

Mariah made a small circle in the dirt with the toe of her shoe. "I miss my momma, too, but I don't go runnin' off cause of it."

Annika stilled, a silent prayer for wisdom forming in her heart. "When people lose someone they love, it affects them in different ways."

"What do you mean?"

"When I lost my parents, I cried for days. I wondered if I'd ever be happy again." The memory of that dark time passed over her like a cloud hiding the sun. Five years was long enough to lessen the pain, but not to wipe it out completely.

Mariah looked up at her, sympathy filling her eyes. "You lost both your momma and your papa?"

Annika nodded.

"What happened to them?"

"They died in a carriage accident when I was seventeen. It changed everything for Sophia and me. We had to leave our home, find jobs, and learn to live on our own in a very big city. It was hard, but we made it through by clinging to each other and to the Lord."

Mariah leaned back against her. "I'm sorry about your momma and papa."

Annika swallowed past the tightness in her throat and wrapped her arms around Mariah. "Thank you, Mariah. I'm sorry you lost your momma. I'm sure she loved you very much."

Mariah sat quietly while Annika finished the last section of her hair. Finally, she released a soft sigh. "My momma used to brush my hair just like this."

Tears burned Annika's eyes, and she bent and kissed the top of Mariah's head. "Well, I'm happy I can do it for you."

Hoofbeats sounded in the distance. Annika looked up. Three men rode across the pasture toward the house.

"Here they come!" Mariah jumped up.

Mr. Simms rode in the lead on a big black horse. Annika's heartbeat sped up as she searched the other men's faces. The one on the left was stocky, gray-haired, and had a grizzled beard. The other was middle-aged with dark brown skin and eyes and a drooping moustache. Neither of them looked anything like Daniel or Mr. Simms.

Mariah ran to her grandfather. "Did you find my papa?"

Mr. Simms dismounted and passed his reins to the older man. "Sorry, not yet."

Mariah trudged back to the porch, her shoulders drooping.

Daniel jogged over from the barn. "Any sign of Chase?"

His father shook his head, looking more irritated than worried. "We rode out past Marshall's Creek and talked to the men working out there, but they haven't seen him." He stomped up the steps and strode past her into the house. Mariah followed him inside.

A chill traveled through Annika, and she pulled her sweater more tightly around her. Where was Chase? When would he come back? He'd seemed eager to meet her in the letters they exchanged. Why had he taken off on the day she was due to arrive? She turned to Daniel. "I don't understand."

He was quiet for several seconds, the muscles in his jaw jumping. "Me neither."

"What happens now? Will your father keep looking for him?"

He took off his hat and ran his hand through his dark hair. "We'll find Chase. You can be sure of that."

Chapter 4

Daniel carried a load of firewood into the sitting room and stacked it on the hearth. That should keep the fire blazing for a couple more hours and give them time to enjoy the evening together.

He glanced around at the cozy scene. Annika and Mariah sat side-by-side on the settee holding a book between them. A lantern on the end table nearby gave off enough light for Mariah to practice her reading. His father sat in the large chair on the right of the fireplace with his newspaper and pipe.

His niece scrunched her face as she focused on the book. "The man. . .can see the cat in the. . .tree."

Annika smiled and nodded. "Very good. Try the next line."

"The cat will not. . .come down. What. . .will the man do?" Mariah huffed and lowered the book. "He's gonna have to climb up there and carry that old cat down, that's what."

His father chuckled and lowered his newspaper. "Sounds like you ought to be writing those stories rather than reading them."

"Well, I could make a better story than this." She closed the book and set it beside her on the settee. Her eyes lit up. "Maybe Uncle Daniel could read now."

"Well, I don't want to interrupt your lesson."

Annika looked up and sent him a shy smile. "I think we'd all enjoy hearing the next chapter of *The Adventures of Tom Sawyer*."

Daniel nodded and took the book from the mantel, pleased that Annika as well as Mariah was enjoying the story. He hoped it would ease the worry lines around her eyes and distract her from her concern for Chase. Seven days with no word was wearing on all of them, but she had to be feeling it more deeply.

He settled into his chair and opened the book, determined to do his best to fill the next hour with a lively story and hopefully lift everyone's spirits.

On Thursday afternoon, nine days after Annika had arrived at the Simms's ranch, Annika and Mariah carried two empty laundry baskets outside to the clothesline. Annika set her basket down, scanned the rolling pastureland, and searched for any sign of Chase, but there was none. Where could he have gone? What if he never came back? What would happen to her then?

Her parents had taught her that worry was a sin, so she

did her best to catch her anxious thoughts and turn them into a prayer. Pulling in a deep breath, she reminded herself that God knew where Chase was and when he was coming home. Her duty was to trust God and make the best of her situation.

The scent of fresh air and sunshine drifted from the clean cotton sheets dancing in the brisk breeze. Annika tested one of the sheets for dryness. She nodded and plucked a wooden clothespin off the line, then dropped it in her apron pocket. "Pick up that corner, Mariah."

The girl lifted one side to keep it off the ground while Annika unpinned the other. "Uncle Daniel said it might snow soon. I sure hope so."

Annika looked up and searched the blue sky. The few wispy clouds overhead didn't look as though they carried snow, but she'd come to trust Daniel. His years of working on the ranch had taught him common sense and life skills one couldn't learn at school. It amazed her to see the way he could tame a wild horse, mend a broken fence, nurse a sick calf, and even coax a tired and cranky seven-year-old into finishing her supper.

Yes, Daniel was a fine man—smart, patient, and caring.

Too bad his father didn't seem to appreciate him. Why did he overlook Daniel's efforts and continually talk about Chase? Was he trying to convince her she'd made a wise choice by accepting his older son's proposal, or was this always his habit?

Some days she wished she could give Mr. Simms a good shake and make him notice all that his younger son did around the ranch. Even though she'd only been there a little over a week, she could see how much his father's uncaring attitude hurt Daniel.

Lord, help them all see how much they need each other.

She put those thoughts aside and glanced at Mariah. "So, it sounds as though you like the snow."

Mariah nodded and grinned. "Last year, Uncle Daniel and I had a snowball fight, and Grampa took us for a sleigh ride."

She couldn't help noticing Mariah hadn't mentioned her father very often the last few days. She sent off another prayer for Chase as she placed the folded sheet in the basket. "When the snow comes, maybe I can teach you how to make a special treat."

"What kind?"

Annika took the next sheet off the line. "It's a delicious candy called Sugar-on-Snow. You make it by pouring hot maple syrup over some clean snow."

Mariah's eyes widened. "Your pour syrup outside on the snow?"

Annika chuckled. "We usually bring the bowl of snow indoors."

"I never made that before."

"I'm sure you'd like it. Do you think your Uncle Daniel—"

The sheets on the line parted, and a man in a dark gray hat poked his head through. "Hello, ladies!"

Mariah spun around. "Papa!" She dropped her end of the sheet in the dirt and jumped into his arms.

He laughed and twirled her around, then tossed her up in the air.

She screamed with delight and dropped back into his arms. "Where've you been? Grampa's been looking all over for you."

"Oh, don't worry. I'm home now."

Annika stared at her future groom. Dust covered his face and clothes, but it couldn't hide the shadows under his bloodshot, gray-green eyes or the scraggly, reddish-brown whiskers on his chin and upper lip.

"Oh, Papa, I missed you." Mariah gave him a big kiss on the cheek.

He set her down and looked Annika over with a lazy smile. "Well now, you must be that gal from Chicago. What's your name, darlin?"

She blinked and swallowed. How could he forget her name after the letters they'd exchanged?

Mariah took his hand and tugged him closer. "That's Annika, Papa. She came all the way out here on a train to marry you."

"Mariah!" Daniel charged around the end of the clothesline, worry etched on his face. "Are you all right?" He caught sight of Chase and skidded to a halt.

"Hey there, brother." Chase staggered over and slapped Daniel on the shoulder. "How ya doing, Danny boy?"

Daniel glared at Chase. "Where've you been?"

"In town and around, takin' care of a little business."

"It's been nine days, Chase."

"Don't worry. I'm fine. . .fine and dandy." He turned and

41

sauntered back toward Annika. "You sure are a quiet little bird, aren't you?" He laughed and slapped his leg like that was the funniest joke he'd ever heard.

She tried to form a reply, but her mouth suddenly felt as dry as desert sand.

"Well, you might not talk much, but you sure are pretty." He wiggled his brows. "I really know how to pick 'em, don't I, Daniel?" He reached for her. "Come here, sweetheart. Show me what—"

Annika froze.

"That's enough!" Daniel grabbed his brother's arm.

"Hey, what ya doin? I wanna talk to my bride."

"You aren't talking to anybody until you sober up." Daniel hauled his brother off toward the barn.

Mariah looked up at Annika. "What's wrong? Where's he takin' my papa?"

Annika shivered. "It's. . .all right. He and your uncle just need to talk."

"You're a skunk! You know that? A dirty, rotten skunk!" Daniel punched his fist into his palm to keep from busting his brother's jaw.

Chase leaned back against a stall door and chewed on a piece of straw. "Why are you so riled?"

Daniel whirled around and faced his brother. "You take off for nine days and never tell us where you're going. We have to search over half the territory, not knowing if you're dead or alive. Finally, you show up drunk at three in the afternoon. You upset your daughter and insult your future bride; then you act like there's nothing wrong!"

"Ah you're just mad 'cause you had to do my chores while I was gone."

Daniel clenched his fists. "Oh, I'm mad all right, but it's not the extra work or the worry. It's the way you're hurting Mariah and Annika."

Chase scoffed. "I don't even know that gal. I've got no power to hurt her."

"That *gal's* name is Annika. Did you catch it this time? Annika! And you've got more power over her happiness than you know."

"What kind of name is that? German? I thought Pa said she was from Chicago. Well, she better speak English, or I'm not wasting my time with her."

Daniel glared at his brother, wishing he could kick him all the way to Cheyenne. "You have got to be the most small-brained, stubborn fool I ever met!"

Fire flashed in his brother's eyes. He spit out the straw and pushed off from the wall. "I'm not listenin' to any more of your insults."

Daniel hustled after him and grabbed his arm. "Hold on."

Chase growled and pulled away. "It ain't gonna work. I can't stay around here and marry that gal."

He'd better think fast, or his brother was going to climb on his horse and disappear over the hills again. "I thought you cared about Mariah."

Chase stalled in the doorway. "Of course I do."

"You'd never know it from the way you're acting."

Chase swung around and clenched his fists. "You better take that back."

Daniel stepped closer. "It's true, and you know it."

All the starch drained out of Chase, and his eyes glittered with shame. "I love Mariah, but every time I look at her, I see Eliza. I can't take much more of that."

"That's not her fault. She needs you to stick around and do what's right instead of running off every time you and Pa have a fight."

Fire smoldered in Chase's eyes. "I can't abide living in the same house with that man. He's always riding me about taking over the ranch. But there's only one way to do things—his way! Well I'm tired of it!"

"I know he's hard to deal with, but he just wants you to stop running wild and face up to your responsibilities. He doesn't mean to anger you."

Chase huffed and crossed his arms. "You should'a heard him yellin' at me in town yesterday."

"What? He talked to you yesterday?" Why hadn't Pa told them he'd found Chase in Laramie?

"That's right. He told me I'd never inherit one acre of this ranch unless I came home and got ready to marry that little gal."

Daniel sighed and ran his hand down his face. Poor Annika. What had she gotten herself into? Would Chase marry her just to lock in his inheritance? What kind of marriage would that be?

"Listen, Annika's a sweet girl with a good heart." Maybe if he kept repeating her name, it would sink in and his brother would remember. "She's been working real hard to learn how we do things around here. And she's real good with Mariah. She's been teaching her how to read and knit. I think she'd make a fine wife."

Chase scowled. "Not sure I can marry some gal Pa picked out for me."

"Don't hold that against her."

He shook his head. "You think she's strong enough for ranch life? She don't look like she's got enough meat on her bones to make it through winter."

The worry in his brother's eyes hit Daniel hard. He'd wondered the same thing. If Chase married Annika and lost her as he had Eliza. . . His stomach twisted. He straightened and shook off those fearful thoughts. "She seems strong and healthy, but none of us has a guarantee on tomorrow. We've all got to put ourselves in God's hands and trust Him to carry us through whatever's ahead."

"Don't know why I should trust God. He hasn't done me any favors lately."

Daniel studied the lines sin and sorrow had cut in his brother's face, and he felt as though they sliced into his own soul. He loved his brother. Seeing him struggle was hard, maybe harder than going through it himself. But he'd never make the same mistake Chase had by trying to overcome his problems without God's help.

"You're wrong, Chase. God's done more for you than you realize."

"Like what?" He clamped his jaw and narrowed his eyes.

"He's kept you alive and given you a chance to have a home and a family. I'd say those are pretty big favors for a man who's been running away from God and breaking most every commandment in the Good Book."

His brother's face hardened. "Don't preach at me, Daniel. I don't want to hear it."

"Maybe not, but someone's got to tell you the truth. You need to surrender to God and drop that load of grief and bitterness you're carrying, or it's going to destroy you and hurt all the people who love you."

Chase snorted. "Not many people on that list."

Daniel clamped his hand on Chase's shoulder. "I'm on it, right up there with Mariah."

Chase dropped his head and shuddered. "I don't deserve it, Dan, not after everything I've done."

"Chase!" His father strode across the yard toward them, his stern glare slicing a path ahead of him.

Chase turned and nodded to his father. "Pa."

"So, you finally decided to come home."

Daniel winced. Why couldn't his father treat Chase with a little dignity or at least understanding?

"You didn't give me much choice, did you?" Chase and his father locked gazes for several seconds.

"Let me make your *choices* clear. You've got one month to court Annika and convince me you're serious about this, or I'll send you packing myself." His father spun away and marched off toward the house.

Daniel studied his brother's mottled face. If glares could shoot bullets, his father would be a dead man.

❄

Annika pushed aside the curtain of the upstairs bedroom window and bit her lip. Her gaze bounced from Daniel and Chase, standing together by the barn doorway, to Mr. Simms, striding back toward the house. Even from a distance, she could read the tension between the men in their rigid postures and drawn faces.

What had Mr. Simms said to them? Had Chase really been off drinking all this time? Was that what Daniel meant when he hustled him off to the barn and said he needed to sober up? She didn't have much experience with men who had been drinking, but Chase's voice had certainly been loud, and his actions bordered on obnoxious.

How could he be drunk in the middle of the day? That didn't sound like the man who had written to her. This must just be a lapse in his behavior, a way he dealt with his grief over losing his wife.

Grief could make people act in unusual ways. She'd been through that herself when her parents died. But being a woman, she'd had the freedom to cry and pour out her troubles to her sister and friends. It must be harder for a man like Chase, especially when his father was such a stern, strong man. Maybe Chase never had been given the freedom to grieve for his wife so he could move on and put his sorrow behind him.

Annika clasped her hands. She was no expert at helping people sort out the deeper issues of the heart, but she could pray that God would help her be a good wife to Chase so he might not need to run off or turn to a bottle for comfort or companionship. Surely the warmth of family and the love of a new wife would be enough to keep him on the right path. But could she learn to love and trust a man like Chase? The bedroom door squeaked opened, and Mariah walked in. "Song Li is all done in the kitchen. How about we bake a cake for Papa?"

Annika let the curtain fall back into place and forced a smile. "That sounds like a nice way to welcome him home."

Perhaps it might also make up for the way she'd acted when he surprised her out by the clothesline. She certainly hadn't made a very good impression, gawking at him without a word of welcome. The next time she saw Chase, she'd greet him with a warm smile and a freshly baked apple cake.

Chapter 5

After supper the men settled in the sitting room by the fire with their coffee.

Annika carried in a warm, cinnamon-scented apple cake. She'd dusted the top with sugar and placed it on a pretty white plate with a scalloped edge, hoping Chase would be pleased with her efforts.

"Something sure smells good." Daniel smiled at her and then winked at Mariah as she brought in the bowl of whipped cream.

"Me and Annika made apple cake, 'specially for Papa."

Daniel chuckled. "You gonna let your grampa and me have some?"

Mariah's grin spread wider. "Of course you get some, too."

Annika placed the tray on the low table by the settee. Mr. Simms sat in the large upholstered chair to the left of the fireplace. Daniel shared the wooden bench on the right with

Song Li. Mariah's small rocker was pulled up close to the settee, where Chase sat on one side, leaving the only empty seat next to him.

She exchanged a brief glance with Chase, and a shiver traveled up her back. He'd changed clothes, washed his face, and slicked back his curly auburn hair, but rough whiskers still covered the lower half of his face. His gray-green eyes held no warmth or invitation. In fact, he had avoided looking at her altogether during supper.

Annika swallowed and focused on cutting the cake. "Who would like some dessert?" The forced lightness in her voice didn't fool anyone.

"Cut me a big slice." Chase sniffed and wiped his nose on his sleeve.

"You want whipped cream, Papa?"

"Sure do."

Mariah added a dollop and passed him the plate. "I helped chop all the apples and mix up the batter."

He nodded to Mariah. "That's nice." Then he glanced at Annika, and his forehead wrinkled for a second. "Thank you, Annie."

Daniel grimaced and looked as though he would correct his brother for calling her by the wrong name, but Annika gave her head a slight shake. Daniel sighed and sat back.

"You're welcome, Chase. Would you like more coffee?"

Chase took a big bite, grunted, and shook his head.

Annika passed plates to the others, and they ate in silence. Annika's spirits wilted like a flower picked and left out on the porch steps in the sun. Even though the fire crackled, spreading its warmth in the room, the temperature seemed to have dropped several degrees. Without Daniel's usual stories and laughter, the atmosphere seemed gloomy and tiresome.

Daniel finally broke the silence. "You girls sure did a fine job with this cake."

Annika looked up, meeting his gaze. Empathy filled his dark eyes, and she forced a smile. "Thank you, Daniel."

Mr. Simms cleared his throat and glared at Chase.

Chase shoveled in the last bite, then glanced at his father and sat up straighter. "Yes, it's real good." But he sounded a bit like a puppet, mouthing words his father wanted to hear. He grabbed his cup and gulped down the last of his coffee. "Well, I think I'll go out and check on the horses."

Daniel blinked and frowned at his brother.

"But, Papa, I was gonna show you how I've been learning to read." Mariah hopped up and took her primer from the basket by the hearth.

"Not now. Maybe later." Chase walked out of the room. A few seconds later, the back door banged shut.

A heavy silence hung over the room. Annika stared down at her half-eaten slice of cake and wished she could dissolve into the floor. Chase obviously didn't enjoy her company.

Song Li got up and bowed slightly to Annika, his expression grim. "You make good cake. I go write to family." He bowed again and fled the room.

Mariah put her primer back in the basket. "I don't feel much like reading."

"That's all right, sweetie," Daniel said. "Why don't you

51

go on up and get ready for bed. I'll come tuck you in after a bit."

Mariah nodded and trudged off toward the stairs.

Annika's heart sank as she watched her go. Poor girl. Couldn't Chase see how Mariah longed to spend time with him?

"That was mighty fine dessert. Thank you, Annika." Mr. Simms got up. "Oh, I almost forgot, I picked up these letters for you when I was in town." He pulled two envelopes from his jacket pocket and held them out to her.

Annika gasped and reached for them with a trembling hand. "Thank you." One glance at the handwriting confirmed they were from Sophia. She clutched them to her chest as though they were gold.

Worry lines fanned out around his old blue eyes. "Hope they bring good news."

"Any news from my sister will be a blessing." She started to open the first envelope then looked up. "I have several letters I'd like to mail to her. Will we be going into town soon?"

Mr. Simms frowned and rubbed his chin. "I think we could go in for church on Sunday if the weather's not too bad."

Daniel glanced toward the window. "I think we're in for some snow soon, Pa."

Mr. Simms nodded. "Long as it's not too deep, we could take the sleigh."

Daniel turned to Annika. "The post office is closed on Sunday. But we could give your letters to someone to mail on Monday."

"Thank you." Annika bit her lip, her face warming. "I was wondering if. . . Well, I don't have any money for postage—"

"I'll take care of it," Daniel said. "And anything else you need, just let me know." Kindness shone from his eyes.

"Thank you, Daniel."

How could two brothers be so different?

Early the next morning, Annika peeked out the kitchen window. Snowflakes fell at a steady pace, covering every rock and dusty patch of dried grass with a powdery white blanket.

Daniel trudged through the snow and tied a thick rope from the barn and outhouse to the back porch so no one would lose his way in the blowing snow. Then he and Mariah went to check on the chickens.

Song Li muttered under his breath while he flipped hotcakes then scooped a heap of scrambled eggs into a bowl.

Annika looked up as Chase entered the kitchen. "Good morning, Chase." She handed him a hot cup of coffee.

"Morning," he grumbled and sat down at the breakfast table.

She tried to engage him in conversation while he ate, but he gave her one-word answers and focused on shoveling in his food.

Finally, he pushed away his plate and rose from the table. "I've got to go outside."

Annika's heart sank. Gripping her coffee cup, she watched

him stomp off and slam the back door. Why did he spend almost all his time out in the bunkhouse or barn?

Friday morning, the temperature rose a bit, and the sky finally cleared. Mr. Simms pushed his breakfast plate aside. "Looks like it would be a good day to go into town. Let's head out as soon as we finish our chores."

Annika's heart leaped. Finally she could mail her letters to Sophia and see if any more had arrived.

Mariah hopped up from her chair and ran to put on her coat. "I'll hurry up and feed the chickens!"

Annika laughed and helped her with her buttons. "Don't forget your mittens. Hold on to the rope and stay out of the drifts so you don't get too wet."

"All right." Mariah pulled her mittens from her pockets and dashed out the door.

Daniel smiled as he watched her go then turned to Annika. "We may not get into town again before Christmas. Is there anything you need from the store?"

Song Li faced them. "I already make list."

Daniel and Annika exchanged a glance. "We'll get whatever you need, Song Li, but Annika might like to make something special for Christmas."

Song Li scowled, but he didn't argue. "I check list." He marched off to the pantry with a scrap of paper in one hand and a stubby pencil in the other.

Annika leaned toward Daniel. "Thank you."

"You're welcome."

"There are a few recipes I'd like to make, and maybe we could get some fabric and yarn. Mariah and I want to make some Christmas gifts."

Daniel nodded, looking pleased. "It's nice what you've been doing with Mariah. She seems real happy."

Working with Song Li, they cleared the table, washed the dishes, and banked the fire in the stove. Then they dressed in their warmest clothes and climbed into the sleigh.

Annika sat in the back seat with Chase, although Mariah sat between them. Song Li placed hot bricks wrapped in cloth at their feet, and Daniel tucked heavy blankets around them before he climbed up front with his father and Song Li. Mariah chatted away, exclaiming over everything she saw as the sleigh flew along the snow-covered road.

Chase barely spoke the entire trip, but Annika was determined to enjoy the beautiful day, no matter how somber and distracted he seemed.

By the time they reached Laramie, the bricks had cooled, and Annika's teeth began to chatter. Her nose felt frozen, and the tips of her fingers were stiff from the cold.

As they pulled into town, they passed the hotel, café, post office, and bank. The one- and two-story brick and stone buildings were smaller than those in Chicago, but most looked relatively new and well kept. Several horses were tied to hitching posts, waiting for their owners to finish their business in town. But only three other sleighs passed as they glided down Second Street.

"Whoa, now." Mr. Simms guided the horses to a stop in front of Iverson's General Store. Mr. Simms jumped down and saw to the horses while Daniel helped Annika and Mariah.

Chase climbed out of the sleigh and tugged up the collar of his coat. He cast a longing glance across the street toward the Silver Nugget Saloon.

Annika's stomach tightened. "Shall we go into the store?" She smiled up at him and took his arm. He nodded, then walked up the steps and opened the door for her.

A small brass bell jingled overhead as they stepped inside. The delightful scents of nutmeg and fresh-cut wood greeted her. Her eyes widened as she looked around. Shelves filled with every kind of food and household item she could imagine covered the walls. Glass jars holding lemon drops and peppermint sticks stood next to the cash register. Baskets of apples, walnuts, potatoes, and onions sat on the floor in front of the sales counter. Bolts of cloth and baskets of thread and notions covered the far wall.

Mr. Simms introduced Annika to Ed and Jane Iverson and their daughter, Mary. Then he joined three other men seated near the potbellied stove, who were discussing the price of livestock and the effects a hard winter might have on their herds.

Daniel spoke to Mr. Iverson about a rifle he hoped to order.

Song Li read his list to Mrs. Iverson. The shopkeeper quickly packed the items into a wooden crate.

"Come on, Mariah, let's see if we can find the fabric and ribbon we need for your dress." She took the girl's hand, led her to the back of the store, and looked at the material on display. As Mary measured and cut three yards of white fabric for them, Annika glanced over her shoulder.

Chase stood by the front window gazing outside, hands in his pockets, shoulders sagging. Suddenly, he straightened and stepped closer to the window. Two seconds later, he hurried over and spoke to Daniel in a low voice, and then without a word to anyone else, he slipped out the door.

Annika clutched the folds of her skirt. Where was he going?

Mariah tugged on her hand. "How much red ribbon do we need?"

Annika swallowed and turned to Mary. "Two yards should be plenty. Thank you."

"Are you making something for Christmas?" the young woman asked as she unrolled the ribbon.

Mariah's eyes danced. "We're making a special dress for me for St. Lucia Day, but don't tell my papa. We're gonna surprise him."

Mary smiled. "Your secret's safe with me. I've heard about that holiday from some other folks." She measured and clipped the ribbon. "I remember they made some special buns and needed saffron. I think we still have some if you'd like it."

"Thank you." Annika followed her to the front of the store. While Mary checked through the spice jars, Annika glanced out the front window, searching for Chase.

She didn't have to look far. Across the street between the saloon and the café, a pretty young woman with long dark hair and a tattered brown cloak stood with Chase. The woman was obviously upset about something. Chase placed his hand on her arm and leaned toward her, his posture tense.

Annika's stomach dropped like a bucket tossed in a well. Who was she? What was Chase saying to her?

Chase shook his head, then turned away and strode back toward the store, his mouth set in a jagged line. The woman called to him, but he didn't look back. Her face crumpled, and she turned and fled down the street, disappearing into the small opening between the saloon and the café.

Annika gulped and glanced around the store. Had anyone else seen Chase and the woman? What should she do—ask him about her or pretend she hadn't seen them?

Before she could decide, Mary held up a spice jar. "Here it is! How much do you need?"

Annika blinked. "Oh, just two teaspoons or so."

Mary nodded and spooned a small amount into a little paper envelope.

Daniel turned and looked at her. A frown creased his forehead. He crossed to meet her. "Are you all right?" he asked in a low voice. "You look almost as white as that material." He nodded to the folded fabric on the counter.

"I'm fine." But her voice trembled.

Chapter 6

Daniel grabbed the pitchfork, scooped up a pile of dirty straw, and tossed it in the wheelbarrow. Mucking out stalls wasn't his favorite way to spend the afternoon, but it sure beat being cooped up inside all day. Too much time sitting by the fire with Annika and Mariah had left him feeling fractious and out of sorts.

Strange, he usually enjoyed the slower pace of winter with more time to read, relax, and repair things that had broken since last winter. But everything seemed different now that Annika had arrived.

It wouldn't be so bad if she and Chase were growing closer and making plans for their wedding, but his brother continued to treat her like a distant cousin, never taking her hand and rarely sitting next to her in the evening. More than six weeks had passed since their father had given Chase the ultimatum, but he still hadn't pressed Chase to follow through on the marriage plans or even confronted him about his standoffish attitude. Even when they'd all taken the day off to celebrate Thanksgiving, Chase had not seemed to enjoy their celebration or his time with Annika.

So what was his problem? How could he not want to marry Annika?

Daniel shook his head and heaved more straw on the pile. The whole situation was about to drive him crazy!

The barn door squeaked open, and Annika stepped in. She looked around and smiled when she saw him. "Afternoon, Daniel."

His chest tightened, and a strange sensation flooded through him. He shook it off. "Afternoon."

"Have you seen Chase?"

"He and a couple men rode out to check the cattle up north past Grier's Peak."

"Oh." Her smile faded and little lines creased the area between her golden brows. "When do you think he'll be back?"

Daniel leaned on the pitchfork. "Maybe not till suppertime."

Pressing her lips together, she turned away and paced across the barn. Then she spun around and marched back, determination in her steps. "Teach me to ride."

"Right now?"

"Yes!" Her bright blue eyes sparkled with life. For the first time, he noticed the pale freckles dusting her nose and cheeks. They looked almost like cinnamon sprinkled on apple pie, sweet and tempting.

He swallowed and looked away. "Well, I wouldn't mind

teaching you, but it's awful cold out for riding lessons."

She laid her hand on his arm. "I don't care about the cold. Please, Daniel, I need to learn."

The warmth of her hand melted through him. He stepped back and leaned the pitchfork against the wall. "What's your hurry?"

"That seems like the only way I'm ever going to catch up with your brother." Her voice cracked, and she quickly looked away.

Daniel's heart clenched. He was going to have to talk to Chase. Couldn't he see how much Annika wanted to please him? She'd even get on a horse, though she was terrified of them, just to win his approval.

He straightened. "All right. I'll teach you, but you've got to go change first. Those skirts will just get in the way."

Annika's cheeks flushed a pretty pink. "What shall I wear?"

Talking to her about changing clothes seemed awfully personal, but there was no way he could teach her to ride in that outfit. "Eliza had a split skirt. Check the trunk in Chase's room. It might be a bit big, but you'll probably find a belt in there, too."

Her smile resurfaced, and her eyes glowed. "Thank you, Daniel." She stood on tiptoe and kissed his cheek. Then she turned and dashed out the door.

Heat burned Daniel's face as he stared after her. The sensation of her soft lips brushing across his cheek lingered, making his heart gallop.

Why'd she have to go and kiss him like that?

❄

Less than ten minutes later, Annika brushed her hand down the brown wool split skirt and tried to smooth out the wrinkles. Daniel was right, the skirt was several inches too big around the waist, but she cinched it in with a leather belt.

Wrapping her blue knit scarf more tightly around her neck, she tucked the ends into the front of the jacket. Then she followed the frozen path to the barn.

Her stomach quivered as she pushed open the side door. The thought of getting on a horse again after so many years made her want to turn around and run back into the house, but she had to do this and prove to herself and Chase that she could be a rancher's wife.

Daniel stood in the center of the barn by a huge bay mare, tightening the cinch strap of the saddle. He looked her over with an appreciative smile and nodded. "That's better."

Heat flooded Annika's face. "I hope Chase won't mind my wearing Eliza's clothes."

Daniel frowned slightly then shook his head. "I think he'll be pleased to see you ride."

"I hope so." She sent him a shy smile.

"Come on over and meet Lady Jane." He patted the horse's neck. "She's a good horse, steady and gentle."

"She looks. . .big."

"She's actually one of our smaller horses."

Annika moved closer, but several feet still separated her from Lady Jane. She looked at the animal's big brown eyes, and fuzzy memories of her childhood in Sweden returned.

She'd loved riding before the accident, but weeks in bed recovering and her mother's anxious response had squelched her desire. She bit her lip, still hesitant to touch the horse.

"It's all right. Give me your hand." He gently guided her as she stroked the horse's neck.

She pulled in a slow, deep breath and relaxed.

Daniel was so kind and caring, always going out of his way to make her feel a part of the family. How many times had he sat with her, listening to her talk about how much she missed her sister? And every morning he carried in extra firewood to lighten her workload. He always seemed to be watching out for her, making her feel safe and protected. Even her two older brothers had never treated her with that much care and attention. Why didn't Chase treat her like that?

She cast a sidelong glance at Daniel. He had deep brown eyes, a fine straight nose, and a firm square jaw. He wasn't bold and flashy like Chase. Instead, he had a quiet strength that inspired her trust and confidence.

He looked down at her, and his hand stilled. His gaze grew more intense and hovered over her face, seeming to take in each detail.

Her stomach fluttered, and her heartbeat sped up. For one second she imagined he was going to lean down and kiss her.

She stepped back. What was she thinking? She'd always had an active imagination, but this was pure foolishness. Daniel didn't think of her like that. She needed to put a harness on her thoughts and keep them in line, or she was going to be very sorry.

She patted Lady Jane's side, willing her heart and breathing to slow down. "She seems very gentle. I'm sure I can ride her."

He cleared his throat. "All right." Then he helped her mount.

For the next hour, she held on tight and tried to follow Daniel's directions. He worked with her in the barn and then took her out to the corral. She focused on staying on the horse and tried not to let her thoughts drift back to those moments in the barn with Daniel. She was promised to Chase. She must not let her affections shift to Daniel. That would only lead to heartache and discomfort between all of them. Her fingers grew cold and stiff inside her gloves, but she didn't complain.

Finally Daniel called her over. "You look mighty chilled."

"I'm all right." But a big shiver raced through her, negating her words.

"We can work on it again tomorrow."

Annika gave in and nodded.

He led her back into the barn and helped her dismount. His warm hand lingered on her waist for just a moment. "You did fine. With a little more practice, you'll be ready to ride wherever you want."

"Thank you, Daniel." She didn't look at him. She didn't dare. Instead, she turned and hurried toward the side door, scolding herself all the way.

Just as she reached for the door, it flew open and smacked her in the face. Her head jerked back, and a thousand white stars exploded around her like the fireworks on

Independence Day, and then they rained down and burned into darkness.

At the sound of Annika's muffled cry, Daniel whirled around. She crumpled to the ground like a puppet whose strings had been cut.

Chase stood in the open doorway with his mouth agape. "What. . .what happened?"

Daniel ran to Annika, his heart pounding like a runaway train. He grabbed her limp hand and searched her pale face. A red bump on her forehead was already rising. He looked at his brother. "You big lout. Look what you did!"

Chase stared at her, his eyes wide. "Is she still breathin'?"

Daniel scowled at him. "Yes, but she's out cold."

"It's not my fault. I didn't even see her." Chase squinted at Annika, and his face grew red. "Hey, why's she wearing Eliza's clothes?"

Daniel scooped her up and clutched her to his chest, struggling to keep his anger under control. "You really are an idiot, you know that?"

"What? Why are you mad at me? I didn't knock her out on purpose."

Fire flashed through Daniel. "Don't say another word." He elbowed his brother out of the way and stepped through the door.

"Well, she shouldn't be poking around in my trunk and taking Eliza's things without askin'," Chase called after him.

Daniel clenched his jaw and carried Annika into the

house. As he passed through the kitchen, Song Li looked up from chopping carrots. His mouth dropped open.

"Get me some snow and a towel. Bring them upstairs."

The cook hustled off.

Mariah met him coming up the stairs and gasped. "What happened?" The look of fear in his niece's eyes tore at him.

"She'll be fine. She just hit her head." He prayed it was true as he laid her on her bed.

Mariah followed him into the room but hung back.

He gently brushed Annika's soft blond hair back from her forehead. The goose egg was growing bigger by the moment. "Go tell Song Li to hurry up with that snow."

Mariah turned and ran from the room.

He rubbed Annika's hand and called her name, but she didn't respond. A cold knot twisted in his stomach. What if that smack on the head was harder than he thought? What if she didn't regain consciousness? "Come on, sweetheart. Wake up." He rubbed her hand again and whispered another prayer.

Her eyelids fluttered, and she slowly opened her eyes. "Daniel," she whispered. "What happened?"

Relief washed over him. "You ran into the door and got knocked out."

She slowly lifted her hand to her forehead.

"Whoa, be careful. You've got quite a bump there."

Song Li bustled in carrying a bowl of snow. He scooped some into a cloth and handed it to Daniel.

"This will help keep the swelling down." Daniel placed the cold cloth on her forehead.

"Thank you," she whispered then closed her eyes, still looking pale.

Chase leaned his head in the door. "How's she doing?"

"She's awake," Daniel said, "but she's going to have quite a knot on her forehead."

Chase turned his hat around in his hand. "I'm sorry, Annika. I didn't know you were on the other side of that door."

Daniel huffed. Well, at least he got her name right this time. He motioned for his brother to come closer.

As Chase approached, Daniel nodded toward Annika, hoping he'd get the message he needed to take over her care.

Chase gave him a pained look but pulled up a chair and sat next to the bed.

Bile burned in Daniel's throat as he strode out of the room. His brother had better change his attitude and start treating Annika right, or he was going to take him out to the barn and teach him a lesson he'd never forget.

Then he remembered how he'd almost kissed Annika, and a load of guilt dropped onto his shoulders. He had no right to be upset with his brother. He'd just about crossed the line and kissed the woman promised to Chase.

A slight headache returned each day the following week to remind Annika of her run-in with the barn door. And if the headache was not enough, each time she looked in the mirror, the purple shadows under her eyes and lump on her forehead brought it all back.

Her hopes to look pretty for Chase were dashed, and she ducked her head whenever he came in the room. He had been a little more attentive after the accident, but soon he returned to spending most of his time outdoors or with the ranch hands, only coming in for meals and when it was time for bed.

Annika had almost grown accustomed to Chase ignoring her, but when Daniel started treating her in a similar fashion, she thought her heart would break. He'd given her one more riding lesson, but he'd kept his distance and avoided conversation. Whenever her thoughts drifted back to that time she thought he was going to kiss her, she scolded herself again and pushed those thoughts away.

She and Mariah retreated to their room for a good part of each day to work on their Christmas preparations in secret. But the truth was she didn't want to face either brother, and for totally different reasons.

"Tell me about St. Lucia Day." Mariah wrapped her doll in a small blanket Annika had made.

Annika smiled and looked up from hemming Mariah's new white dress. "Lucia was a young woman who lived in Rome about a hundred years after the time of Christ. She is remembered for her strong faith and the way she used to go out early in the morning to give food to the poor. She wore a wreath of candles on her head to light the way. In Sweden, people celebrate her feast day on December 13, and the oldest girl in the family portrays Lucia. She wears a white dress with a red sash and a wreath of candles on her head. And she brings special buns and coffee to her family early in the morning. It reminds us we can bring Christ's light and love into the darkest times."

"And I will be our Lucia!" Mariah announced, her face glowing.

"That's right. We'll make the buns this afternoon and get everything ready. Then tomorrow morning you will be Lucia."

Mariah jumped up and danced around the room with her doll.

Annika laughed, and memories came flooding back. She and Sophia had traded off being Lucia every other year. She would never forget the joy that filled her when her mother placed the wreath of candles on her head and handed her the tray filled with fragrant buns and steaming coffee.

Annika and Mariah spent most of that afternoon in the kitchen preparing the saffron-infused Lucia buns. Mariah stood on a stool and helped Annika knead the dough. After it rose, Mariah tucked raisins in the curls of each S-shaped bun. Their sweet fragrance filled the house as they baked.

While they waited for the buns to turn golden-brown, Mariah and Annika wove pine branches into a wreath for Mariah's head. Finding a way to secure the candles to the wreath stumped them for a few minutes. They finally decided to take Song Li into their confidence, and he found some wire to secure the four white candles to the wreath. Now everything was ready for their St. Lucia Day celebration.

The next morning, before the first rooster crowed, Annika

and Mariah climbed out of bed. With hushed laughter and whispered words, Annika placed the new white dress over Mariah's head and tied the red ribbon around her waist. Then they crept downstairs to the kitchen and stoked the fire to warm the buns and make coffee.

"Where did you put the wreath?" Mariah asked, her eyes reflecting the glow of the lantern on the table.

"In the pantry on the bottom shelf," Annika whispered.

Mariah tiptoed off to find it.

"Be careful," Annika called in a soft voice.

Mariah returned with the small evergreen wreath made from pine branches they had clipped and woven together the day before.

Annika placed it on Mariah's head. "There. You make a beautiful Lucia, but you have to promise to be calm and walk slowly."

"I will. I promise." She sneezed, and Annika passed her a handkerchief to wipe her nose.

Annika frowned slightly, hoping Mariah wasn't coming down with a cold. "Good girl." She kissed her cheek. "Remember, we want to surprise your father, but we don't want to burn the house down." She reached for the pan of warm buns on the back of the stove.

Footsteps sounded on the stairs.

Mariah gasped. "Uncle Daniel, go back to bed!"

Annika's hand stilled. My, Daniel certainly looked handsome, even with tousled hair and an unshaven face.

He stopped midway down the stairs and squinted at them through sleepy eyes. "What are you girls doing up so early?"

"It's St. Lucia Day!" Mariah announced.

He padded down the steps in his stocking feet and peeked over Annika's shoulder. "Mmm, those sure smell good."

"If you want some," Annika said with a teasing grin, "you'll have to go back to bed."

Daniel cocked his head. "Sounds like a fun idea, especially if you'll bring 'em to me."

Annika's cheeks flamed. She stepped away and took a plate from the shelf with a trembling hand. "I guess you can come upstairs with us if you're quiet."

Daniel grinned. "I'll be as quiet as a fox sneaking up on a hen."

Annika filled the coffee cups and set them on the tray with the buns. Daniel's gaze remained fixed on her, making her stomach flutter. "All right. We're ready."

"But what about the candles?" Mariah pointed to her wreath.

"We'll light those just before you go into your father's room."

Mariah nodded and rushed toward the stairs. Her wreath slipped, and she slowed.

"Let me take the tray for you." Daniel's fingers grazed Annika's.

Tingles raced through her.

"Annika, I—"

She looked up, and his tender gaze rested on her.

"Pssst!" Mariah leaned over the railing. "Come on! We've got to hurry before the sun comes up."

"We're coming." Annika's voice quivered, but not as much as her knees. Lifting her candle, she took a deep breath and followed Mariah upstairs.

Daniel walked just behind her, but she didn't look back. What had he intended to say? Had she truly seen affection in his eyes, or was her imagination playing games again? He was probably just grateful she'd helped Mariah with this fun surprise.

Mariah stopped by Chase's door, beaming an angelic smile.

Annika carefully lit the candles in her wreath, and a warm glow spread around them, pushing back the darkness.

"Here you go." Daniel gave Mariah the tray and opened Chase's door.

"Good morning, Papa!" Mariah walked toward the rumpled bed. "It's St. Lucia Day, and I made a surprise for. . ." Mariah stopped and stared.

Annika's stomach dropped. The bed was empty. Chase was gone.

Chapter 7

It took Annika well over an hour to calm Mariah. Through her tears, she complained of a headache and stomachache. So Annika climbed back in bed with her, holding her close while they both cried for all Mariah's broken dreams. Finally, Mariah fell asleep. Annika tucked the quilt around her and slipped out of the room.

Down in the kitchen, Song Li slowly stirred a pot of oatmeal and muttered in Chinese.

"Did Daniel and Mr. Simms go looking for Chase?"

"No. They go out to work. They say he not come back till he ready."

Annika slumped in the chair. Ready for what? To run the ranch? To marry her? Would he ever be ready?

How could this happen? Hadn't she prayed and asked God to lead her from the beginning? She'd stepped out in faith, trusting God, Mrs. Mayberry, and Chase with her future. And look where that had gotten her—stuck out in the middle of Wyoming, waiting to become the bride of a man who didn't want her. Was she that unlovable?

Tears stung her eyes, and she wearily pushed her long blond hair back from her face. She'd been so distracted this morning she hadn't bothered to braid it and wrap it around her head as she usually did. She must be a sorry sight.

But it didn't matter. Chase was gone, and so was her hope of being a bride, a wife, and a mother. What would she do now?

Song Li touched her shoulder. "Sorry Chase no like you."

Annika pressed her lips together. He meant to comfort her, but his words tore at her heart. It was true. Chase didn't love her. He didn't even like her. And there didn't seem to be anything she could do to change his mind.

Song Li huffed. "He foolish man. Very foolish."

Annika looked up.

Compassion flowed from Song Li's dark eyes. "You make good wife."

She swallowed against the tightness in her throat. "I'm not so sure about that."

He patted her shoulder. "Song Li see. Song Li know."

A strange moaning cry and a wild thrashing sound came from upstairs.

Annika stared at Song Li, trying to make sense of the noise. Then she turned and ran up the stairs, following the frightening sound. "Mariah?" She dashed down the hall and into their room.

Song Li's steps pounded right behind her.

Mariah jerked and thrashed wildly on the bed, eyelids fluttering.

Annika gasped and ran to her. "What is it? What's wrong with her?"

Song Li shook his head. "I not know. Maybe falling sickness." He bunched up the blankets around Mariah so she wouldn't hurt herself.

Her thrashing finally slowed.

Song Li laid his hand over her forehead. "So hot!" He pulled off the heavy quilt and fluffed the sheet to let in some cool air.

Annika dampened a towel in the washbowl and gently wiped Mariah's forehead, but her face was still flushed and burning. "Mariah?"

She moaned softly but didn't open her eyes.

"She need doctor," Song Li said in a hushed voice.

"I'll stay with her while you ride out to find Daniel and Mr. Simms."

Song Li's eyes grew large. "I not know where they go! I no ride horse! You go!"

Annika shivered. Should she try to find the men or ride to town? The road to Laramie was snow-covered and most likely impossible for her to follow. But she had to get help for Mariah. "Keep her as cool as you can."

Song Li nodded and wiped the girl's forehead.

Annika grabbed her cape and ran down the stairs.

Daniel shifted in the saddle and gazed out across the snowy

hills. A chilling wind blew through the valley. He pushed his hat down and tightened his scarf. That stopped the draft down his neck, but it did nothing to keep his mind from the troubles surrounding his family.

How could Chase take off again? There was no excuse for his brother's heartless attitude toward Mariah and Annika. He didn't deserve such a sweet bride or loving daughter.

Memories from the morning filled his mind—Annika dressed in her long white nightgown with that blue shawl wrapped around her shoulders and her long blond hair flowing down her back. Watching her prepare that tray and light the candles almost did him in. If Mariah hadn't interrupted him, he'd have told Annika exactly how he felt about her.

He had no idea if she had feelings for him. Well, there was that quick kiss on the cheek in the barn the day he'd agreed to teach her to ride, but that seemed more out of gratefulness than anything else. Could she grow to love him the way he loved her? If she did, what would his pa say? And what about Chase? Well, he was tired of waiting for his brother to follow through on the plan to marry Annika.

"Doesn't look like there are any more strays out this way," his father called. "Let's head back to the house and get something to eat."

Daniel nodded. With a gentle nudge of his knees, he urged his horse forward. As they reached the top of the next rise, he spotted someone riding their way.

His father tipped his hat back. "Who's that on Lady Jane?"

Squinting against the sunlight reflecting across the snow,

Daniel pulled in a sharp breath. "It's Annika."

"What's she doing riding out this far from home?"

Daniel kicked his horse to a gallop and rode toward her. His father followed.

"Daniel!" Her blond hair blew in the wind as she raced to meet him. The crazy girl wore no hat or gloves. Her cheeks were wind-whipped red and her hands practically blue.

"What's wrong?" Daniel called, reining in his horse.

"It's Mariah. She needs a doctor."

"What happened?" His father demanded, pulling his horse to a stop beside her.

"She had some kind of convulsion or seizure. She's burning up with fever." Tears flooded Annika's eyes.

"I'll ride to Laramie for the doc. You two head home." His father spurred his horse and galloped toward town.

"I was so scared. I didn't know what to do. Song Li said he couldn't ride for the doctor. None of the men were in the bunkhouse, so I saddled Lady Jane, but I didn't know the way to town. I followed your horses' hoof prints and prayed I'd find you—" Her voice choked off in a sob.

Daniel swung down from his horse and reached for Annika. She slid off the horse and into his arms. He held her close while she cried and shivered. "You're freezing."

She sniffed and looked up at him, tears lacing her eyelashes. "I didn't want to take time to dress any warmer. Oh, Daniel, I'm so worried about her."

"She'll be all right," he said, pushing the words past his clogged throat. "You did fine coming out here by yourself." He took off his scarf and put it over her head, covering her ears and crossing it under her chin.

"Come on. You can ride with me." He tied her horse behind his then boosted her up in the saddle. He sat behind her and pulled her back against him. "Put your hands inside and tuck them under your arms."

With one arm wrapped around her, he held her close and rode toward home. Annika soon relaxed against him, and he breathed in the sweet scent of her hair. At last the ranch house and barn came into view.

Daniel rode up to the house and dismounted, then helped Annika down. He tied the horse to the railing and followed Annika inside. "Why don't you warm yourself by the fire? I'll check on Mariah."

Annika headed for the stairs. "I'll be fine."

They found Song Li in the bedroom hovering over Mariah.

Lines creased Song Li's brow. "You bring doctor?"

"Pa went for him." Daniel took off his hat and leaned over his niece. "Mariah?" But she didn't answer. His stomach clenched, and he shot Annika a glance. "How's she been, Song Li?"

"She not talk. Fever still high."

Annika touched Mariah's forehead and nodded. She drenched the cloth in water and gently wiped the girl's face and neck. "Song Li, can you dump that water and refill the pitcher?"

He grabbed the bowl and pitcher and fled the room.

Annika looked up at Daniel. "We need to pray."

He nodded and bowed his head, but his throat felt too

tight to speak. Annika slipped her hand in his, and new strength flowed through him. He pulled in a deep breath. "Father, we ask You to have mercy on Mariah. Please bring her fever down and heal her of this sickness."

Annika squeezed his hand. "Father, please watch over Mariah. Bring her back to good health. And help us trust You now and always. In Jesus' name, amen."

Through the next hour, Daniel paced the room, prayed, and watched Annika tenderly care for Mariah. Every few minutes he glanced out the window toward the road, searching for his father and the doctor. Surely he should've been able to reach Laramie and bring him back by now.

Finally, he saw three riders approaching. "Here they come."

Annika crossed to the window and looked out. She gripped the windowsill. "Chase is with them."

They exchanged a glance, and Annika returned to Mariah's side.

Emotions stormed through Daniel. Mariah needed her father, but he hated to see Chase return. He quickly shook off that selfish thought. It was better this way. As soon as Mariah was better, he'd tell Chase how he felt about Annika.

Chase pounded up the stairs. "Mariah!" He ran through the doorway and tore over to the bed.

Pa and the doctor followed him in.

"Oh, Mariah, I'm so sorry I wasn't here." His voice tore from his throat.

"Step aside now, Chase. Let me take a look at her," the doctor said.

Chase moved back and turned to Annika. "Pa told me how you rode out to find him. Thank you." He crushed her to him in a tight hug.

She slowly lifted her arms and wrapped them around him.

He held her close and rocked her slightly back and forth. "I'm sorry, Annika. So sorry."

Daniel stared at his brother holding Annika. His chest constricted, and he felt like a boulder rolled over him, crushing out his breath.

He clamped his jaw, then turned and walked out of the room. There was no way he could stay here and watch Chase take Annika and make her his own.

❄

Annika spent the afternoon nursing Mariah, trying to keep her as cool and comfortable as possible. But Mariah's condition didn't change. Chase came in for a few minutes every hour, and Mr. Simms checked in often. It wasn't until suppertime she realized she hadn't seen Daniel for quite a while.

As the room grew darker, she lit the lamp on the table.

Song Li brought her a plate of stew and corn bread. "You not eat all day." He scowled at her. "Eat now, or you get sick."

Annika took the plate and thanked him. "Where's Daniel?"

Song Li turned away and straightened Mariah's covers.

"Song Li, I asked you a question."

The cook spun around. "He go hunting."

"Hunting? In this weather?"

Song Li shrugged and hurried out the door, a guilty look on his face.

What was going on? Why would Daniel leave when Mariah was so ill?

She set aside the plate and checked Mariah once more. She was still warm but resting peacefully.

Annika hurried downstairs and passed through the quiet kitchen. Maybe Chase or Mr. Simms could explain where Daniel had gone. She heard the two men talking as she approached the sitting room.

"I'm sorry, Pa. I know I should've said something sooner."

"How can you just up and decide to marry some gal you met in town when you've got a bride out here at the ranch waiting for you."

Annika froze. Surely she'd misunderstood them.

"It wasn't my idea to bring Annika here. That was all your doin'. If you'd let me pick my own bride, we wouldn't be in this mess."

Annika gasped then strode into the sitting room. "I can't believe this. Who wrote the letters?"

"That would be me." Mr. Simms's moustache twitched. "I'm sorry. I thought when he met you, everything would work out fine."

Chase stared at her, a pinched expression on his face.

She grasped the back of the settee. "So you never wanted to marry me?"

He hesitated then shook his head. "It's nothing

against you. I've been courting a woman in Laramie since September."

Suddenly, Annika remembered the young woman who had spoken to Chase that day they'd gone into town.

"She's a real sweet gal. Her pa died last summer. He was a miner. She'd already lost her ma years ago, so she came into town looking for work."

His father groaned. "Don't tell me she works at the Silver Nugget!"

"No, she works at the café, but that's no life for her. We want to get married so she can live out here with me."

"Why didn't you tell me before?" Mr. Simms demanded.

Chase straightened. "Her name's Angelica Morales. She's Mexican."

Mr. Simms's face flushed. He turned away and braced his hand on the mantel.

"She's a good woman, Pa. I love her. It shouldn't matter where her parents came from."

Mr. Simms turned to Annika. "I never should've written those letters." He sighed and rubbed his forehead. "We'll buy you a ticket back to Chicago tomorrow. That way you'll be home by Christmas."

Annika stared at him. Home? She had no home in Chicago. She'd given up the room she and Sophia rented. Sophia and Lars lived in northern Illinois with another family until their parsonage could be built next spring. Her brothers lived in Sweden, and she had no money to pay her passage back to her homeland. Where would she go? What would she do?

Chapter 8

Daniel trudged through the snow to a small hunting cabin halfway up Grier's Peak. He and Chase used it each fall when they hunted elk, antelope, or whitetail deer, but he'd never come up this late in the year. He wouldn't be here tonight if there was anywhere else he could go to get away from Annika and Chase.

But leaving the ranch didn't blot out the image of Chase taking Annika in his arms. That tormenting memory sent a searing pain through him each time it returned.

"Why, Lord? Why did I fall in love with Annika when she was promised to my brother?" He struggled against the unfairness of it as he built a fire and tried to warm his hands.

It wasn't right. Chase would crush her spirit and heap a load of burdens on her shoulders unless he changed. Closing his eyes, Daniel clasped his hands while he wrestled with his conflicting feelings. He had to stop thinking of himself and how he hated to lose Annika. If he truly loved her, it was time he put her needs first.

He bowed his head. "Oh Lord, for Annika's sake, help Chase become a better man and a loving and faithful husband. Protect her and bring her all the love she deserves."

A sense of calm settled over his soul. He'd won the first battle, though he knew many more would come.

He could never stay at the ranch and watch Annika and Chase together. It would be too hard. He'd have to head west and make a new life far from Annika and the rest of his family.

❄

Song Li burst into the sitting room. "Come quick! Mariah wake up."

Annika hurried upstairs with the men right behind her. As soon as she entered the bedroom, she could see that Mariah's coloring looked better.

Chase rushed to the bedside, nearly knocking Annika out of the way. "Oh, darlin', are you feelin better?"

"Papa!"

"That's right, darlin. Your papa's here, and he's never leaving you again."

Mr. Simms and Song Li huddled around, while Annika stood back, no longer feeling a part of the family. But Mariah called for her.

Song Li brought a bowl of broth, and Annika tenderly fed it to her. They left Mariah in her care, and not long after, the girl settled back in bed and fell peacefully asleep.

Annika's eyes burned as she tucked the blanket around Mariah. Would Chase's new wife continue teaching her to read? Would she help her learn to knit or sew or bake cookies? Who would help her finish the Christmas gifts?

And what about Daniel? Mr. Simms and Chase had no idea where he was hunting or when he would return. As she thought of never seeing him again, she felt like a flower crushed in the road by a hundred wagon wheels.

Oh Lord, this is too much to bear. Please carry it for me.

With an aching heart, she lifted the lid of her trunk and began packing. They'd leave the ranch tomorrow morning by nine so she could catch the ten-thirty train headed east. Heaven only knew what would happen to her then.

❄

The jingle of sleigh bells filled the air as Annika and Mr. Simms sped down the road toward Laramie.

Mariah had begged to go along and see Annika off at the station, but Chase felt it would be too upsetting for her, especially since she was still recovering. So Mariah and Annika said a tearful good-bye at the ranch. Chase and Mr. Simms stood nearby looking grim. Song Li cried and fled the kitchen, clutching a dishtowel to his mouth.

She stared across the snow-covered landscape feeling as numb and frozen as the stream they'd just crossed. So much had happened in the last twenty-four hours that she could barely take it in.

How could she be leaving Wyoming? The thought of returning to the crowded, busy city weighed her down, but not as much as leaving without saying good-bye to Daniel. If only she could have seen him one more time.

Mr. Simms flicked the reins, and the horses picked up their pace. He glanced up at the overcast sky as they entered Laramie. "Looks like we're in for some more snow."

Annika lifted her face as the first few flakes drifted down in a lazy dance then flew past the sleigh. She pulled her coat more tightly around her, trying to keep out the cold wind.

Mr. Simms rounded the corner and approached the train station. "Whoa, now," he called to the horses, and the sleigh glided to a stop. They climbed down, and Mr. Simms made arrangements for her trunk. They walked inside, and he purchased her ticket.

In five days she'd be back in Chicago. What would she do then? Who would take her in? Where would she find a job? A shiver passed through her, and she gripped her bag.

Annika glanced toward the windows. "You don't need to stay. I can wait in the station until the train comes."

Mr. Simms's silver brows dipped. "I wouldn't feel right leaving you here alone."

"I'll be fine." The truth was she didn't think she could take one more extended good-bye.

"Looks like the storm is picking up. I suppose I should head back."

Annika nodded, her throat feeling tight and dry.

He removed his hat and looked at her with sorrowful eyes. "I'm truly sorry for the way things turned out. I just wanted to help Chase. I hope. . ." He stopped and cleared his throat. "You're a sweet girl, Annika. You deserve a good husband who'll love you and take care of you."

"It's all right," she said, forcing out her words. She thought of Mariah and how much she loved her. "A parent will do just about anything to help a child."

He nodded and sent her a sad smile. Then he placed his hat on his head and walked out the station door.

Annika sank down on the bench and blinked back her tears. Now she was all on her own.

Chapter 9

Daniel rode to the top of the hill and reined his horse to a stop. His heartbeat kicked up as the barn and ranch house came into view. Gripping the reins, he debated his decision a few more seconds. Should he ride on past and avoid the pain of seeing Annika with Chase, or should he stop and say his final good-bye to his family?

He shook his head and huffed out a disgusted breath. He couldn't put them through the same worry they'd experienced when Chase up and left without a word. How could he think of heading west without knowing Mariah was on the mend and Chase was finally treating Annika as he should?

He spurred his horse to a gallop and headed for the house. When he walked inside, he found the sitting room empty. He straightened his shoulders and entered the kitchen.

Song Li looked up from stirring a big pot on the stove. He nodded to Daniel, his expression somber.

Chase sat at the table drinking a cup of coffee, but Annika was nowhere in sight.

"Welcome back," Chase said. "How was the hunting?"

"Not good." Daniel shook his head. "How's Mariah?"

"Better. Her fever broke last night. Doc says she needs to stay in bed, but it's not easy keeping her there." Chase chuckled and took another sip of his coffee.

Daniel glanced toward the steps. "Is Annika upstairs with her?"

Chase's smile faded, and he exchanged a wary glance with Song Li.

"What?" Daniel's gut clenched. "She's not sick, is she?"

"No." Chase stood and put his coffee cup in the sink.

"Well, where is she?"

Chase turned and faced him. "She's on her way to Laramie to catch the ten-thirty train to Chicago."

"What! You're sending her back?"

"That's right." Chase snatched his hat off the table and jammed it on his head.

Daniel grabbed his arm. "But you're supposed to marry her!"

"I can't. I met a gal in Laramie, and I've been courting her since September." Chase stepped back, as though he expected Daniel to take a swing at him.

Daniel's jaw fell slack. "You're not marrying Annika?"

He shook his head. "I know you and Pa want me to, but I can't do it. I love Angelica. We're getting married as soon as Pa settles down and gets used to the idea."

Daniel stared at Chase for a second, and then his face

split into a big grin. He gripped his brother's shoulders. "You just made me the happiest man in Wyoming!" He turned and dashed toward the back door.

"Hey, where are you going?" Chase called.

"To Laramie! I've got to beat that train!"

"But you'll never get there by ten thirty."

Daniel jumped on his horse. "Watch me!"

Annika sat on the hard wooden bench and stared at the huge snowflakes swirling past the station window. Her thoughts drifted back to the ranch. Was Mariah still improving, or had her fever returned? Was Chase spending time with her, or had he left her alone in her room? Surely now that he'd revealed his reason for spending so much time in Laramie, he'd be more open with his family and give Mariah the attention she longed for.

Please, Lord, let it be so. She needs her father's love so much.

Her thoughts shifted to Daniel, and her heart grew heavier. Was he safe and warm? Had he returned from his hunting trip? Was he sorry she'd left? Would he miss her even a little? Tears clogged her throat, but she refused to let them fall. Instead she swallowed and clasped her hands tightly in her lap.

The truth was clear now. She loved Daniel. But she'd never know if he returned her affection. She'd be back in Chicago soon, and Daniel would return to his life on the ranch. Chase would bring his new wife home, and they'd all settle in together and forget about Annika. She'd be just an uncomfortable memory—that mail-order bride who'd arrived unexpectedly and been sent home when no one wanted her.

A terrible pain stabbed her heart, and she squeezed her eyes shut.

The stationmaster cleared his throat as he stepped out from his office. "The train should be here any minute. It's running a little late because of the snow."

Annika lifted her head and thanked him, but her voice came out in a choked whisper.

He nodded and sent her a concerned glance, then crossed the room to add coal to the stove. "This storm looks like a bad one. But don't worry. The train will plow right through. You'll be back in Chicago before you know it."

That was exactly what she was afraid of.

The station door burst open. "Annika!" Daniel strode in, snowflakes covering his hat and shoulders.

She gasped and rose on trembling legs. "Daniel. . .what are you doing here?"

He rushed across the room and took her in his arms. "Thank the Lord you're still here." His voice was rough with emotion.

Her tears finally overflowed. He'd come all this way in the storm just to say good-bye. But now that he was here, how could she ever make herself get on that train and leave him. She stepped back and looked up at him with a trembling smile. "Thank you for coming. I didn't want to leave without saying good-bye."

"Good-bye?" He stared at her. "No, please, don't go."

"I can't stay. Chase is marrying someone else."

Daniel clutched her shoulders. "Then stay and marry me."

Annika stilled. "What?"

He took hold of both her hands. "I love you, Annika Bergstrom. I have from the first day you stepped off the train, but I. . ." His voice choked off, and he looked at her through glistening eyes.

"Oh, Daniel." She flung her arms around his neck.

Laughing, he picked her up and spun her around. "I take it that means you'll stay and marry me?"

She nodded, still struggling to believe the love shining in his eyes. "Yes, Daniel! Yes!"

Chapter 10

C hristmas Day arrived bright and clear with a fresh snowfall covering the ground.

Inside the Simms's house, happy preparations gave way to a merry celebration. Mariah wore her St. Lucia dress and served buns and coffee to the family early that morning.

A happy glow filled Annika's heart as she lit the candles around the house and on the small pine tree they had decorated with dried fruit, straw figures, popcorn, and cookies.

After breakfast Mr. Simms read the Christmas story as they all sat by the fire. Then Annika and Mariah gave handknit scarves to each of the men. Chase delighted Mariah by giving her a beautifully illustrated book titled *Young Folks Christmas Book*. Song Li gave the family a Chinese tea set.

Daniel presented Annika with a lovely gold locket. Her heart nearly burst with joy as he fastened it around her neck.

In the early afternoon, Chase brought Angelica Morales to meet the family. Her dark laughing eyes and warm smile delighted everyone, even Mr. Simms. She presented each person with a little tin of homemade cookies.

Angelica gave Mariah a little doll she had fashioned for her. Mariah promptly named her Angel and carried her everywhere, even seating her at the table for Christmas dinner.

"This is the nicest Christmas we've had in a long time." Daniel winked at Annika then slipped his hand into hers under the table.

Her stomach fluttered, and she smiled at him. What a blessing to be chosen and loved by such a fine man.

"It certainly is," Mr. Simms added. "The best part is seeing everyone together around the table." He smiled at Chase and Angelica, then at Annika and Daniel. Finally, his warm gaze rested on Mariah. "Merry Christmas, everyone. Let's pray."

Annika bowed her head and held tightly to Daniel's hand.

"Dear Heavenly Father, we thank You for Your kindness and goodness to our family. Thank You for healing Mariah and for bringing such fine wives for my sons. You've blessed us, and we're grateful. Help us remember the best gift of all, Your Son, Jesus. Let us welcome Him into our hearts today and always. Amen."

Annika lifted her head and glanced around the table, basking in the knowledge she had a special place in the family now. She looked across at Angelica, and they exchanged a smile. Right then, Annika made up her mind to do all she could to help the young woman feel accepted and welcome.

Mr. Simms shook out his napkin. "Well, what are we waiting for? Song Li, bring on the feast!"

The cook carried in a big platter of glazed ham. Soon bowls of mashed potatoes, green beans, beets, spiced plums, and applesauce covered the table. Laughter and lively conversation filled the air as they enjoyed the special meal.

When it was time for dessert, Annika brought in a big bowl of rice pudding sprinkled with cinnamon. "This is a special Swedish tradition."

Chase frowned. "It looks like rice pudding."

Angelica's eyes flashed, and she nudged him with her elbow.

"Well, it is rice pudding, but there's a surprise in someone's bowl," Annika said as she passed them around the table.

Mariah's eyes grew large. "What is it?"

Annika's cheeks grew warm. "There's an almond hidden in the pudding, and Swedish tradition says whoever finds it will marry soon."

Mr. Simms chuckled. "Well, eat up, and let's see who gets the prize!"

They all dug into their bowls, while Chase and Daniel teased each other about finding the almond first.

"I'm too young to get married," Mariah said, "but I sure like this pudding."

Annika laughed then crunched down on the almond. "Oh my. . .I got it!"

Laughter and cheers rose around the table.

Daniel grinned and lifted his coffee cup. "Here's to my beautiful Christmas bride. Almond or no almond, we're getting married next Sunday." Then he leaned closer and kissed her tenderly. "Merry Christmas, sweetheart."

His kiss left her breathless. "Merry Christmas," she finally whispered. Then, with her heart overflowing, she lifted a prayer of thanks to God for His faithfulness.

All the time, even when she couldn't see it, God had been working on her behalf, bringing everything together to give her the desires of her heart—a loving husband and wonderful family.

What an amazing blessing—what a wonderful plan.

Carrie Turansky lives in central New Jersey with her husband, Scott. They have been married for over thirty years and have five young adult children and three grandchildren. Carrie leads the women's ministry at her church, teaches Bible studies, and enjoys mentoring younger women. When she is not writing or spending time with her family, she enjoys reading, gardening, trying out new recipes, and walking around the lake near their home. Carrie and her family spent time in Kenya as missionaries, giving them a passion for what God is doing around the world. Carrie has authored several novellas for Barbour and two novels for Steeple Hill Love Inspired, including her latest release, *Seeking His Love*. She enjoys hearing from her readers. You may contact her through her Web site: www.carrieturansky.com.

THE PRODIGAL GROOM

by Vickie McDonough

For this my son was dead, and is alive again;
he was lost, and is found.
And they began to be merry.

<small>LUKE 15:24</small>

Chapter 1

Christian woman seeks an honorable Christian man
to marry. I'm eighteen with brown hair and dark
brown eyes, 5'4", thin and prefer to live in a town.
Can cook, sew, and clean.
I have no dowry, but I'm a hard worker and
can read, write, and converse well.

Council Bluffs, Iowa, November, 1882

That one, right there. She's the one I want."

Jolie Addams looked up from the sweet face of the baby she'd been rocking and found a gnarly finger belonging to the orphanage's benefactor pointed in her direction. She swallowed hard and clutched the child closer to her bosom. Why would Lloyd Richter, a man old enough to be a great-grandfather, want the seven-month-old orphan?

"Miss Addams"—Florence Tuttle, director of the Council Bluffs' Foundlings' Home, peered over the top of her spectacles at Jolie—"put the child in her bed and come to my office immediately."

Jolie rose and watched Miss Tuttle and Mr. Richter meander away, as the orphanage director updated him on the recent additions to the home. With twenty-seven children, the home was near bursting at the seams. Miss Tuttle had reminded Jolie numerous times that she'd have to leave the orphanage she'd grown up in once she turned eighteen, but she had hoped to make herself so useful that the woman might keep her on as a worker.

Her sigh lifted little Deborah's wispy blond hair. Jolie tucked the baby in her bed for her nap and covered her with a blanket. She glanced around the infant ward, making sure all seven babies were sleeping, and then she tiptoed out. They wouldn't miss her for a short while. She sincerely hoped that Mr. Richter didn't want to adopt Deborah. The contented child with an easy smile filled an empty place in Jolie's heart, and she'd dread seeing her leave, especially with that creepy, old man.

Her hand trembled as she knocked on Miss Tuttle's door a few minutes later. The dreary hallway mirrored her mood. Hard as it was to lose one of the youngsters she'd grown to love, she couldn't begrudge any a chance for a normal life with parents who adored their child. But *Mr. Richter*?

"Enter," Miss Tuttle's harsh voice ordered.

Jolie had been in the director's office only a few times, and each time she'd left in tears. The first time had been the day her father dropped her off after her mother had died trying to birth Jolie's only sibling. The last two times had been to receive punishment for not cleaning as thoroughly as Miss Tuttle thought she should.

Jolie stood immobile in the doorway to Miss Tuttle's office, unable to get her feet to obey her mental command to move. Her whole body quivered, but not from the chilly room.

"Come on in, Miss Addams, and have a seat."

Mr. Richter had settled into one of the two chairs sitting in front of Miss Tuttle's desk. His leering eyes followed her, making her feel dirty. Why was he gawking at her?

She scooted around the far side of the chair so as not to have to squeeze between them and be close enough that the man could touch her. Perching on the edge of the seat, she held her hands tightly in her lap.

Miss Tuttle looked at some papers on her desk then glanced up. "As you well know, most girls leave the orphanage by age sixteen to marry or find employment. You'll turn eighteen at the end of November and can no longer stay here. Of course, you must be gainfully employed so you can support yourself and not be a burden on the community."

Jolie's heart crimped. "I'm a burden?"

"Hmm, well, all you orphans are a huge responsibility." Miss Tuttle said *orphans* as if it were a nasty word.

Jolie sifted through her confusing thoughts. She hadn't asked to be an orphan. And hadn't she earned her keep by working from sunup to well past dark? Hadn't Miss Tuttle earned a salary for heading up the children's home? And what did Jolie's age have to do with Mr. Richter adopting Deborah?

She peeked sideways and caught him watching her. His upper lip lifted into more of a snarl than a grin, revealing crooked yellow teeth and crinkled lips. He smelled of medicinal liniment. White hair hung out from his nose, and the hair on his bushy eyebrows looked an inch long. Liver spots dotted his wrinkled skin. Bile seared Jolie's throat, matching the burning in her stomach.

Miss Tuttle ran her tongue over her upper teeth and made a sucking noise, drawing Jolie's gaze back to her. "Mr. Richter is in need of another housemaid and has requested your services. Pack your things. You leave with him today."

Jolie's mouth dropped open, but she quickly snapped it shut. Her heart stampeded, and she gripped the arms of the chair with white fists. "W—what happened to Eloise? Isn't she still Mr. Richter's maid?"

Miss Tuttle's mouth swerved upward to one side. "Miss Flannery is no longer working at the Richter Estate. You will take her place."

A fog surrounded Jolie's head. She was to leave? Today? "B—but what about the babies? If I go suddenly, they'll all be distraught and will cry, and you know how that disturbs you."

"Hmm. . .that is true. I suppose you'll need to train someone to take your place." Miss Tuttle rested her chin in her hand with the index finger framing her cheek. Her eyes lifted upward, and her mouth pulled up on one side. "I suppose Helena will do. I'll give you a week to train her."

Jolie's mind raced. "I. . .uh. . .need more time. There's

much involved, and the babies need to get familiar with her."

"Now see here. I'm in need of a maid right away." Mr. Richter rapped his cane on the floor.

Miss Tuttle studied the man. "Yes, I'm aware of that. Perhaps you could find some temporary help by some other means."

Mr. Richter scratched his balding head. "I suppose I could do that, although it is quite inconvenient."

Miss Tuttle nodded, and her gaze swerved back to Jolie. "Miss Addams, I'll give you until your birthday to train Miss Carver to take your place with the infants, but on that day, you'll be expected to move to Mr. Richter's estate."

"W–what happened to Eloise?" Jolie remembered Eloise crying in the night because she was being sent to work for Mr. Richter. She'd been afraid and uneasy to leave the children's home, but Jolie figured that was a normal reaction to such a big change in her life. Now, she understood what Eloise had felt. Something wasn't right about the wealthy man sitting beside her. Yes, he donated large sums of money to keep the orphanage running, but one young woman after another had gone to work for him and was never heard of again. She swallowed hard and stared out the large picture window, the gloomy room's only redeeming quality. What had happened to her four friends who'd worked for Mr. Richter over the past few years?

Miss Tuttle waved her thin hand in the air. "Never you mind about her. The girl's work was. . .unsatisfactory, but I'm sure you will do much better."

Mr. Richter cackled and bounced his head, sending chills

charging up Jolie's spine. She'd never work for this man. She had several weeks to come up with another plan, but the one she'd already set into motion was her best option. "May I be dismissed, ma'am? I don't like to leave the little ones alone too long."

Miss Tuttle nodded, and Jolie shot to her feet. "Just you be ready come your birthday. Mr. Richter will send a carriage to collect you."

Jolie nodded and hurried from the room without looking at the man again. Still trembling, she peeked in on the sleeping babes and then scurried upstairs to the large room where the older girls slept. With the school-age children in class at the local schoolhouse and the few other older girls engaged in their duties, nobody was in the bedchamber.

Jolie pulled out a loose brick behind her bed and stuck her hand in the small cavity she'd discovered one night. She removed two letters from the wall and held them to her chest. They were her only hope for a new life, and though she'd wavered in her decision, her mind was now made up. She'd written to Mrs. Mayberry's Matrimonial Society for Christians of Moral Character, offering herself as a mail-order bride.

Rebekah, a close friend who'd gone to work for a kind widow, had mailed the letters for her and received the response. Miss Tuttle would never have allowed Jolie to communicate with Mrs. Mayberry. The first letter she'd received gloriously stated the benefits of using such a screening society. Only the most upright gentlemen were allowed to solicit for brides. Most lived in Western states and were ranchers or businessmen looking to marry and raise a family.

She shuddered. How could one marry a stranger? What if he turned out to be someone like Mr. Richter? Her stomach swirled at the thought. And yet, wouldn't the unknown be better than being in that slimy, lecherous old man's clutches day after day?

Spreading out the crumpled letters, she reread Mrs. Mayberry's scrolling script. She listed four men who were looking to marry: two California ranchers, a widower with three small children who lived in Wyoming, and a store owner from Nevada. Such faraway places, and yet the thought of traveling out West tickled her adventure bone.

She'd never been around animals of any kind, especially big ones, such as cows and horses. She scratched through the ranchers' names and stared at the other two. A man with children or a store owner? She loved children. But was she ready to be a mother? She slowly circled the store owner's name—Hiram Peavey. Maybe if she married him, he'd let her have nice things—a ready-made dress and new shoes. And even if he didn't, she'd surely help him out at the store and would get to handle all those lovely things. She drew another circle around his name. At the very least, she'd be married, tending her own home and not someone else's.

Jolie stood and walked to the window, staring down at the bare yard where the children too young to attend school were raking leaves and stacking kindling. She could do this. Marrying a stranger was preferable to working for Mr. Richter. Her gaze lifted to the heavens. *Lord, show me what to do. Mr. Richter frightens me half to death. Surely, it's not Your will for me to work for him. Is marrying this store owner Your way of escape?*

She watched the children below, working, toiling, instead of playing like three- and four-year-olds should. All her life she'd worked hard, scrubbing dishes, raking leaves, weeding gardens, and tending orphans. Was it too much to hope to have a place of her own?

December, 1882

Clay Jackson studied the young woman sitting across from him on the stagecoach.

When they'd first left Elko, Nevada, she'd tried to read but had soon given up. The stage bounced and jostled so badly on the rough trails that the woman had a hard time staying on her seat, much less keeping a novel steady. Every once in a while her big, brown eyes met his, and she'd turn away, a becoming pink coloring her cheeks.

"I'd offer to sit beside you and help you hold on, but I doubt you'd agree."

Her eyes widened, and her gaze darted away like a spooked hummingbird.

He chuckled and was tempted to tease her some more, but he was a changed man. Given another day and time, alone with a pretty young woman like her, he'd have pressed his interest. But no more. He lifted his chin and stared out at the barren countryside. God had come into his heart and changed his life. He wasn't the wild child who'd left home three years ago. He was a new man. He only hoped his father would give him a second chance like his heavenly Father had.

He glanced at the woman again and decided she couldn't be all that old. He doubted she'd even reached her twentieth birthday. Why would she be traveling alone out here in the wilds of Nevada?

"My name's Clay Jackson."

She flashed him a half-smile and dropped her gaze.

"We haven't even reached the midway point yet. It'll be a long trip without conversation."

"You mean it will take another six hours? Why, we won't even arrive in Cedar Springs before dark."

"Probably not, since the sun sets so early these days."

She pulled her worn travel coat tighter. "But how can the stage travel at night?"

He shook his head. "Normally, it can't."

She opened her mouth and shut it several times. "But. . . nobody told me that. I can't—uh, I can't stay alone overnight with. . ."

Strange men. He finished her sentence in his mind. "I said normally it couldn't, but I wouldn't worry none. There's a full moon tonight, and by the time the sun sets, we'll be close to town. We should make it fine."

He hoped for her sake they did. Where was her father or escort? Didn't she know how much danger she was putting herself in traveling alone in this rugged country?

He shook his head. She wasn't his concern, but at least she had nothing to fear from him. He leaned back, pulled his hat over his eyes, and crossed his arms, determined to put the lovely vision from his mind. He had his own worries. Would Pa grab the nearest rifle and shoot him for coming home? Or would he do as the father in the Bible had done when his prodigal son had returned home—kill the fatted calf and rejoice?

Clay huffed. Not likely.

Chapter 2

Jolie breathed a sigh of relief when the man across from her covered his face with his hat and went to sleep. How he could rest with all the shaking and shimmying, she didn't know, but at least he no longer watched her with those engaging eyes.

Odd how his stare made her feel all warm inside, instead of frigid and frightened like Mr. Richter's had. Perhaps it had to do with his being a handsome man, with dark hair and eyes the color of blueberries. Her heart had startled when she'd first glimpsed their vividness.

She stared out the window at the barren Nevada landscape so different from the flatlands of Iowa. She'd been delighted to catch her first glimpse of the snow-covered mountains as she rode the transcontinental railroad west. She relished the pine-scented air, and even the birds were different here. She laid her head back like the other passenger, but it bounced and rocked to the left and back.

Weariness made her limbs heavy, but sleep wouldn't come. Her nerves were on fire.

Would Mr. Peavey be at the depot in Cedar Springs to meet her? Would he be young or old? Tall or thin? How would she recognize him? What would he expect of her?

She took a deep breath. "Stop being a ninny," she whispered to herself. The road leveled out and became smoother. Jolie laid back her head again, and this time it wasn't shaken half off her neck. Her eyelids closed, and her body relaxed.

A loud noise jolted her awake. At the blast of gunfire, she sprang to the window and peered out, her breath coming in quick bursts.

"Robbers!" The coach driver yelled.

"Fool woman. You want to get shot?" Mr. Jackson, now in her seat, yanked her backward.

She fell into his lap, arms flailing. "Unhand me."

He grabbed her arms, pinning them to her side. "Stop it. I'm trying to help."

A bullet ricocheted off the doorframe, sending splinters of wood flying. Her captor threw her to the dirty floor between the seats. Gunfire erupted from inside the stage as Mr. Jackson fired his revolver at their attackers. She covered her head. The odor of gunpowder mixed with the scent of dirt and wood.

What had she gotten herself into?

The stage seemed to pick up speed, and Jolie was jostled in all directions, unable to regain her balance enough to even sit. Mr. Jackson stepped on her leg, and she jerked, nearly knocking him on top of her.

"Lie still," he snapped.

Shots fired all around. She peered up and saw light shining through a hole in the door. Glory be, it must have just missed her head. Would she even live long enough to meet her husband-to-be? "Father in heaven, help us."

"Amen," Mr. Jackson yelled.

His gun fell silent, and Jolie peeked up again. He wrestled to stay on the seat and reload his weapon at the same time. His bullets suddenly flipped out of his hand and showered down on top of her. The carriage bounced and shook as if a madman drove it.

"Hold on," yelled the driver.

Jolie glanced at the window. Trees whipped past in a blur, and her heart flew up to her throat. The horses' hooves thundered down the road, and the carriage creaked and groaned.

"Whoa! Whoa!" the driver yelled.

The floor slanted as the coach careened down a steep hill. Mr. Jackson slid off the seat and landed on top of her, pinning her down.

She pressed her hand against the door, trying to brace herself. The stage rocked viciously back and forth then gradually slowed and rolled to a halt. Jolie dared to breathe again. Dared to move. But she could hardly catch a breath or budge with Mr. Jackson's large body weighing her down. She pushed against his back, trying to lift him up, but he was too big. Too heavy. Why didn't he move?

"Mr. Jackson, could you please get off of me." She jerked her legs and shoved his shoulder, but when she got no response, she lifted her head up. A large red circle stained the left shoulder of Mr. Jackson's shirt.

"You folks all right?" the driver asked.

"I'm fine, but Mr. Jackson looks to have been shot. And I'm unable to move."

The coach creaked as the driver shook the door and finally jerked it open. He peered in, rubbing his scruffy beard. "Looks like you two had a rough ride."

"We've got to get Mr. Jackson out and see if he's still alive." Jolie tugged at her skirt, but it was firmly held in place by the man's body. "Are the robbers gone?"

The driver nodded. "Shot two of 'em, and the other rode off like he was chasin' the wind." The man shook his head. "They killed my shotgun rider, Fred. Don't know what they were after. I ain't hauling no payroll this trip."

He slapped his hat against his leg. "M'name's Bill, in case you was wonderin'."

"I'm Jolie Addams. Do you think you could get Mr. Jackson off my legs so I can check his wound?"

"Reckon I could do that." He put his arms under the wounded man's and pulled him out the door, dragging his feet behind. Jolie sat up and reached to help, but the unconscious man's feet dropped to the ground with a jarring thud. Mr. Jackson didn't even blink.

Fearing for his life, she hurried out of the stage and glanced around. Not so much as a house met her gaze. A light breeze whipped at her thin coat, sending a chill into her bones. At least the ground wasn't dampened with snow.

She turned her attention to Mr. Jackson, who now lay under the wide arms of a tall pine. Grimacing, Bill flexed his arm. He tugged his sleeve tight, and Jolie noticed a blood stain. "Oh, you're hurt, too."

He waved his hand in the air. " 'Tain't nothin'. Just got grazed a bit." He stood with his hands on his hips studying the area. "It's just about as far back to Elko as it is to Cedar Springs. And we got us a problem."

Jolie glanced up. "What kind of problem?"

"One horse has a gash on its leg, and another is limping. We could ride to town, but it's a far piece for you and him. Too bad he had to get himself shot. I'll have to go for help."

"Y—you mean you'd leave us here alone?" Jolie's gaze skittered around the tree-lined valley surrounded by tall, snow-capped mountains. "Aren't there wild animals out here?"

Bill shrugged. "Some, but they shouldn't bother you. I can leave my pistol if'n yer worried."

Jolie glanced toward the stage. "Mr. Jackson had one, but I think he dropped it when he got shot."

Bill strode toward the coach and leaned into it. He pulled out the gun and held it up. "Found it. Same caliber as mine. That's good." He removed some bullets from his pocket and loaded the gun then handed it to her.

She wrinkled her brow. "I don't know how to shoot a weapon."

Bill scratched his chin. "Just aim and pull the trigger. It ain't hard."

Jolie eyed the gun, doubting she'd have the nerve to shoot anything. "You wouldn't have a medical kit, would you?"

Bill grinned, his leathery face creasing at the sides of his eyes. "We do indeed, but there ain't much in it." He turned and limped back toward the stage.

Mr. Jackson moaned, drawing Jolie's gaze to him. She reached toward him then pulled her hand back. She'd never touched a man before, other than to allow one to help her onto the stage or up steps.

Bill returned and dropped a small weathered box beside her. He lifted the lid, and she peered inside. Just a few rolls of bandages, but that would save her from tearing up her only nightgown.

"I. . .uh. . .do you suppose you could help me get Mr. Jackson's arm out of his shirt?"

Bill nodded and did as requested, and then he stood. "He's gonna need a doctor. . .unless you can dig out that bullet yerself."

Jolie felt her eyes go wide and shook her head. "I'd only thought to bandage the wound in hopes of stopping the bleeding."

Bill scratched his chin. "I've gotta go fetch help."

Jolie tossed her loose hair over her shoulder and watched him stride toward the coach.

He climbed up and then back down with a canteen and a coat in his hand. He slipped the coat on and handed her the canteen. "You two will need this more'n me. I'll do my best to get back soon, but it may be morning. Once he comes to, y'all ought to get back in the coach. Might be a bit warmer than out here after the sun sets—and uh"—he rubbed his chin and gazed at her—"it could protect you from varmints, too. I'll unhitch the horses then head out."

A million questions formed in Jolie's mind as she laid down the canteen and gun Bill had handed her. He quickly unhitched the horses, but the stage driver was mounted and gone before she thought to voice any.

She glanced at her patient then looked around. She was in the middle of nowhere. Not a building in sight, only trees, shrubs devoid of their leaves, and dried, yellow grass. The only sound she heard was the wind swishing through the tall trees. They had no food or blankets, only some lukewarm water.

Her gaze lifted heavenward. "What do I do, Lord? Help us."

Clay fought the cobwebs and shadows, clawing his way toward the light. Toward the voice. He blinked, and a bright blue blur took shape. The sky?

His head ached, and his shoulder felt as if someone was holding a branding iron to it. He reached toward it, only to have his hand grabbed.

"Don't. You've been shot."

Aw, there was that voice again. The one that had led him back from the darkness. His blurry vision cleared, and he remembered the young woman from the stage. "How bad is it?"

She nibbled one side of her lip, causing his stomach to do strange things. Her big brown eyes looked worried, and he turned his head to see his shoulder. He tried to move his arm, and fingers of fire clutched him in their blazing grasp.

He ground his teeth together.

"I've. . .uh. . .tried to tend your wound, but it would be easier if you could sit up."

He nodded and pushed up with his good arm, clamping down his jaw to keep from crying out. She made haste, applying a fresh wad of cloth to his wound and then wrapping the bandage around his chest and over his shoulder. Her warm breath teased his neck, and this close, he could see gold specks in her brown eyes. She helped him back into his shirt, but when she went to button it, he swatted her hand away. "I can do it."

She sat back, looking hurt. Moving away, she reached for the canteen, allowing him time to fumble with his buttons until he got them fastened. "Would you care for some water?"

He stared at her, wondering who she was and where she came from. She hadn't told him earlier, before the attack. "What's your name?"

"Jolie Addams." Her lips turned up in a faint smile, and she held out the canteen.

Jolie—an unusual name, but it fit her. He took a long swig from the canteen and handed it back. She set it down beside a gun lying in the dirt—his gun. "Let me see that."

Surprise sparked in her gaze, but she picked up the weapon with her thumb and forefinger as if it were something vile. They just might need that gun before the night was over. He took it from her and flipped open the cylinder, noting the refilled cylinder.

Gazing around, he took in their surroundings. Three of

the horses grazed nearby, but the stage looked sound. They could spend the night in there and have some means of protection. "What happened to the driver?"

"He went for help," she called over her shoulder as she walked toward the coach, her long brown hair swaying behind her. Since she'd had it up before, he assumed she must have lost her hairpins in the accident. He watched her open the boot and rummage around in it, finally pulling out a worn satchel. She found a brush and a small tin box and then walked behind the stage.

"Don't wander far. There are dangerous creatures around these parts."

She didn't respond, but he watched underneath the coach and saw her stop.

He scooted over and laid his head against a tree. A stabbing pain shot through the upper part of his body every time he moved. A man needed to be healthy to work a ranch. How was he going to prove himself to his father now?

Chapter 3

Jolie patted her hair, feeling a bit more in control now that it was properly pinned up again. She helped Mr. Jackson to the coach and propped him against the side while she climbed in and set the canteen on the seat. She turned to assist him, but he frowned and ignored her outstretched hand. She stepped back but didn't sit, in case he needed her more than he thought. The man had lost a fair amount of blood, and from accidents the orphans occasionally had, she knew that made people unsteady.

He grabbed hold of the doorframe and hauled himself up. Grimacing, he held his left arm tight against his body and dropped into the seat. Sweat beaded his temple, and his breath sounded ragged.

"I. . .uh. . .should probably check your bandage."

He nodded and undid the top three buttons of his shirt.

Jolie peeked at the bandage and blew out a sigh. There

was some blood on it, but the patch wasn't saturated.

"You'd better close the shades to preserve what warmth there is in here. At this high elevation, December nights can be quite cold."

Jolie nodded and slid over to the window. Before she closed the final shade, securing them in the dark, she stared at the deep blue of twilight where the sun had already set behind a tall peak. Her hand trembled as she lowered the last shade.

What would Hiram Peavey say when he learned she'd spent the night in the wilderness alone with a man? Jolie sat on the seat across from Mr. Jackson, her whole body shivering. Her stomach grumbled, complaining of the lack of food. If only she'd thought to save a bit of her lunch for later.

"I know we're strangers, but you should sit over here. As cold as it will get, we'll need each other's body warmth. Did you find anything we could use for a blanket?"

Jolie touched her flaming cheeks. She shook her head then realized he couldn't see her. "No." She'd already helped him back into his jacket. "I have another dress we could use."

She heard what sounded like a snort on the other side of the stage.

"Get it, and come over here."

She slid across the wide seat and found her satchel in the corner where she'd put it earlier. Fishing around, she located her dress. That was the easy part. How could she sit so close to a stranger—and in the dark? Would he be a gentleman?

"You don't have to worry about me bothering you. Moving causes pain, and besides, I'm a Christian."

She'd heard stories of so-called Christian men who'd done horrible things but also knew of others who seemed kind, like the pastor where she'd attended church with the orphans. Jolie shivered on the cold leather seat. Though the temperature had seemed mild for winter when the sun was shining, she could already tell it was getting colder.

"C'mon, don't be shy." She thought she heard him pat the seat.

Taking a deep breath, she crossed the coach and sat down near the window. Cold air seeped in the sides of the shades, and she shivered.

Mr. Jackson chuckled. Jolie felt his hand grasp her arm and jumped. He grunted and tugged her toward him.

Her heart fluttered like the wings of a caged bird, and she fought the urge to flee. But the darkness and unknown outside of the coach equaled the fear of that inside. *Please help me, Lord.*

Once he'd tugged her up close, Mr. Jackson wrapped his good arm around Jolie's shoulders.

She sat stiff and trembled.

"I was serious. Don't be afraid of me, Miss Addams. I promise to be a gentleman."

As the heat of the man's body warmed her side, she began to see the sense of his suggestion and relaxed. The man smelled of leather and dust, and yet there was something appealing about it. Jolie held her dress against her chest and sat up straight, not wanting to relax her head back against his arm. Thinking was difficult with him so close. She spread the dress she'd planned to be married in over their legs and pulled her coat together tighter. If only she had buttons to fasten it shut, but she'd long ago used them to mend coats belonging to younger orphans.

"Why are you traveling alone?" he asked.

"I'm. . .uh. . .going to Cedar Springs—to get married."

"Ah, a mail-order bride, I presume."

She nodded then answered. "Yes, I am."

"Weren't there any intelligent men back where you lived?"

Confused by his comment, Jolie blinked in the dark, wishing they could open the shades and allow the full moon to shine in. "I'm sure there were, but I didn't know any men at all. I was raised in an orphanage."

❄

Clay winced. No wonder she was desperate enough to do something so drastic. In an odd way, he could sympathize with her. Hadn't he been an orphan of sorts the past three years, estranged from his father?

He relaxed his right arm against her stiff shoulders. No wonder she was so skittish. She'd probably never been close to a man before, and now she was in one's arms. Maybe if he talked, she'd relax. "My father owns a ranch just south of Cedar Springs. I've been gone three years and am returning home."

She was silent for a few moments; then he heard her take a deep breath. "Why were you gone so long? Do you live somewhere else?"

Clay clenched his jaw. Why hadn't he considered where

that trail would lead? "Let's just say we had a falling-out, and I left."

"My father left me at the orphanage in Council Bluffs, Iowa, when I was five, after my mother died."

His arm tightened around her at the forlorn sound of her voice. What kind of a father would abandon his child? "I'm sorry."

He felt her shrug. "It was a long time ago."

For a while she didn't say anything, but he could hear her breathing. He thought about how she looked. She wasn't a beauty. Her hair was a medium brown, just like his saddle, but those eyes—they drew him in, made him want to protect her. Now he knew why her clothes were so shabby. They were most likely someone's castoffs. Had she ever had a new dress? He fingered the one lying across his legs and noted the fabric was just as thin as the dress she wore. She'd freeze in the frigid Nevada winters in the thin fabric.

"Why did you leave home, if I might ask? I mean, I can't imagine having a home and leaving it."

The tremble in her voice made him pause. He'd had a home, a family, but had taken everything for granted. It took losing it all for him to realize that. He allowed himself to think of his older brother for the first time in a long while. He'd adored Clint, but unlike his brother, Clay couldn't seem to do anything right. He was more bookworm than rancher. "I guess it all started when my brother died."

Miss Addams gasped. "Oh, I'm sorry. You don't have to talk about it if you don't want to."

For some reason, sitting here in the dark with her, he

wanted to get it off his chest. He hadn't told anyone what happened, and though he'd given the burden to God, it still ate at him sometimes. Why not tell a woman he'd never see again after they were rescued? "Clint died trying to break a rogue horse. He was always my pa's favorite, because he was far better at ranching than me. I. . .uh. . .guess you could say I fell off the wagon after that."

The accident had been his fault and had broken Clay's heart. Somehow, he must not have saddled the mustang properly, and Clint broke his neck when the saddle came loose and he fell off. Clay laid his head back, remembering how he'd started drinking, gambling, and picking fights to drive away the pain—until his father finally told him to either stop his carousing or get out. Clay left.

"But you said you were a Christian."

"I am. Now. I sowed a lot of wild oats before meeting a man who set me on the straight and narrow."

"And now you're going back home. I will pray things go well with you and your father."

Her comment humbled him and also warmed his spirit, knowing she, too, must be a believer. "Are you warm enough?"

"Yes."

"Good. So, tell me, who are you marrying in Cedar Springs? Maybe I know him."

"He's a store owner—Hiram Peavey."

Clay's grip tightened on the woman as he remembered the cowardly, sniveling man. He couldn't believe the man had lasted through another three years of Nevada winters.

He was always whining and complaining, so much so, that folks dreaded having to buy supplies. But his was the only general store in town.

"Is something wrong? Do you know Mr. Peavey?"

He knew him all right, but what could he tell her? That the man would probably make her run the store and labor from sunrise to sunset while he tipped his cup at the saloon? That Hiram was a stiff-necked hypocrite who wouldn't want a woman who'd spent the night alone with another man, even if it was all perfectly innocent? Why, Lord? Why did You have to bring this sweet woman all the way here just to marry that scoundrel?

Chapter 4

J olie's shoulder bumped the stage driver's arm as the wagon jostled down the mountain road. Eyes closed, she lifted her face to the morning sun, finally feeling the warmth creep back into her body after the long night. Mr. Jackson had been the gentleman he'd promised, though his soft snores, occasional moans, and nearness had kept her from drifting into a deep sleep.

He groaned as the wagon dipped down and back out of an especially large rut in the road.

She twisted in the seat and stared down at his pale face. "How is he, Doctor?"

"I'm fine," Mr. Jackson growled.

Dr. Gates touched his patient's forehead and nodded. "He lost a fair amount of blood, but the bullet came out easy enough and there's no fever, so far. That's always a good sign." He smiled. "You did a real nice job tending his wounds, ma'am. You most likely saved his life."

Mr. Jackson grunted as if disagreeing.

"Thank you." She faced forward again and studied the wide valley that opened up before her. Mountains touched the sky on every side of them, but with this being December, the grass was dead and yellowed, and no wildflowers colored the barren land. Up ahead, she could see the makings of a small town. Weathered buildings promised civilization and food. And her husband-to-be.

"That there's Cedar Springs, ma'am. Ain't much of a town, but those of us who live in these parts are thankful we have it." Bill waved his hand toward the crop of buildings. "Used to be a big mining town, but much of the silver in this area has played out."

"Mr. Jackson mentioned there was a store. What else is there?"

Bill grinned. "Ol' Hiram Peavey was fit to be tied that you didn't arrive last night. He was all set to marry up with you right on the spot."

Jolie shivered. Now that she was getting close to marrying, her anxiety level was climbing faster than Todd Bennett could shinny up the pine tree in the orphanage's back yard. Would her husband be kind? Handsome? Would he think her plain? Boring? What if she couldn't abide him? What if he thought she was a burden to him? She swallowed hard. "Could you tell me a little about Mr. Peavey and his store?"

Bill nodded. "Ain't all that much of a store. Hiram sells tools, some canned food, coffee, of course. He's a strange little man. Mostly keeps to himself, except spending several nights a week down at the saloon."

Jolie's heart dropped. He was a drinking man? Mrs. Mayberry had assured her that she'd checked out Mr. Peavey's references and that he was an honorable, Christian man. Had he deceived the owner of the matrimonial society that she'd written to? But how could references be forged?

She nibbled the inside of her lower lip. What could she do if she found Mr. Peavey too repulsive and not the Christian man he purported himself to be? Had she come all this way for nothing?

The wagon rolled into town, and Jolie's heart sank further. Only a dozen structures, mostly dull, weathered gray, formed Cedar Springs. How could she live out the rest of her days here? She'd mostly stayed close to the orphanage and hadn't ventured around Council Bluffs since she never had money, but this town didn't even have a church.

A man standing in front of the barber/dentist office let out a whoop, and people poured out of the buildings, all looking at them. She wanted to be anywhere else in the world but here, and yet she'd accepted Mr. Peavey's money to travel to Cedar Springs, and by tonight she'd most likely be his bride. A shiver charged down her spine.

A medium-tall man with the frame of a broom handle pushed his way to the front of the crowd of dirty, bearded men. "Let me by. That there's my mail-ordered bride."

Jolie held her hand to her chest. Why, he had to be in his mid-thirties, and his pointed nose reminded her of a fox. What had she gotten herself into?

A picture of Mr. Richter formed in her mind, and she

strengthened her resolve. She could do this. She had no other choice.

The driver helped her to the ground, and needing something to do, she hurried around to the back and retrieved her satchel.

Mr. Jackson was sitting up, still looking pale in his tanned face.

"How are you feeling?" she asked.

He stared at her, his once-lively blue eyes now dulled with pain. "Like I've just busted a whole heard of mustangs."

"Well, at least you're home now and can rest." With the doctor on one side and her on the other, they helped him to stand.

Mr. Peavey sauntered past the wagon and stared at her then at Mr. Jackson. "Just what's going on here?"

"Hiram, you know Clay Jackson?" The doc looked at the two men.

Hiram nodded. "What's he got to do with my bride?"

"She saved his life. That's what."

Hiram paced in front of them. "I don't like that she was alone with him all night."

"Nothing happened," Jolie hurried to say. The whole crowd pressed in around them, and she didn't see a single woman. Just long-haired, bearded men in dirty clothes. Every man wore a stained hat, and the pungent odor of moldy onions wafted her way.

Her knees trembled, and her fingers on Mr. Jackson's arm shook. He lifted a hand and pressed it against hers as if reassuring her.

Hiram crossed his arms and shook his head. "Clay Jackson has a reputation as tall as a lodgepole pine. I ain't marrying no woman what spent the night with the likes of him." He spat on the ground. "I want a pure bride not a tainted one."

Jolie gasped and held her hand over her mouth.

Mr. Jackson glared at the man, standing nearly a head taller than Mr. Peavey. "Nothing happened, Hiram. We sat close to stay warm, and she tended my wound. That's all."

Murmurs resounded through the crowd, and Jolie heard the words, "bare chest" and "slept together." She backed up against the wagon, horrified that they believed the worst about her.

Hiram shoved his hands to his hips. "You owe me fifty dollars, Clay."

"What for?"

Mr. Peavey waved a boney hand at her. "For her. That's what how much I sent her for traveling expenses. I don't want no sullied bride. You can have her."

Heads nodded, and the murmuring grew louder.

"I'll take her if you don't want her," a black-haired beast of a man called out.

Jolie clutched the front of her coat. What would become of her?

The stage driver held up his hand. "Listen up. If Hiram don't want her, it's only fair that she marry Clay."

"What?" Both she and Mr. Jackson said in unison.

Shouts rang up. Someone yelled, "Go on, marry her, Jackson. Do right by her."

Jolie released his arm and sat back against the wagon. While she'd much rather marry Clay Jackson than Hiram Peavey, she hardly wanted a husband who was forced to marry her.

The roar of the crowd grew, and the people pressed in against them. For once, Jolie wished she was a weaker woman and could faint and make this nightmare disappear. What would become of her?

Mr. Jackson's jaw tightened, and he stood, albeit wobbly. "I'm a changed man now. I came home to patch things up with my pa, not to get married."

Jolie winced at his comment. A fat lot of help he'd be.

A shot rang out, and all eyes swerved toward the noise. The crowd parted to allow two men through. The man carrying the rifle had a husky build. His white hair was peppered with strands of black, but his neatly trimmed beard was all gray. A younger man, tall and slender with dark brown hair and kind gray eyes, followed.

"I'm Jake Hennings, the only lawman in this town. And this here's Reverend Marks. What's going on?"

Hiram started ranting. "That there's my mail-order bride, but she spent last night alone with Clay Jackson and doctored his bare chest. I demand Clay pay me the money I'm out 'cause I cain't marry her now."

The sheriff rubbed his beard and eyed each one of them. "Good to see you again, Clay. Is what he said true?"

Clay nodded and fell back against the wagon, his arm touching Jolie's. "I told them nothing happened, but no one believes me."

132

The sheriff turned his gaze on Jolie. "What have you got to say, ma'am?"

She swallowed hard, wishing she'd never written those letters to that matrimonial society. "He was shot, sir. I tended his wound to save his life. That's all that happened."

Hiram spat on the ground. "That ain't so. They cuddled together all night." He muttered a curse and started pacing again. "I'm out a passel of money."

The pastor's eyes were the only sympathetic ones in the crowd. Did everyone else believe she was a wanton woman?

The sheriff rubbed his jaw. "So, you don't want her, Hiram?"

He shook his head and curled up one corner of his mouth. "But I want my fifty dollars back."

Jolie reached into her handbag and pulled out the money she hadn't spent. "Here's fourteen dollars and some change. I'll pay back the rest as soon as I can find employment."

The whole crowd broke out in laughter, and she looked around.

"The only women's work in this town is at the saloon," a dirty man with a shaggy beard said. He fingered his whiskers and stared at her. "Then again, the Lucky Star could use a new female. Can ya sing?"

Jolie's cheeks flamed, but her chest ached. *Please, God, save me. I can't work in a saloon.*

Clay Jackson pushed to his feet again. "Now see here, Miss Addams is an honorable woman. I won't have you all talking bad about her."

The pastor stepped forward. "So, are you willing to marry her then?"

Jolie's gaze shot to Mr. Jackson's. He scowled at her until she looked away and stared at the dirt in the road. How had things gone so wrong?

❄

Clay ground his back teeth together. How had his homecoming turned into a forced wedding at the end of a shotgun? Neither he nor Miss Addams had done a thing unsavory. They were just trying to survive the cold December night.

The last thing he needed was a bride. But she looked so lost—so afraid—that his heart was tempted. And he bet she'd just given every coin she had to that weasel. He studied her again. She wasn't beautiful, but there was a wholesomeness to her. Would his father receive him better if he returned with a wife?

Foolish thoughts those were. He didn't even know if he'd have a home once he returned to his family's ranch. And if his father turned him out, he had no job and no means to support a wife.

The pastor awaited a response.

Clay looked around the crowd of rough men. Some were farmers or ranchers, but others were rough miners come down from the mountains for the weekend. If he didn't marry the girl, what would become of her in such a rugged town? Marrying her was the last thing he wanted, but he was a Christian man now. How could he walk away and leave her to the wolves. She was so young and naive. So innocent. A desire to protect her welled up within him. But was marrying her the right thing?

"We need your answer, Clay." The pastor's intense gaze compelled him to agree.

Clay found himself nodding his head, even though his heart wasn't in compliance.

Both the pastor and the sheriff grinned. "All right then, let's have a wedding."

Clay glanced sideways at the bewildered girl. What if she didn't want to marry him? "Don't you think you should ask Miss Addams if this is what she wants?"

The sheriff rubbed his beard. "Oh, uh, I reckon we oughta. So, ma'am, would you be willing to marry this man? Or would you prefer someone else?"

Her frantic gaze bore into Clay's and clawed at his heart. The poor thing was scared to death. She'd probably rather marry a fence post than him, but she gazed around the crowd and then slowly nodded.

"Great!" The pastor pulled a book from his jacket pocket. A Bible. "You two move closer together. You can stand, can't you, Clay?"

He gritted his teeth and pushed up from the wagon, the loss of blood making him weaker than a newborn foal. If only he hadn't procrastinated and had taken an early stage like he'd planned, then none of this would be happening. "I can."

Miss Addams stood beside him, looking like a hummingbird that would flit away at any moment. His heart went out to her. None of this was her fault. What must she be thinking?

They quickly repeated the vows the reverend spoke, and then he pronounced them man and wife. Mr. and Mrs. Clay Jackson. A unified cheer rang out from the crowd, and then it began to disperse.

Hiram continued to pace. He suddenly stopped and stared at Clay. "What about my money?"

Clay had always detested the despicable man, who was less than ethical and was only out to earn a coin. He could hardly believe Hiram had parted with enough money to buy a mail-order bride. He reached into his pocket and tossed two double eagles on the ground.

Hiram dove on them like a hawk on a mouse.

Clay turned to Bill. "Could I borrow your wagon to get out to Bar J Ranch? One of our crew can return it in a day or two."

The driver nodded. "I'll tell Hank over at the livery. Just return it to him."

Clay shook the man's hand.

"You reckon you can drive all the way to your ranch? I could go along if you need some help," Reverend Marks offered.

"I'll be fine, but thank you."

The reverend nodded his head toward Clay's bride. "Take good care of her. I feel in my gut that the hand of God had a part in all of this."

Clay turned to his wife, holding back a sarcastic huff. The waif's dark brown eyes reminded him of a spooked deer's. Something inside him gave way. He was married. This woman now belonged to him, and he'd made an oath before God to care for her. Was it possible God had actually thrown them together?

He shook his head, receiving a frown from his wife. Well, he sure hoped God had a home for them somewhere if his pa sent him packing.

Chapter 5

Jolie stared at the white-topped mountain in front of her, thankful that the ground they rode over wasn't snow-covered. These mountains weren't as steep and jagged as the Rockies, but rather flat or rounded with no trees.

The sun now shone directly overhead, but Mr. Jackson had made no mention of getting lunch before they'd quickly driven out of town. Nope. Her new husband had just climbed in the wagon with the doctor's assistance, and she'd tossed her satchel in the back and shinnied up the other side of the buckboard before he could drive off without her, which she was certain he would like to.

She rearranged her skirts, trying to grasp hold of the concept that she was married. No longer was she Jolie Addams, but Mrs. Clay Jackson. In spite of the rushed wedding, she liked the flow of her new name, Jolie Jackson. Peering sideways, she studied her husband. He was a handsome man with his hair, black and shiny as a raven's wing, and those teasing blue eyes that were now laced with pain. He hadn't shaved this morning, and the stubble on his cheek gave him a rugged, dangerous look.

They hit a rut in the road, and he grimaced.

"Would you like me to drive the wagon?" she asked.

His gaze skimmed over her, but it didn't give her the creeps that had crawled down her spine at Mr. Peavey's appraisal. "Do you even know how?"

She shrugged. "What's to know? You hold the reins and stare at the horses' rumps."

His mouth quirked up. "It also helps to know where we're going."

"Oh, well, you can direct me."

He tossed the reins in her lap, leaned back in the seat, and settled his hat over his eyes. Crossing his arms, with the good arm supporting the one in the sling, he slouched down as if he intended to nap. "Just stay on this road, and you'll come to a burned-out tree. Turn left and go a couple of miles, and you'll see the entrance to the Bar J Ranch."

Jolie stared at the wide valley. Not another person was in sight, other than her husband. The emptiness of it set her nerves on edge. Before she started on this journey, she'd always lived in the city, and she'd never dreamed America was so big. Just getting from Council Bluffs to Cedar Springs had taken several days of riding the train and then the stage.

A flock of slowly circling birds drew her attention. Vultures? Were there wolves out here? Bears? She swallowed hard. "W–what if I need a gun?"

"This is a peaceful valley, Miss Add. . .uh. . .Jolie. If you require a gun, just wake me up."

How many times would Mr. Jackson slip up before he remembered she was his wife? She halfway felt sorry for him. He hadn't asked for any of this. He'd been as much a victim as she, but he'd agreed to marry her, and for that she'd be eternally grateful.

She remembered the leering gazes of the men in town and shivered. *Thank You, Father, for rescuing me from that mob. Thank You for my husband. Please show me how to be a good wife.*

What did a wife even do? Cook, probably. Clean and do laundry. She was an expert at mending, but she knew nothing about caring for a husband. She peered at him again. What would he expect of her? Would he be kind? Cruel?

A lump lodged in her throat. Forcing such thoughts away, she studied the area. Spring had to be beautiful here, with multi-colored wildflowers freckling the bright green grass that was now yellowed and bent from December's chill. And the air smelled so much fresher, not tinged with the scent of coal from the trains or the many businesses in town. The openness of the valley both frightened and exhilarated her. Maybe she'd be free to discover herself here, instead of cowering to Miss Tuttle's every whim. At least she was free from Mr. Richter.

They traveled on for what seemed like hours, and she finally turned at the burned-out tree. Her throat grew parched, and her stomach complained like Miss Tuttle when breakfast was late. Up ahead, a large boulder jutted up from the ground like the tip of a mountain that hadn't had enough strength to break through the thick grasses. Bar J was painted on the side of it with an arrow pointing to the right. She steered the wagon in that direction, anxious to see her new home. Would it be merely a shack? Or a warm log cabin? *Please, Lord, not a soddy or a dugout.*

The ground started to rise a bit, and the mountain grew bigger the closer they got to it. Jolie saw movement in the distance. She squinted, holding her hand over her eyes, and noticed a man riding toward them on horseback. He held a rifle across his lap, keeping his gaze on them. As he drew closer, she could see that he was an older man, with silver blending into his dark hair. The sun had baked his skin to a dark tan, and his deep blue eyes roamed back and forth between her and Clay.

He pulled close and reined to a stop. His dark brown horse with a white diamond on its forehead pawed the ground. "Can I help you folks?"

Clay stiffened at the sound of his father's voice, but he didn't remove the hat that covered his face. Would his pa recognize him anyway? A part of him wished—hoped that he would.

"We're looking for the Bar J Ranch," Jolie said. "Could you please direct me to it, sir?"

"You're on it now. Have been for a spell."

"Oh."

"What business do you have here?"

Jolie didn't say anything, and Clay felt her stare. He was

a scoundrel for forcing her to face his father alone. But as much as he'd ached to return home, he'd admit only to himself that he was scared. What if his father turned him out?

"We have business with Mr. Jackson. Could you please take me to him?"

The old man grunted, and Clay almost grinned. The sound was so familiar. "What business do you have with him?"

Clay sighed and straightened, removing his hat. "Afternoon, Pa."

His father's blue eyes grew wide before he regained control and schooled his expression, but Clay had seen hope in his eyes. It was the same hope that warmed his chest.

"What are *you* doing here?" His father rubbed his palm down his gray stubble. He had aged a lot in the three years that Clay had been gone.

"Didn't you get my letter?"

"I got it but didn't think you'd show."

Clay held out his open palm. "The prodigal has come home. Are you gonna kill the fatted calf?"

His pa grunted again and stared at him with those cold blue eyes. He pointed a finger at Jolie. "Who's she? Not one of your conquests, I hope."

Jolie gasped, clutching her hand to her chest.

Clay shot to his feet. "Don't you talk about her like that. She's my wife."

His father's mouth dropped open for a moment before his glare returned.

Clay wobbled and fell back onto the seat, unable to silence the moan that crept out at his hard landing. Pain sliced through his chest and arms, and he groaned.

His pa spat on the ground, a disgusted look hardening his face. "Drunk as normal, and I see you've been fighting. I suppose it was too much to hope you'd changed."

"No, he's—"

"Don't make excuses for him, ma'am. I know all too well what he's like."

Disappointment seared Clay. His pa wasn't even going to give him a chance to prove he had changed. He was condemned because of his past indiscretions. He should have known his stubborn father wouldn't accept him home with open arms.

His pa worked his jaw, as if what he was about to say was painful. "You can stay a short while." He glanced at Clay and his gaze narrowed. "Not because you're my son, but because of her. And if you expect to stay here more than a few days, you'd better straighten up. I'll have no drinking on my ranch."

His ranch. That sure made things clear. He wasn't welcomed in his own home—the house he'd been raised in. His father still thought the worst of him. He could argue that he wasn't drunk, but his pa wouldn't believe him. Clay shook his head. God may have changed *his* heart, but his father's was still as hard as a blacksmith's anvil.

❅

Clay pulled the reins from Jolie's hands, and she cringed at the tension between father and son. What had happened to create such a rift between them? She watched Clay's father gallop off. Was he not happy in the least to see his son again? "Can I ask what happened between you two?"

Clay shrugged. "Doesn't matter. It was a long time ago."

She held her hands in her lap, wanting to say more, longing to comfort him, but she sensed he wouldn't welcome her efforts. Whatever had happened, time had done little to dull the discord between father and son. Why wouldn't Clay let her tell his father he'd been shot?

Clay's jaw looked rigid, but the pain in his eyes signified hurt more than anger. She reached out and touched his arm. "I'm sorry, Mr. Jackson."

He swung a surprised glance her way. "Might as well call me Clay, or things will get confusing with there being two Mr. Jacksons, and besides, Pa might get suspicious of our marriage if you don't call me by my Christian name."

"What do you mean he might get suspicious?" Was Clay ashamed of her? Sorry that he'd agreed to marry?

"I'd prefer Pa not know how our marriage came about."

"Oh." She hung her head. How would she endure the next days. . .weeks. . .in such a union?

"Hang on." He sidled a glance her way. "Don't get the wrong idea. It's just that there's enough rough ground between Pa and me without him thinking I'm not doing right by my own wife."

Jolie blinked, trying to make sense of his words. "Are you embarrassed about our wedding?" *Or me?*

Clay shook his head. "You have to admit our wedding was. . .uh. . .rather unconventional."

Jolie nodded.

Clay turned in the seat, laid the reins across his lap, and rubbed the back of his neck. "Look, I never planned on getting married, at least not anytime soon. But I made a pledge before God and you, and I intend to keep it. I reckon we can get along well enough, if we give it a try."

Jolie laid a hand on her chest. "So, you don't wish to be rid of me?"

He shrugged, and a gleam lit his eye. "Right at first I did, but having a wife just might be a good thing."

Good thing? How? She wanted to ask, but they crested a rise, and she sucked in a deep breath at the lovely sight before her. Atop the next hill, a broad two-story log home rose up. Smoke curled up from one of the two chimneys, as if welcoming them home. A ways behind the house and down the hill was a barn and several out-buildings nestled in a wide valley, surrounded by treeless mountains. Several had taller peaks with snow covering them. Jolie's heart soared like the hawk she watched circling the valley. Had she finally come home?

Clay pulled the wagon to a stop near the house and handed her down. He climbed to the ground, wincing and holding his shoulder. He must be exhausted. Since his shooting, he hadn't gotten any decent rest. He grabbed Jolie's satchel, and she nearly tugged it from him, but she didn't want him loosing face with his father any more than he already had.

A wide porch with a view of the valley beckoned to her as she climbed the stairs. She could see herself sitting in one of the rockers in warmer weather mending clothes or shelling peas.

They stepped inside, and she gazed around. The great room was two stories tall, and off to one side, a stairway led to the second floor. You could walk down the open hallway to what she assumed were the bedrooms and still look down over the railing and see the people downstairs. Never had she seen the likes of it before.

A warm blaze danced in the fireplace, drawing her. She held up her hands, warming them and studying the room. "You have a lovely home."

Clay watched her, his head cocked. "It's your home, too—for as long as Pa lets us stay."

Jolie smiled. *Please, Lord, mend the rift between Clay and his father, and let us stay here.*

A shuffling sound upstairs drew her attention. Clay's father strode out of one door at the end of the open hallway, carrying a load of clothes, and into another. They watched as he returned to the first room and exited again with an even bigger pile of things in his arms.

"Great."

She spun around and looked at her husband, wondering about the snide tone of that single word. "What's wrong?"

"Looks like Pa is moving out of the big bedroom. I suspect he's going to give it to us."

Jolie swallowed hard. She hadn't considered where they'd sleep. For some reason she half expected to have her own room.

Clay leaned down near her ear. "It would hardly look right if we didn't share a bedroom. I promise not to bother you—for now."

She stared at him with wide eyes. What did that mean?

She wrung her hands together and took her satchel from him. If only she had some clue what went on between a man and a woman, but she'd had no one in her life to teach her such things. Her hands trembled, and she hoped her husband would honor his vow.

Chapter 6

Jolie poured her father-in-law another cup of coffee then set the pot back on the stove. She walked over to the window and stared out. Overnight, a light snowfall had blanketed the land, making everything fresh, just like her new life.

Had Miss Tuttle been enraged when she'd discovered her missing? She grinned, thinking how she'd outsmarted the woman. One thing was for certain, nobody would find her up here. As soon as she could borrow some paper, she would start sending letters to the Council Bluffs mayor, telling him what was going on at the children's home. She may be free, but there were plenty of other children she dearly loved who weren't.

"It's warmer over here by the stove."

She smiled over her shoulder at Clay's father then took a seat at the table. The older man hadn't said much at breakfast, just scooped in the ham, eggs, and biscuits she'd made like he hadn't eaten in weeks. It blessed her to do such a small thing to make him happy.

He scowled and stared at her. "How long that no-good son of mine and you been married?"

Uh oh. "Um. . .not too long. In fact, we just got married. Would you like some more eggs? There's more left in the pan."

He shook his head. "Don't know what a pretty little thing like you sees in him."

Jolie longed to restore peace and laid her hand on the man's arm. "Please give Clay a chance. I think you'll see he's changed."

"Humpf! He can't even get up at a decent hour."

She'd promised not to tell his pa that he'd been shot or how their marriage had come about. "The past few days have been difficult for him."

"And what about you?"

She shrugged, knowing she'd skirted out of one trap and into another. "How long have you lived here?"

He stared into his coffee. "We moved here when the boys were young."

She wondered if he knew that he'd referred to both brothers.

"Those were good times, when my Ella and Clint were still alive."

"I lost my mother when I was just four. She died in childbirth." Jolie couldn't tell him that her father had left her at the orphanage because he couldn't work and take care of her. Was he even still alive?

"Losing Ella was hard, but I had my boys—and then

Clint had that accident. I lost two sons that day. Some days I wonder why I even stay here. But where else could I go?"

Jolie's heart ached for the man who had lost so much. But maybe she could help him heal. Maybe Clay could. She offered a smile and noticed her husband coming down the stairs. "At least now you've got Clay back."

Mr. Jackson shook his head. "That boy's been nothing but trouble ever since his brother died."

Clay's lips pressed into a thin line, and he turned and strode toward the door. He yanked his coat off a hook and slapped his hat on his head, not even giving her a second glance. He stomped outside and slammed the door.

Mr. Jackson jumped and looked over his shoulder. "Guess he heard me. Well, good. He needs to know where I stand. I'm not housing and feeding no moocher."

Jolie jumped up and hurried to the window, but Clay must have gone around back, toward the barn. She longed to go to him, to comfort him, but would he even welcome her presence?

Mr. Jackson cleared his throat and stood. "There's a trunk in your room that holds some of Ella's things. It don't seem like you have warm enough clothes for being up this high. Help yourself, if you've a mind to. Though you may have to take them up some since Ella was taller than you."

She smiled at him. "Thank you. That's very kind. Are you certain it won't bother you if I wear her clothes?"

"No bother. I reckon me and Clay will be in for lunch. Might be nice to have some soup or stew, if you're of a mind to fix some." He snagged another biscuit off the plate. "And these are delicious."

He strode for the door and put on his heavy coat. "I may have problems with my son, but I want you to know that you're welcome here. I hope you'll make yourself at home."

"Thank you, Mr. Jackson. That's very kind of you."

He grunted, just like she'd heard Clay do on several occasions. "Call me Will or Pops, not that Mr. Jackson stuff." He shoved his hat on and went out the back door, letting in a frigid blast of air.

Standing close to the stove, she crossed her arms and stared outside. Was it possible for them all to start anew? "Please, Father, show me how to help Clay and his father. Heal their relationship."

Clay strode toward the barn, his anger raging like a prairie fire. Why had he thought returning home was such a great idea? He should have known his father hadn't changed. That the old man still blamed him for Clint's death.

No, he hadn't said that, but Clay could feel his censure all evening last night. He knew his pa wished that he'd died instead of Clint, and he'd gladly give his life if it would bring his brother back. Clint had been his best friend, his confidant, and partner in crime. It had been Clint who'd comforted him when their ma died, not their father.

He yanked open the barn door, relishing in the familiar scents. Hay, horses, and leather. This had been his refuge when life in the house became unbearable. *Give me patience,*

Lord. And forgive me for my anger toward Pa.

"Well, well. So the prodigal returns home. Hoping for a fatted calf, were you?" Drake Gruber leaned on a manure fork and narrowed his eyes at Clay.

He'd hoped his pa had gotten rid of the troublesome foreman. The man was pure trouble and had done everything he could to set brother against brother, but Clay's bond with Clint had been too strong for this man to destroy. Clay pushed aside his anger and nodded. Sometimes being a Christian was downright hard to do.

"You're looking good, Clay." Farley, his pa's second-in-command, nodded and returned to spreading fresh straw in a stall.

Drake scowled at the man then set aside the manure fork and walked up to Clay. "Things been goin' good here. I hope you don't plan on causing problems."

Clay stood almost nose to nose with the man. "Just remember whose land this is, Drake."

"Last I checked it was your daddy's."

Clay winced, wanting to punch the cocky smile off the man's face, but he was a better man now. He stepped back. "Be that as it may, you're still the hired help—and that can always change."

The barn door opened, and Clay jumped back. His father strode in and looked around. His pa glanced from man to man then focused on Drake. "You got some work to do?"

Drake nodded but glared at Clay. Turning his back, Clay crossed the barn to the stall where his mother's horse, Spice, still stood. The bay mare stuck her head over the gate and nuzzled him. Did she remember him? He smoothed her black forelock, halfway surprised his father still had the horse. "You care if I take her out for a ride, Pa?"

"We work around here. If you can ride, you can check the herd."

Clay nodded and reached for a curry comb, eager to be on horseback again. He'd lost his horse in a card game shortly after leaving home and still missed the gelding. He'd been a good horse, and Clay hoped his new owner treated him decently.

"I heard Clay has his own mare up at the house," Drake said to Farley.

Clay clenched his fist and marched toward the man.

His father stepped in his way, holding up his hand. "There'll be no more talk like that, Drake. That woman is decent and kind. She's my daughter-in-law, and you'd best remember that if you don't want to draw your walkin' papers."

Drake nodded, but Clay could tell he didn't like being put in his place. He returned to the stall and finished brushing down Spice. Saddling the horse one-handed wasn't easy, but he managed. He sure wasn't asking anyone in the barn for help. He walked the mare outside then stared at the house. His wife was up there.

He smiled, remembering last night. Jolie had been in her nightgown and under the covers before he'd gone to bed. She'd slept so close to the edge of the big bed that she'd fallen off twice. At least that's how many times he heard her before he fell asleep. Resting in a good bed in his own home had felt wonderful, and he'd overslept. He sighed. Seemed like he couldn't do anything right.

Jolie came out the front door, carrying a bucket. Her coat flapped in the light breeze, and she looked around. He led the horse in her direction, still unable to believe he was married and she belonged to him. He couldn't explain the powerful desire to keep her safe that had welled up in him. They'd need a plan, in case staying here didn't work out. But he had no idea what that could be. He'd done ranch work all his life, but it was hard for a man with a wife to find a ranching job.

She smiled as he drew near. "I was going to wash the dishes, but I need more water. Do you have a well or a creek nearby?"

"A creek—or if there's enough snow, we just melt it."

She looked around the ground. "Guess I'd better check the creek. Which way is it?"

He nudged his chin at the large log home. "Other side of the house, down the hill."

"Oh, well thanks."

"Did you sleep well last night?"

His wife's eyes widened, and her cheeks grew red—and not from the chilly air, he suspected. She shrugged. "Well enough, I suppose. I'll just be fetching the water now."

"Do you know how to shoot a gun?"

"What? Um. . .no."

"You shouldn't go anywhere around here without protection. I'll walk with you to the creek." He took the bucket and hung it over the saddle horn.

She glanced around, as if she expected a mountain lion to jump out at any moment.

He bit back a smile. "Most of the times it's no problem, but it's best to be on the safe side, especially in the winter."

She scooted over beside him, looking all around. "You have a lovely home."

"Thank you. It's good to be back, even though Pa is less than enthused to have me home."

"Give him some time. He'll see how you've changed."

Clay shook his head. "How do you know if I'm any different?"

Jolie looked up at him. "I know you're a good man, Clay. If you weren't, you'd never have allowed yourself to be coerced into marrying me."

He shrugged. "I couldn't very well leave you to that mob. Besides, I was in a weakened state."

"I don't think that made any difference."

Clay had to admit he liked his wife. She seemed sweet and caring, and she wasn't bad to look at with that mass of brown hair and those penetrating eyes the color of coffee, with just a speck of milk added.

"You didn't get any breakfast. Could you come in and eat before you go wherever you're going?"

"I thought I'd take a short ride and see how things have changed. You wouldn't want to go, would you?"

Jolie eyed the horse and shook her head. "I haven't ridden a horse since I was a young child."

"This is Spice. She was my mother's horse, and she's as gentle as they come. We can ride together."

Jolie pulled her cloak together, half looking like she'd run back to the house. He reached out and fingered the worn piece of fabric. "You need something warmer than this."

"It's all I have."

"One of these days we'll go back to town, and you can order some new things."

She shook her head. "This is fine. I don't want to be any trouble."

He started to say she wasn't trouble until he remembered the state of his bank account. Who was he to be making promises?

"I suppose I could go on a short ride while the water heats."

Clay grinned, his heart warming. "Great. Let's get the water then."

Chapter 7

Clay eyed his wife, riding beside him on Spice, while he rode a black horse from his father's stable. In just one short week, Jolie had gone from riding double with him and clinging to the saddle horn with both hands to riding alone, although she did still maintain a tight grip on the horn with one hand most of the time. She gently rocked in time with the mare's slow gait, and her eyes roved the landscape.

He sighed. Already she was tugging at his heartstrings, making him wish she'd married him because she wanted to and not because she was forced to. The light breeze picked up a strand of saddle brown hair that had come loose from her braid and blew it across her face. Using two fingers, she tucked it behind her ear. Clay longed to run his hand down her hair, to see if it was as soft as it looked, and he enjoyed watching her eyes light up when she saw something new.

Days spent with Jolie were a joy, but the nights were

driving him crazy with her sleeping right beside him and him unable to touch her. He rubbed his hand across his jaw, forcing himself to think of something else.

Cold water. That's what he needed.

"Let's go this way. There's something I want to show you."

Jolie followed his lead, as they wound up a trail that would take them to the crest of the nearest mountain if they went all the way up. But that wasn't their destination.

"How are things going with you and Pa?" he asked.

Jolie shot a glance his way and then refocused on the trail. "All right, I suppose. He still asks lots of questions, but I try to divert his attention onto something else if it's a question I don't want to answer."

"Pa is tenacious, that's for sure."

She grinned and nodded. "And stubborn. How long will it take him to see that you've changed?"

He clamped down on his back teeth. "Stubborn is an understatement. Once you get on my father's bad side, it's almost impossible to redeem yourself."

"Well, I think you should keep showing respect to your father and honoring him, even when he belittles you. Allow God to redeem you."

There was wisdom in his wife's words, but doing what she said wasn't easy. A man could only take so much of his father putting him down.

Guilt heaped onto Clay's shoulders. He needed to remember how much God had forgiven him. After his brother's death, he'd become a drunk, a gambler, and even spent time with the wrong kind of women, but none of those things dulled the ache of his brother's death. Only giving his heart to God had silenced the roar of the pain. He didn't deserve Jolie or reconciliation with his father, but his heart craved both. God forgave him and sent His own Son to die for him, so how could he not forgive his own father? The truth was—his pa didn't know him now and was still judging him by how he used to be.

Give me patience with him, Lord.

"I think your father wants things to be better between you two, but he's afraid to show it. He lost his whole family, and now that you're back, he's afraid to open his heart again for fear he'll get it stomped on."

Clay grunted. It sounded as if he and his pa had the same fears.

Jolie looked at him. "I know this is hard, Clay, but you need to repair your relationship with your father, or you'll never have peace in your heart."

"How did you get to be so wise?"

She shrugged one shoulder, her cheeks turning a rosy pink. "Guess it comes from mediating disagreements between children at the orphanage."

Clay studied her profile. Her nose was straight, and her slightly full lips begged for his attention. He cleared his throat. "Just how old are you, anyway?"

"I turned eighteen the end of November."

Clay lifted his hat and ran his fingers through his hair. She was older than many brides in the West but still seemed young to him. He was only six years older, but he'd seen the hard side of life. Jolie was sweet. Innocent. She intrigued him, and he longed to know more about her. "What was life like in the orphanage?"

She frowned. "Lots of work."

"Didn't you go to school?"

"Yes, but only for a few hours a day. Miss Tuttle felt we'd be better suited for life if we learned practical tasks. We worked fixing meals, cleaning the building, doing laundry, mending clothes, gardening. My last job was to tend the babies. I loved that task." A gentle smile lifted her lips.

Clay ached for the young girl who'd probably had no childhood. He longed to make life easier for her, but being a rancher's wife was hard work. At least she didn't have to cook for their rowdy hands, since Farley was a decent hand with a spatula.

As they rode up the next incline, he kept his eye on his wife's face, anticipating her expression at the upcoming view. Jolie gasped, delight filling her eyes, and he wasn't disappointed.

Jolie held her hand over her mouth as her eyes took in the serene setting. A beautiful lake, unbelievably blue, nestled in the lap of a mountain. Several pine trees surrounded the lake, enhancing the beauty.

"We call it Jackson's Hole."

A smile twittered on Jolie's mouth. She cast Clay a teasing look. "I thought that was in the Wyoming Territory."

He chuckled. "Well, this is our version. Pretty, isn't it?"

She nodded. "Can we go down to the water?"

"You think you're ready to ride down that steep trail?"

Jolie studied the path winding down to the lake. Her riding skills were improving, and she learned from the start that if she didn't want to spend her days in the house, she needed to learn to ride. What had really surprised her was how easy it was once she lost her fear and how much she enjoyed it. When she was on Spice's back, she felt free for the first time in her life. "I'd like to try if you think I can do it."

He gazed at her, a soft smile tilting his lips. "I think you can do anything you set your mind to, Mrs. Jackson."

Her heart somersaulted at his first reference to her married name. He guided his horse onto the path, and she followed, her heartbeat kicking up a few notches at the steep downward slant.

Clay glanced over his shoulder. "On the steepest part, lean back a bit and let your horse have her lead."

She wasn't sure what that second part meant, but she leaned back a little and tried to relax. Spice was sure-footed and didn't seem to have any trouble on the incline. Jolie closed her eyes and held on to the saddle horn, hoping they'd be down soon and wishing she'd never suggested they visit the lake. Cold air stung her nose and cheeks, but she loved being outside. At the orphanage, she rarely had time to enjoy nature.

Clay chuckled. "You can open your eyes now."

A blush warmed her cheeks, but any embarrassment quickly fled as she took in the gorgeous view. "I imagine there are people who'd be willing to pay a goodly sum to see such a beautiful sight."

Fresh mountain air filled her lungs, and she longed to taste the water. She slid her leg over the horse's rump, dropped to the ground, grabbed Spice's reins, and walked toward the lake.

"Hey, where you goin'?" Clay jumped off and followed her. "Just let go of the reins. The horses won't go anywhere."

She questioned the wisdom of turning her horse loose this far from the house but figured Clay knew what he was talking about. At the water's edge, she pulled off a pair of gloves that had belonged to her husband when he was younger and swirled her hand in the frigid water. She took a sip and stood. "I wish you could have built your house up here so we could see this view each morning."

"That would be nice. Maybe someday we can build a new one."

Jolie shook her head. "That's not practical when you already have such a lovely home."

"So, you like it here?"

She turned toward him, unable to keep a grin off her face. "I love it here."

He cocked his head. "Not too cold for you?"

"It's cold, but if you wear enough clothes, it's bearable."

"I see my old coat fits pretty well."

"Yes. Thank you for letting me use it." She heard a tapping sound and spun around. "What's that?"

He leaned his arm around her and pointed to a nearby tree. "See that black-and-white bird? That's a sapsucker. Some folks call them woodpeckers."

"Oh, it's so lovely with that red head and yellow chest."

"That's a male. God made many male animals colorful so they could attract a mate."

She turned back to face him. "Truly?"

Clay nodded. "Kind of odd, isn't it? With humans, it seems He did things the other way around and made women the pretty ones."

He stood there studying her. Did he find her pretty? Miss Tuttle had always commented on how plain Jolie was and that she wouldn't likely find a husband, but she'd proven her wrong. Even if their marriage had been hasty, Clay could have said no.

Her gaze roved his face, and she longed to touch him. To caress his cheek. Would it feel soft or bristly? Did a wife take such liberties?

She loved her husband's deep blue eyes, almost the same color as the lake. Suddenly, her lack of knowledge overwhelmed her, and she ducked her head.

"What's wrong? Did I say something that upset you?"

She shook her head. "No. It's just that. . ." She nibbled her lip, unsure if she should voice her thoughts or not. Would they anger Clay? Disappoint him?

He lifted her chin with two fingers. "Tell me."

She glanced at his handsome face then back at the water. "I just feel so. . .inadequate."

"In what way?"

She shrugged. "I don't know how to be a wife. I don't even know what a wife does other than cook, clean, and sew."

"That's a big part of the job." He smiled down at her. "But it's also a wife's duty to please her husband."

She studied his boots again, her heart thumping. "I don't know how to do that."

"Would you like me to teach you?"

Her gaze shot up to his. Was he teasing? The sincerity there told her he wasn't. Working up her nerve, she nodded.

Clay's wide smile was worth pushing aside her fears. "All right then, let's get started."

He pulled off his gloves and removed his arm from the sling, then reached out, capturing both of her hands. He rubbed his thumbs on her skin, sending chills skittering up her spine. "First off, a married couple is allowed to touch each other. Like this."

After a few moments, he dropped one hand and lifted his palm to her cheek. He caressed her face and ran his calloused thumb over her bottom lip, stealing away her breath. "And like this."

Her knees started wobbling, but she liked his gentle touch.

"Now, you try it."

With a shaky hand, she touched his cheek, dragging her fingers from the soft upper part to the bristly lower half. She grinned. "You feel like a porcupine."

Clay chuckled. "And how many of those have you felt?"

She looked away. "None."

"Would you mind if I show you more?"

Jolie shook her head, wondering how much faster her heart could beat without it bursting from her chest.

A smile lit Clay's eyes. "Married couples often hug. Like this."

He pulled her to his chest, and she stood stiffly, but as he ran his hand over her hair like she'd done to many orphans, she began to relax. Sucking in a daring breath, she leaned her face against his coat. It smelled like the cedar chest he'd found it in. He tightened his grasp, not enough that she felt trapped, but rather protected—and special. She closed her eyes. No one had ever made her feel cherished before. Her heart opened, and she knew it would be an easy thing to love this man.

He sighed, as if he, too, enjoyed hugging. She'd often embraced the children in the orphanage, but this was so different. She rarely allowed herself to love a child, because too many times people would come and adopt her favorites, and though she was happy for them, the ache of never seeing them again had forced her to harden her heart. Maybe now she could fully open it and love her husband. She wrapped her arms around his waist.

Clay sighed into her hair. He, too, was a person who'd had little love, at least since his mother died. Did he feel what she did?

He leaned back a ways, his warm smile making her stomach do odd things. "There's one more thing I'd like to teach you today. I'd like to kiss you, if that's all right."

Jolie eyes widened. She'd known girls at the home who'd kissed boys. They all seemed to enjoy it, except the few that had been forced. She should probably say no, but her curiosity was pushing her to agree. She nodded her head before she could change her mind.

Clay smiled and released his hold on her, only to gently

capture her face between his hands. He tilted her head back and leaned down, his breath brushing her face like a feather. Her heart thundered, and she didn't know what to do with her hands. His lips touched hers, caressing her mouth softly at first and then with more intensity. Her hands found his arms, and she accepted all he gave. Then, he pulled back suddenly, gazing into her eyes.

Her breath came out in short bursts, as if she was afraid, but he hadn't frightened her in the least. In fact, she'd enjoyed their time together very much.

Clay lifted his hat and ran his hands through his hair. "I guess we oughta head back."

He marched toward the lake and knelt down, splashing cold water on his face as if he was trying to wash off her kisses. She hung her head and plodded back to her horse. She must have done something wrong. Or maybe she hadn't pleased him. Maybe she didn't have the makings of being a good wife.

Chapter 8

Clay whistled as he carried three logs under his arm and dropped them into the fuel box. His "wife" lesson had been fun. Teaching Jolie to accept his touch was something he looked forward to. She was an unexpected blessing from God and had sneaked in and stolen a piece of his heart. Falling in love with her would be as easy as falling off a horse—and far less painful and more enjoyable.

He peeked at her where she stood cutting out biscuits with a glass dipped in flour. She was a decent cook and an excellent housekeeper, but he'd never met a woman so naive. So innocent. She'd been quiet since their ride, and he couldn't help wondering if he'd spooked her. If he'd come on too strong. Next time, he'd try to take things slower.

The front door creaked, and his pa walked in and stomped his boots on the floor. "It's snowing again." He glanced at Clay and scowled. "You done any work today?"

He nodded. "Yes, sir. I'm filling the fuel box now, and

earlier, I took Jolie for a ride to help her learn the lay of the land."

His pa grunted, belittling his efforts. Clay turned away, not wanting him to see the hurt in his eyes. He'd like to see him up and working with a bullet hole in *his* shoulder. The man was just cantankerous enough that he probably would.

His pa poured himself a cup of the coffee that Jolie kept warming on the back of the stove. He lifted his head and sniffed. "What's for supper tonight? Sure smells good."

"Rabbit stew. One of the hands trapped a half dozen and gave us two of them."

"That will taste good."

Clay strode outside for another load of wood. With his arm still in the sling, he could only manage a pitiful amount. He sighed and stared out at the valley, not wanting to go back inside while his pa was there.

How could he get his father to see he was a different man now? "Help me, Lord. Show me how to handle my father. What to say to him. Help me to love him, even when he's unreasonable and crotchety and just plain mean." He sighed hard, rubbing his jaw. "Restore us as a family. Please, Lord."

❄

Will leaned over Jolie's shoulder and snagged a biscuit. "I can't seem to get enough of these, missy."

She turned, spoon in hand, and smiled. "I'm glad you enjoy them, since biscuits are my specialty. I must have made thousands of them."

He scowled. "I'm sorry you had to grow up in that home. Ain't no way for a child to have to live."

Jolie shrugged. "I survived and found myself a good husband."

Will rubbed his jaw then glanced out the window. "Clay does seem different. He's not the hothead he used to be, even when I say things I shouldn't."

She set her spoon down and crossed to where he stood and laid her hand on his arm. "I didn't know Clay back when he was. . .wild, but I can tell you he's treated me far better than I'd ever expected."

He grunted, and she bit back a smile. "Well, that's one thing good he's done. What did he do to his arm? Seems like it oughta be better than it is after a week's time."

She watched Clay struggle to lift a load of wood that would challenge a man with two good arms. He wanted to impress his father, she knew that. He should be taking it easy and healing instead of working so much. Making a rash decision that she hoped would set Clay and Will on the road to reconciliation, she said, "He got shot."

Will's eyes widened before they narrowed. "What'd he do, cheat at cards and make someone mad?"

"No, the stagecoach we were on got robbed. Clay got shot defending us."

Will stood a bit straighter and stared at his son again. Then he ran his hand through his hair and muttered something she couldn't hear. "And I've been pushing him to work. When did that happen?"

"The night before we arrived."

"Why didn't he tell me?"

"He didn't want pity. He hoped you'd welcome him home because he's your son. He's trying to prove to you how much he's changed."

Will stood with his hands hanging loosely at his waist. "I was so mean to him."

Jolie reached out to him again. He was family and hurting, and maybe touching him would help. "He wants your approval so badly, Pops. I truly believe Clay is different. If you knew everything that had happened between him and me, you'd understand."

"Then tell me."

She shook her head. "I can't. I've already broken one promise to Clay by telling you about his wound." Scurrying across the room, she returned to her cooking. "He'd be upset with me if he knew."

"I won't tell him."

Jolie started dishing up the stew. "Supper is ready." She set two bowls on the table and winced. Will was still watching Clay. She cleared her throat. "I've been meaning to ask you if you have any special family traditions for celebrating Christmas. It's only a few weeks away."

"Ain't celebrated since Clint died. That first Christmas afterwards, I wasn't in any shape to celebrate. I rode off and didn't return until late that night. Clay was gone by the next season."

"Oh." Jolie couldn't keep the disappointment from her voice. This was her first Christmas as a married woman, and she'd hoped to make it special. She'd already started knitting some new socks for Pops and a scarf for Clay, but she could still give them their gifts. And maybe she could find something special to cook.

Will walked to the front door and stood there with his hand on the knob. "Ella had some glass doodads somewheres that her grandfather sent her from Germany, along with some handmade ornaments. If you want to try and find them, I guess I could find a tree for you to hang 'em on."

Jolie clapped her hands and squealed, flew across the room, and hugged Pops's neck. He patted her back; then they heard Clay's footsteps. She moved out of the way, and Will opened the door.

Clay stood there, his cheeks red from the cold and sweat dotting his forehead, a large load of wood under his arm. His gaze went from her to his father. "What is this? A welcoming committee?"

❋

Jolie pulled a beautiful quilt out of one of the two huge trunks in the bedroom she shared with Clay. It smelled of cedar, and she couldn't help wondering if the piecings had come from clothes that Clay and his family had worn years ago. If only the quilt could talk. What stories it could tell her.

She laid it aside then pulled out three dresses, two of which were wool and would keep her warm this winter. Holding a dark green one up in front of her, she stared at her expression in the mirror. "You'd make a lovely Christmas dress, with a few alterations."

Setting it aside, she dove down through men's and boys'

clothing to toddler and then infant size. She held up a tiny gown, trying to imagine her over-six-foot-tall husband that small.

Footsteps sounded down the hall then Clay strode into the room. "What's that you've got?"

"A baby gown. It must have been yours or your brother's."

He shook his head. "I was never that little."

Jolie chuckled. "I'm guessing you were. Why else would these baby clothes be in here?"

He cocked his head, a teasing grin on his face. "Why are you looking at baby things?"

Jolie spun around, certain her cheeks were bright red. "I was looking for the Christmas decorations." She hastily stuffed the clothing and quilt back into the trunk and shut the lid then forced herself to face her husband. "Your father thought they might be in these trunks, but they weren't. I don't suppose you know where they'd be."

He shook his head and wiggled his brows. "No, but I'm hankering for another *wife* lesson."

Splaying her fingers across her chest, she tried not to gape at him. If he'd been displeased by their first lesson, why would he want to try again? Did he think she could improve enough to satisfy him? She hung her head and turned her back to him.

He crossed the room and rested his hands lightly on her shoulders. "What's wrong, Jolie?"

She shrugged but didn't say anything.

He gently turned her around. "Tell me what's the matter."

She studied his worn boots, thinking that she needed to polish them soon. Did one even polish Western boots?

His finger lifted her chin. "Didn't you like hugging and kissing me?"

Oh, *she* liked it all right. It was the most wonderful thing she'd ever experienced. She lifted her shoulders again and lowered them, embarrassed to voice her inadequacies.

"Jolie, please. Tell me what's got you upset."

She blew out a sigh. He'd probably nag her until she told him. "I did like it, but I don't think you did."

"You're wrong about that."

His blue eyes blazed with sincerity, but she was confused. "Then why did you wash off my kisses?"

His eyes sparked with surprise, and then mirth danced around his lips. Suddenly he threw back his head, and laughter filled the room.

It took him so long to compose himself that Jolie's embarrassment turned to anger. She shoved her hands to her hips and then decided to leave him to his humor. She marched past him, tears of mortification burning her eyes, but he grabbed her arm and pulled her against his chest. She pounded on the solid, muscled surface, but he didn't let go. "Stop laughing at me. I can't help it because I don't know how to do those things right."

His chest still vibrated with his chuckles, and tears ran down his cheeks. "I'm trying, honey."

She pursed her lips and stared up at him, swiping at her tears. "Just what's so funny?"

Clay shook his head. "Darlin', I washed my face in that

frigid water because our time together nearly made my blood boil."

"Oh." She frowned at him. "Is that a good thing or bad?"

He smiled wide. "Good. Very good."

His gaze roved her face, making her squirm. Nobody had looked at her like that. Clay made her feel as if she were someone special. She relaxed in his arms.

His head lowered, and his soft, warm lips met hers. He hugged her close, sending her senses into a tizzy. Her heartbeat sped up, and a butterfly war loosed in her stomach. This was where she belonged—in her husband's arms.

Too soon he pulled back, his forehead resting on hers. "Did that feel like an unsatisfied man?"

She shook her head and allowed the smallest of smiles. She could get used to this hugging and kissing stuff.

"I just thought of something. It seems like we stored some boxes out in the barn. I can go check and see, but first I need to talk to Pa."

Jolie nodded. "I have a little time before I need to prepare lunch, so maybe I'll head on down there and take a treat to Spice."

Clay shook his head, but a smile graced his handsome face. "You're gonna spoil that mare."

Feeling bolder now that she knew he enjoyed his time with her, she decided to tease him a bit. "I'm going to spoil you, too."

The smile he gave her set her heart pounding again. "I certainly hope so."

Jolie nearly skipped her way to the barn. Life here was

so much different from the orphanage. If only Clay and his father could reconcile, everything would be perfect.

In the barn, she gave Spice a lick of sugar and patted the mare's neck. Her gaze roved the barn, searching for crates that might hold the Christmas decorations. "Why would anyone put glass ornaments in the barn, huh, girl? You think maybe Pops was trying to forget about his old life?"

She glanced at the closed barn doors. "Can I tell you a secret?" A warm shiver heated her cheeks. "I think I'm falling in love with Clay."

The barn door rattled, and she jumped back into the shadows of the barn, halfway feeling guilty for voicing her affection out loud. She ducked behind a barrel and waited. What if that were Clay, and what if he'd heard her?

Drake and Farley led two horses into the barn, and Jolie slunk down further and pulled her skirt out of sight. Both men, but especially the foreman, made her uncomfortable. Clay said he'd be down soon, so maybe she could hide until then.

One of the men slammed a stall gate hard and cursed. She leaned sideways to where she could see between the side of the barrel and Spice's stall.

"Why'd Clay have to come home now? Just when I was ready to put my plan in action."

Farley shrugged, uncinched his saddle, and set it on a saddle block. "Rotten timing, all right."

Drake did the same and slapped his horse on the rump. The poor animal jumped and trotted into its stall. Jolie felt sorry for the creature.

Drake rubbed the back of his neck. "Until Clay rode up

in that wagon with that gal of his, I thought for certain he'd been killed in that stage attack. I'm gonna have to find that lowdown polecat I hired and take care of him. The man took my money but didn't deliver the goods."

Jolie gasped and slapped her hand over her mouth. Will's foreman had hired someone to kill Clay? How did he even know Clay was returning?

She remembered Clay mentioning a letter to his father. Drake must have seen it, or else Will mentioned it to him.

"Well, well, look here, Farley. There's a little mouse hiding behind the oat barrel." Drake grabbed her arm and hauled her up.

"Ow! Stop it! You're hurting me." Her heart beat as fast as it had during the stage robbery.

Farley rubbed his whiskery chin, looking sorry to see her.

Drake snarled. "Guess you decided to come down where the real men are, huh? That Clay Jackson not satisfy you enough, sweetheart?" He leaned toward her, licking his lips.

Jolie fell back against the barn wall. "Leave me alone. Will and Clay won't like you bothering me."

"Ohhhh, I'm so scared. I can take that old man and that one-armed brother-killer any day. Let me show you what a real man is like." He shoved her up against the wall and kissed her neck.

Jolie's breath caught in her throat, and she turned her face away. While she welcomed her husband's affections, this man frightened her. Drake took her chin, forcing her to face him. His stale breath stank. She shivered, drawing a grin from him.

"Relax, sweetheart."

She looked past Drake, pleading with her eyes for Farley's help. The older man backed up, as if not sure what to do.

Then the barn door opened, allowing in a blast of bright sunlight. A tall silhouette filled the door.

"Clay! Help—" Drake's hand slammed over her mouth, filling it with the taste of salt and dirt. Her heart hammered like the orphans banging their cups for breakfast.

Clay strode toward her. "What's going on in here?"

Chapter 9

C lay hurried toward the back of the barn, his fist clenched. "Somebody going to answer me?"

Farley slithered back like a frightened weasel. Drake cursed then released Jolie, and she slid down the wall.

Clay's anger boiled.

Drake lifted his chin and glared at him. "I told her what she needed was a real man." He lifted one corner of his mouth in a cocky smile.

"Why you!" Clay grabbed a hay fork and swung the handle at Drake. He had to get the man away from Jolie.

The foreman lunged back and snatched up a shovel, waving it back and forth in front of him. "Why'd you come back? Wasn't it enough that you killed your brother? Now you've gotta ruin my plans?"

Clay grimaced at the accusation then frowned. "What plans?"

"He hoped with you and your daddy out of the way, he

might inherit the ranch," Farley said.

"Shut up, you fool," Drake ground out.

Clay glared at the infuriating man. "Like I said before, Pa and me are family. He would have left the ranch to me, even if I hadn't showed up."

Drake snarled like a rabid wolf. "You don't know that. I've served that cranky ol' man for years and deserve more than beans and cornbread and that paltry pay he gives us. He's no better than you."

Clay growled and lunged for the foreman.

Drake swung and knocked both the fork and shovel from their hands.

Jolie pushed away from the wall, and Clay hoped she'd stay back. *Help me, Lord. I've only got one fighting hand.*

Jolie screamed, drawing Drake's gaze. Clay took advantage and planted his fist in the man's cheek. Drake went down, but Farley jumped onto Clay's back and pummeled him in his wounded shoulder. Clay cried out and slammed backward into a barn support. Spice and the other horses squealed, prancing in their stalls. Farley went limp, and when Clay stepped forward, the ranch hand fell to the ground.

Drake lurched up and growled, running toward Clay. His head landed in Clay's midsection, knocking him down and stealing his breath. Drake drew his gun.

Jolie raised her hands to her mouth. "No!"

"You shoulda stayed away, Clay. You and your brother thought you were such hot stuff with your Pa owning this ranch. My own pappy threw me out, but no more. I aim to have this ranch for myself." He pointed the gun at Clay and cocked it. A look of pride wiped away Drake's glare. "Since you're about to die, you might as well know I'm the one who rigged the saddle on that horse your brother rode. All I had to do was slit some strands on the cinch, so that they broke loose when the horse bucked. An ingenious plan, if you ask me."

Clay glared at the man then cast a sad look at Jolie that said he was sorry. "What are you waiting for?"

Drake shrugged and grinned. "Just enjoying the moment, I guess. But I'll enjoy my time with your wife a whole lot more."

Fear clutched Clay's heart. He let out a yell and kicked Drake's feet out from under him at the same time a gunshot rattled the barn.

His pa strode in the front door and headed for him. He bent and helped Clay stand. "You all right, son?"

Clay nodded. "Thanks. You saved my life."

"No thanks needed. I should have gotten rid of that skunk years ago." His pa nudged Drake with his foot, and the foreman moaned. "Guess he'll live, but we should probably get him into town. I want Doc to look you over, too. Make sure that wound is healing well and that you didn't reinjure it again."

Clay cast his gaze at Jolie. "You told him?"

She nodded but looked like a frightened bird that might flit away any second. "I felt he ought to know."

"Did you also tell him we were forced to marry?"

Jolie's eyes widened, and she shook her head. "No, I didn't."

"Oh." Clay's gaze roved between her and his pa.

"What does that mean?" his father asked, his expression unreadable.

"Could we talk about it later? It'd be best to get these men tied up before they come to. I don't think I'm up to another fight."

His father pursed his lips and nodded. "Good idea." He laid his hand on Clay's shoulder, surprising him. "At least you now know you weren't responsible for Clint's death."

"You heard that?" Clay pressed his lips together and stared up at the barn roof, fighting tears. For so long he'd borne that immense burden. All he could do was nod.

Ten minutes later, the wagon was hitched, and Farley and Drake were loaded in back.

"I'll take these two coyotes to town," his pa said.

Clay shook his head. "Not alone, you're not."

His father looked him in the eye. "You sure you're up to it? You've been working too hard for a man who recently got shot. I'm sorry. You should have told me about that."

Both surprised and elated at his father's concern, Clay smiled. "I'm going with you. It's just a wagon ride."

"Then Jolie would be alone all night, and she's been through enough."

Clay longed to take her in his arms, but he'd been busy.

"I'll be all right," she said as she crossed her arms over her chest, but her eyes said something else. She'd been frightened in the barn, and he'd all but ignored her.

Clay strode toward her and pulled her against his chest, hugging her tightly. "You're all right, darlin'. These men are going away and can't hurt you ever again."

She lifted her hand to his cheek. "You're my hero. God sent you twice to rescue me."

Clay huffed a laugh, trying to make light of the situation. "I think Pa did the rescuing today."

A smile glimmered in his father's eyes, and he glanced up at the sky. "Looks like the weather may hold. Why don't we all go? That way Jolie can get whatever supplies she may need at the store."

She shivered in Clay's arms. "Worried about seeing Hiram Peavey again?" he asked.

"Him and the rest of that town."

"Pa and I will be with you. Don't be afraid. You're a Jackson now."

She smiled. "I'm never afraid when I'm with you. And I would like to purchase a few things to make a special Christmas dinner for the two men in my life."

Epilogue

Christmas Eve

J olie lay back on Clay's arm and watched the flames dancing in the fireplace. Pops had already headed to bed after complimenting her on the fine meal she'd cooked. Her life was as full as the Christmas stockings hanging on the mantel. Presents lay under the small tree that Will had brought in this morning, but the glass ornaments hadn't made it onto the tree this year. She would continue her search in her spare time, determined to find them by next year.

Clay rubbed his belly. "Oh, I don't think I can climb the stairs. What say we sleep on the bear rug tonight?"

"Not me." Jolie smiled. "That thing stinks."

Clay cuddled her closer and kissed her head. "Well, darlin', if you're not sleeping here, neither am I."

She snuggled against his chest. "Who would have thought that a trip West to be a mail-order bride would have ended in a forced marriage to another man?"

"God did. He knew just what I needed."

"Mmm. . .me, too."

"I love you." She trailed little kisses up Clay's chin and cheek. He'd taught her how to be a wife—in all ways—and she looked forward to pleasing him and making him happy, because when she did, she also was happy.

Her heart flooded with love for the husband God had given her. She laid her head on his chest again, and his soft snores tickled her ear. "Thank You, Lord, for blessing this orphan and giving me a family and a home."

Award-winning author **Vickie McDonough** believes God is the ultimate designer of romance. She loves writing stories where the characters find their true love and grow in their faith. Vickie has had 18 books published. She is an active member of American Christian Fiction Writers, and is currently serving as ACFW treasurer. Vickie has also been a book reviewer for nine years. She is a wife of thirty-five years, mother of four sons, and grandmother to a feisty four-year-old girl. When not writing, she enjoys reading, watching movies, and traveling.

HIDDEN
HEARTS

by Therese Stenzel

Dedication

For Neal. In order to write romance, one has to live it.
Thanks for being my hero!

A threefold cord is not quickly broken.
ECCLESIASTES 4:12

Prologue

I am a young Christian woman of twenty, in posses-
sion of deft housewifery skills—cooking, sewing,
baking, and gardening. I am 5 feet 6 inches tall of
slim stature with blond hair and, despite being of
reduced circumstances, wish to make the acquaintance
of a Christian gentleman, and if suited, matrimony.

November, 1884

As abysmal days went, this one had just gotten worse. Elisabeth Lariby stared at the shattered vase at her feet.

Someone cleared his throat.

She snapped her gaze toward Grimford, her aunt's butler. She took the letter from the silver salver in his hand. "Thank you."

"Shall I clean up the mess for you?"

"No." She heaved out a sigh. How could she have been so clumsy? "I'll take care of it, thank you." She limped into her aunt's office, her big toe throbbing with each step. Reaching over her aunt's desk for her monogrammed letter opener, she peered at the unfamiliar masculine handwriting on the envelope. As she read the missive, it shook so hard she could barely make out the words. "*. . .so I respectfully ask for your hand in marriage.*" Her? A mail-order bride? To a complete stranger from—

"Elisabeth?"

She shoved the letter behind her back.

Her aunt stood in the polished entryway of her St. Louis home, her posture tense with accusation. "Is that the mail?"

"You wrote to find me a husband in—" Elisabeth cut a hard look at the letter again. "Nebraska?"

Aunt Dorothy stepped over the shards of ceramic and closed the double French doors to her office. She stood behind her massive wooden desk with the carved scrollwork. Her first husband had died after only one year of marriage and left her quite wealthy. "You have no money. As of last week. And your *former* fiancé, from the Gatesworth lineage, the only son of one of the most respectable families in St. Louis, has chosen another woman to marry. Your parents are dead—"

"We've discussed this many times." Elisabeth gripped the back of a chair, more from her pulsating toe than intimidation. "Please, Aunty, do we need to go over it again?"

"I had such high hopes for a good match for you, but now it seems you have no prospects for marriage."

Elisabeth bit her lower lip, trying to find the courage to

speak her mind. "Aunty, as you know, Hamilton broke things off only three months ago. I've just turned twenty. My friend Caroline assures me that no one considers a woman at my age to be an old maid anymore."

"You are ruined. This town will never forget such a humiliating event. Your friend is wrong. No one of any standing will have you now."

No one will have me. Elisabeth swallowed back the tightening in her throat.

"Is there a problem?" Uncle Richard, Aunt Dorothy's husband of six months, opened the door and poked his impeccably coiffed silver-haired head through the opening.

Her aunt set a smile in place. She adored her new husband. After being a widow for thirty years, she had found love again and was fiercely protective of it. "Nothing, darling. Elisabeth and I were just having a chat about her offer of marriage from a very nice, Christian gentleman in Nebraska."

Her uncle perused Elisabeth from the top of her head down to her shoes. "Nebraska?"

She squirmed at his lingering gape. A glance out of the corner of her eye told her her aunt had noticed it, too.

"She has no choice." Aunt Dorothy blinked back tears. "She has to say yes."

Elisabeth turned her back on them as she scanned the letter again. *"If you are agreeable to my offer, I look forward to meeting you as soon as you are able to travel."*

She pressed the letter to her chest. Hamilton, with his handsome face and red hair, would soon be a married man. And as much as she tried to dismiss his apology that he had to marry the girl his parents had chosen for him, she couldn't. Shame consumed her insides like a fire burning out of control. She still loved him. Her fingers found the pendant about her neck—the one he'd given to her. Her last link with him.

The only way to forget Hamilton would be to leave town. Elisabeth turned around and straightened her posture. If she wasn't good enough for his family, if her aunt no longer wanted her in her home, if God didn't care that her heart was broken, then she would show them all that someone needed her. There had to be a place where she belonged.

With the weight of her loneliness crushing her chest, Elisabeth folded the letter into a small, insignificant square of paper and turned to face them. "I'll post a reply to him in tomorrow's mail. Soon, I'll be out of your way."

Chapter 1

Elisabeth stood in line near the train doorway as the passengers emptied out and waited for the clogging steam and smoke to clear her view of the Plainsville, Nebraska, platform. She inched forward, clutching her satchel like a stray child instead of a respectable young woman. A woman who was about to meet her husband-to-be.

Please, Lord, not red hair like Hamilton's.

"Miss Lariby!" A vibrant, male voice broke into her thoughts.

But his greeting did not cheer her, because a woman should never arrive on her wedding day with a broken heart.

"Miss Lariby."

Her breathing stilled. The young man calling for her had reddish hair. She held out her hand. "Hello."

"I'm Zane Michaels. I'm mighty glad to meet you." He took her hand and helped her down the steps. "I hope your journey was not too tiresome."

She took in his friendly face and broad, welcoming smile. Clear blue eyes that held no secrets flashed with vigor and expectations. His confidence would have to be enough for both of them. "Mr. Michaels, nice to meet you." Her teeth chattered from more than just the gust of late November air.

"Please, call me Zane. And might I call you Elisabeth?"

Despite the din of the mass of people around them, there was something in his tone—an innocence. A soul that had never known rejection. What made him think marrying a mail-order bride was a wise decision? He had no idea what he was getting for a wife.

Before she could answer his question, the crowd at the station nearly jostled her off her feet.

Zane steadied her with a gentle hand to her back, but his attention turned downward. "Stand still, girls!"

Two curly-haired little girls about ages six and eight stood next to him. One was fair-haired, and the other had chestnut-colored hair.

Elisabeth's throat squeezed until the air was almost gone. Children? She had never fathomed. . . She stepped back from them, her thoughts whirling in a hazy confusion. "I am to be. . . Are they your girls?"

Zane's eyes squinted. He lifted the little girl closest to him into his arms. "In my first letter, I told you about my daughters. Don't you remember? This is Sophia, and my older daughter is Olivia."

Elisabeth's stomach soured. Her legs trembled. She never planned on being a mother. She took a step backward and fell into what seemed like a long, black hole.

❄

Zane held his cowboy hat to his chest as he paced the floor just outside the guest room door. Miss Lariby had fainted at the train station. Was she sickly? Was she disappointed at his plain appearance? He glanced at his pocket watch for the tenth time. How long did a doctor need to—

The door to Miss Lariby's room opened, and Doc Tenberger closed it quietly behind him.

Zane's Scottish housekeeper, Mrs. MacIntyre, stood beside Zane holding a hot pan of shortbread cake wrapped in a towel. "She looked a wee too delicate if ye ask me."

Zane ignored the tantalizing smell of the cake and gripped his hat by the brim. "How is she, Doc?"

"She's resting quietly." The doctor snapped his case shut with a click.

"Good. Good." Zane let out a tumbleweed-sized sigh of relief and tossed his hat on the kitchen table.

"When did you say the wedding was set for?" Doctor Tenberger asked.

Zane shoved his hands to his hips. What was proper in this situation? He wasn't educated in the finer things in life. "Well, I thought today. . .but maybe we should wait a few days to be sure she—"

"You're not worried she's changed her mind about marrying you?" The teasing arch to the doctor's eyebrow sent a fission of annoyance through Zane.

"It would be a good idea for her to get to know the girls, that's all." Zane folded his arms and leaned one shoulder on the wall. What if she had changed her mind? What if his simple manners and straightforward ways weren't up to her fancy, citified expectations? The tension that had eased from his shoulders returned like the blast of a Nebraska blizzard. "You're certain she's not ill?"

"Nope, just plain tuckered out." Doc strode to the door with Zane close behind him. "You sure are going to be the envy of every man in town. Can she cook, clean, and sew as pretty as she looks?"

Zane's chest expanded as he recalled Miss Lariby's letters describing her many domestic skills. "As tasty and as perfect as the crust on a blueberry pie."

"Maybe I ought to look into Mrs. Mayberry's marriage society—er—what was it called?"

Zane drew the doctor away from his housekeeper and toward a writing table. He glanced over his shoulder and lowered his voice. "Mrs. Mayberry's Matrimonial Society for Christians of Moral Character."

"I sure would like to have a bride by Christmas. Did they say if they had any more gals willing to—"

Zane held up his hand. He was determined to keep how he'd acquired a wife from getting around. He dug through his papers on the table and slapped the doctor's chest with the handbill for the society. "Take it."

"Mighty grateful. And thank you again for paying off Widow Tatler's medical account."

"You will keep that and how I met Miss Lariby between us?"

"As silent as the prairie." The doctor paused. "Have you made a decision about buying my parents' homestead?"

"No, not yet."

"Just let me know when you do." Doc Tenberger tipped his hat as he departed.

As soon as he left, Delilah, Zane's sister, whirled through the front door, her steps as brisk as her personality. Her husband, Reginald, paced in dutifully behind her. She unfurled the ribbon securing her feather-sprouting hat and smoothed back her dark hair. "I heard the wedding was canceled."

Zane frowned. Hearsay sure spread fast in this town. "Miss Lariby fainted at the station. So I've decided to give her some time to recover and get to know the girls. I think it would be best to wait a few more days. Maybe we'll have the wedding this Thursday."

"But that's Thanksgiving Day. What about my dinner?" Delilah flounced around and settled on the couch like a ruffled hen on her nest.

"Your goose won't mind. The dinner at your house can be our wedding meal."

Delilah blinked. "But—but that's not fair."

Zane knew his sister loved being the center of attention, but on this special day, his attentions would be fixed on someone else. "Then, dear sister, after our wedding, plan another dinner."

"Will she be hardy enough for a Nebraska winter?" Reginald stretched out his long legs and folded his thin arms. "How well did you say you knew this woman?"

Delilah leaned in. "And does she have any money?"

Zane shook his head at his sister's never-ending obsession with money. But with all the times they'd gone to bed hungry as children, he couldn't blame her. Maybe someday she'd stop her fretting and learn to trust in the Lord as he had. "No money, but everything else a man would need in a wife." Zane's mind lingered on Elisabeth's blond hair, slender frame, and cool gaze. She was prettier than her photograph, with a certain air of grace in her manner, but there was also a distance about her. Perhaps, she was just nervous.

"But, Michael—"

"Delilah! I don't use that name anymore."

She ceased her preening in the looking glass. "It's all right. Reginald knows about our former names. I just don't want anyone taking advantage of you and—and what if you run out of—"

"It's okay, sis." He patted her hand until he saw the panic in her eyes subside. "The Lord has provided for us. We will never go hungry again."

"You promise?"

"I promise."

His sister tugged on her cuffs. "Does she expect you to act classy and educated and spend lots of money on her—"

"No. Look, I appreciate your concern, but I have corresponded with Miss Lariby and know that she's a Christian woman of good moral background." Zane shot a glance at his brother-in-law, who accepted a hot cup of coffee and a slice of cake from his housekeeper. Relieved his mode of acquiring a wife was safely hidden, Zane relaxed onto a slat-back chair. He and his sister shared a lot of secrets from their childhood, but keeping this one from her wouldn't hurt. "And in a few days, she'll be my wife."

Elisabeth, with her beauty and homemaking abilities, would make the ideal wife.

The perfect wife.

Chapter 2

E lisabeth sat up in the large bed and glanced around. The room was much nicer than she expected. She'd heard stories of mail-order brides going West and finding themselves in rundown shacks, but Mr. Michaels's house still smelled of new timber. Thick rugs covered the floor, and a tall dressing mirror stood in the corner next to an intricately carved bureau. He must be a man of some means, although his letter describing his humble clothing store gave no indication of such. At least she could be grateful for that.

Mrs. Mayberry had assured Elisabeth's aunt in her letter that all the men she worked with were Christian and of good character. And although Mr. Michaels had been married before, his wife had been gone for six years. Long enough for him to remarry with no claim on his affections. But could she say the same?

She fiddled with her necklace, which hung limp about her neck, recalling her behavior at the station. Her gasp and disbelieving stare at his two little girls as the air closed in around her must have given them a fright. But her aunt had never told her Mr. Michaels had children. After her parents died in a house fire, Elisabeth never desired a family. Being an orphan at sixteen created the kind of scorching pain she in no way wanted a child of hers to experience. Besides, she hadn't much familiarity with little ones. Had no idea how to raise them. How to be a mother—

A knock at the door sounded.

A large woman, with a round and cheerful face like a pumpkin, sneezed as she trotted into the room. "I'm Mrs. MacIntyre, the housekeeper, and I'm pleased to see ye are awake." Her Scottish burr filled the room, as she flitted a feather duster on the mirror. "I didna' get to dusting yur room, but they'll be time for that later."

Before she shut the door, Elisabeth caught a glimpse of Mr. Michaels pacing in the hallway. Her breath halted. The glimpse of his dark reddish hair still felt like someone poking at a festering wound.

"Mr. Michaels is in a right tizzy to see ye. So if yur not too weary, it would set his mind at ease and give my nerves a rest if ye'd have a cup of tea and a slice of cake with him."

Elisabeth nodded as she tucked her pendant from sight. "Of course, I'll go to him immediately." She wrapped her fringed shawl tight against her throat, determined to keep any drafts at bay.

"How are you feeling this evening?" Mr. Michaels nodded toward a chair as she entered the parlor.

Mrs. MacIntyre set a tea tray down on the side table laden with slices of cake and sandwiches. She shot a hopeful glance between them and then excused herself.

He took a mug from the tray. "Sugar? Milk?"

She nodded.

He put in a spoonful of sugar in her cup and tipped in some milk from a small jug. He carefully handed the mug to her before fixing his own. "Are you—do you still—you haven't changed your mind? Do you still want to marry me?"

The hesitancy in this man's voice touched a chord in Elisabeth. His gallant nature surprised her, as she had assumed all country men walked with a wide swagger and chewed tobacco. Thus far, Zane Michaels had proved to be a gentleman.

"I do." She smiled at her slip. "I mean, yes, I will."

"Would you feel up to a wedding on Thursday?"

She studied her lap. She couldn't return the hopeful gaze in his eyes. "Yes."

"Can I ask why you want to marry me?" His voice sounded hesitant. "I'm sure there were plenty of fellows in St. Louis vying for your attentions."

Her gaze fell. "There was no one."

"Good, good." He glanced around the room. "I can have Mrs. MacIntyre unpack your—"

"No, I can do it—"

"Of course." Silence lingered around them. "I liked your picture."

"Picture?"

"The one you sent with your letter to Mrs. Mayberry. She mailed me the letter and the photo you sent so I could write you back."

Elisabeth's mouth bobbed open. Did she dare tell him the truth?

❄

Elisabeth took a long sip of her tea to summon her courage. She had never written to Mrs. Mayberry. Had no desire to leave St. Louis. Had never wanted to marry a stranger. It had all been her aunt's plan.

Resolved to speak with candor, Elisabeth cleared her throat. "That letter was from my Aunt Dorothy, who I lived with. She was concerned about my welfare, as my parents had perished four years ago in a house fire."

"I'm sorry. I had no idea."

"I hope my aunt included in her letters that my father had lost the family fortune. I have no money. And I don't know how to—"

"I thought the letters were from you." A sheepish grin touched his lips. "They were so. . .sweet and ladylike. I had no idea. But why would she want to send you so far from home?"

"My aunt thought being a mail-order bride would be a good"—she swallowed—"idea."

"So you didn't know anything about me or the girls?" He rubbed the back of his neck.

"No." Was he nervous, too? Disappointed to hear the truth? Moisture touched her forehead. What else had her aunt revealed? Her broken engagement? How everyone in town gossiped that penniless Miss Lariby had coerced a wealthy Gatesworth boy into a betrothal? How Hamilton still loved her, but his parents' purse controlled him? She gripped her porcelain cup, the heat from the tea searing her hands. "I'm not sure what other details she included in her letters."

"Your—her letters were informative and"—a flush of pink colored his face—"womanly."

Elisabeth bit back a smile. His embarrassed demeanor gave her a glimpse into what he might have looked like as a little boy.

"She wrote that you were well-educated. And that you are an excellent cook, a gifted housekeeper and gardener, and a deft seamstress with no options for marriage. Of course, after I saw your pretty face in the photograph, I felt like the luckiest man in the world."

Excellent cook? Seamstress? Elisabeth sat up straighter. Her prosperous upbringing and her aunt's moneyed way of life hadn't trained her for any of those duties. She had a head for figures, but how could that help him? How could she explain that he'd been duped? "Might I ask which picture she sent you?"

His face reddened again as he dug into his inside vest pocket.

She reached for the photograph with both hands. It was taken the day Hamilton Gatesworth asked her to marry him. She'd worn a dress her aunt had especially designed and sewn by a well-known seamstress. Her aunt was thrilled by the attentions of such a prominent St. Louis bachelor to her niece and all the social connections this union would bring her.

Though the picture didn't show the colors of the garment, Elisabeth remembered how the pink silk, edged in spring green, was tied with a width of blue satin at the waist, how the soft fabric felt against her skin, and how sweet the small bouquet of violets resting in her hands smelled. Her soft gaze and the hopeful smile that parted her lips brought back a rush of longing to turn back time.

If only Hamilton had told his parents of their plans to wed. If only he had the courage to leave his position at the family bank and follow his heart. If only she still had the faith to believe that God cared about her situation.

She risked a glance at Zane, who showed no concern that the picture had been cut in half. She wouldn't tell him why. Best to leave the past in the past. But how could she give her heart to a man when she pined for another? He would have to settle for her pretty face. "Why did you want to marry an unknown lady?"

A smile spread across his face like a lantern being lit by kindling. "I wrote in my letters that my girls keep me busy, and I have an active clothing business to run. Your seamstress abilities will be a great help to me there. And then there's the land in Colorado—" He cleared his throat and took a swig of his tea. "I'm occupied more than usual. And to be honest, there are times I get lonely."

Her shawl slipped off her shoulder. "Me, too." The words came out before she could stop them. She covered her mouth with a pretend yawn.

"Then, you're an answer to my many prayers." He set down his cup and stood. "But it's getting late, so I'll say good night."

She stood and secured her wrap around herself. God was behind this marriage? The thought disturbed her as if she'd uncovered a plot against herself. After the death of her parents, she'd drifted from her childhood faith. After all, who could trust a God who would allow such a tragedy?

All she wanted was to find a place to belong. She'd seen a favorable marriage with her parents. And to have the same kind of contented union, she knew she would have to please her husband. But she wasn't sure she had the capacity to make anyone happy.

He lifted her oversized trunk as if it were merely a pile of linens. The ripple under his shirt made his muscles look strong enough to hold up the whole house. "I'll put this in your room, but first I want to tell you something." His brows furrowed an earnest expression. "I will be a faithful husband to you. I'll take care of you. Protect you. Provide for you. I'll welcome any children the Lord would give us." His gaze was steady. "I'm growing to care for you already."

She bit her lower lip as she watched his retreating back. *Oh God, please help me.*

After three days of being a guest, it was time for Elisabeth to start acting as if she belonged in this home. She wrinkled her nose at the smell of the burnt pancakes she'd cooked for breakfast. Could she scrape away enough black for them to pass as edible food? She wanted to give Mrs. MacIntyre, who wasn't feeling well, the morning off. But making pancakes wasn't as easy as the cook at her aunt's house made it seem.

Elisabeth snuck a glance at the two little girls who regarded her with blatant stares as they sat at the kitchen table. She'd just have to try harder.

"We're hungry," the girls said in unison.

"Och, dear." Mrs. MacIntyre sneezed as she lumbered

into the kitchen and pulled back the curtain, flooding the room with morning sunlight. "Forgive my sleeping in. These sniffles have been a wee bit hard to shake."

Elisabeth handed the housekeeper the spatula and stepped back from the stove. She'd never learned how to cook, sew, or clean, as she'd always grown up with servants.

"If ye'll sit down, I'll make up a new batch and get coffee brewing." Mrs. MacIntyre's hands flew around the stove like a woman who knew cookery.

"I made some coffee."

Mrs. MacIntyre sniffed at the pot and promptly tipped it into the sink. "No, ye haven't."

Her throat tight, Elisabeth undid the apron that she'd borrowed from a hook in the kitchen. What was she doing in Nebraska? Betrothed to a kind, albeit naive, stranger who had no idea the secrets she held. She hung up the apron and sat down at the table. The two girls' gazes never moved from her face.

Sophia, the youngest one, popped her thumb out of her mouth, climbed down out of her seat, and held her arms out in front of Elisabeth.

Elisabeth's heart sped up like a bird thrusting itself against a cage. "Do you—do you want me to hold you?"

The girl's dark blond curls wobbled as she nodded.

Elisabeth eased Sophia onto the lap of her dark, burgundy skirt. But the girl scrambled further up and wrapped her arms around Elisabeth's neck as if she knew her mother-to-be needed a hug. Elisabeth buried her nose in the girl's curls and breathed in the sweet smell of freshly washed hair. Tenderness welled in her chest. Could she grow to care for

Zane's girls? Would they accept her?

Sophia's curls tickled Elisabeth's cheek as she snuggled her arms a little tighter. "Do you have a little girl?" Sophia's voice whispered.

A gentle balm eased Elisabeth's loneliness. At the memory of losing her parents, her eyes brimmed with tears. "No," came out in a warble.

The child's head shot back. "Why are you crying?"

"I'm. . ." What could she say? "I'm crying happy tears because soon I will have two new daughters." Hope grew within her. She could learn to love these girls. She could be a mother. If she prayed very hard, would God help her? Did He care?

Both girls shared shy grins at each other, as if they knew of her new decision.

"I see we're having a good morning." Zane paused in the room, his dark red hair glinting in the morning sun.

But learning to love another man would be an impossible task. Even with God's assistance.

"Good to see you again." Zane shook hands with Mr. Thomas Worth. Growing up poor, Zane never thought that the town's banker would ever sit across from his desk. Or that he would ever have a desk.

"I've been wanting to get by and see your new house." Thomas adjusted his spectacles as he took in the fine furniture. "And now I hear you will marry soon. Congratulations."

"Thank you." Zane savored the smell of fresh timber. He was proud of his office and the view out the window that overlooked his land bordered by a row of fir trees. "Miss

Lariby and I will marry on Thursday, and she will make the perfect wife. Now my children will have a mother, and Mrs. MacIntyre will have someone to share the burden of housework, cooking, and childcare with. And with my new wife's seamstress skills, she will also be able to help bring in more mending. My store could use the business."

"So your store is still struggling?"

Zane's shoulders drooped. Running a business with all those numbers to keep track of was harder than he imagined. "It is, but with the land I've sold—"

"God has provided."

"Exactly." Zane nodded. Gold was discovered on land he owned in Leadville, Colorado, and he sold it at an amazing profit. Now, hopefully, his greatest desires could come to pass—to be seen as a thriving, godly businessman and to have the perfect family.

For the first time in his life, ever since his wife died and he and his daughters and Delilah moved to Plainsville, he felt as if he'd escaped his poverty-stricken past. Michael Lane was long gone, and now everyone would finally see Zane Michaels as a success instead of the son of the town drunk forced to beg for his supper. "That's why I asked you to come by today. I respect your godly reputation and discretion regarding financial matters. Last fall, when I came to you needing to know what to do with the $100,000 I received, I was a desperate man. Accounting and keeping track of money have never been my strong points, and you were a great help. I was pleased to do business with the list of banks you recommended."

"I'm glad to be of help. But I hope you know my best

advice was to continue to pray about this financial blessing the Lord has given you."

"That's why I wanted to talk to you again. I've kept a thousand dollars or so in cash at the house, and I've been thinking about setting up some kind of home for widows in town with it. Or maybe build a new school." Zane stood and paced in front of the window. His education stopped at the third grade. He barely knew how to read and write, much less handle this much money. "I just need some more of your wisdom on what to do."

Thomas scratched his graying beard. "Well, first of all, don't be in a hurry to give it all away. And I would highly recommend you put that cash in the bank where it's safe."

Zane nodded. "I'll do that the next time I go into town."

"Fine. Now to your offer. The only widow in town is Widow Tatler. I heard someone paid off her medical debts to Doc Tenberger and gave her an unlimited account at Win's General Store. We built a new school five years ago, that was just before you came to Plainsville, so I think you ought to deposit the funds in the bank and continue to wait on God for direction.

"I appreciate your words." Zane handed him an envelope. "I did hear that our town hall needs a new roof. If you could deliver that to our mayor, anonymously of course, I'd appreciate it."

"Mail, sir." Mrs. MacIntyre walked through the open door and set a bundle of letters on the edge of his desk.

"Good morning, Mrs. MacIntyre." Thomas nodded at her. "Are you pleased by the soon-to-be Mrs. Michaels?"

Zane winced. His housekeeper gave her bold, Scottish opinion whether one wanted it or not.

"She is a lovely lass to be sure, but she dresses too fine and dark for our simple Nebraska ways and keeps to herself as if she's concealing—weel, she does truly care for the girls, and that'll warm my heart every day." She folded her arms around her ample figure as if pleased by her own words. "And maybe soon there'll be a son to carry on the family name."

The new family name. Zane smiled to himself. "That would make my life perfect."

"No life is ever perfect." She clucked her tongue.

Zane frowned. Mrs. MacIntyre had come to live with them after he and his girls had moved to Plainsville and her husband died. She acted as if he and the girls were hers to defend. "Thank you, Mrs. MacIntyre."

As soon as she bustled out of the room, Zane directed his attention back to his friend and mentor.

"Will you tell your new wife about your financial blessing?"

Could Zane ever tell anyone about who he really was? A part of him wanted Elisabeth to know everything about his past, but would she look down on his penniless childhood? How his mother died because of the filth they lived in? Although, over the past two days, Elisabeth greeted him with a smile each morning and offered up her cheek to his daily kiss, there remained a distance between them. And he didn't want her to love him for his money. Maybe she would be more comfortable around him after their wedding on Thursday. "I want to give Miss Lariby some time to adjust to her new life. A wife doesn't need to know everything about her husband."

Thomas stood to go. "Secrets are never a good idea in a marriage, but I'll keep you both in my prayers."

After he left, Zane shuffled through the mail. Most were letters regarding his clothing store. The last letter was addressed to Elisabeth in a strong masculine hand from someone in St. Louis. Her uncle most likely. He tucked the letter in his pocket. He'd give it to her later. Tomorrow was his wedding day, and he had a lot on his mind.

Chapter 3

Elisabeth gripped the small bunch of violets Mrs. MacIntyre gave her just before entering the chapel for her wedding.

"I grow the wee flowers in my windowsill in my bedroom." Mrs. MacIntyre's Scottish brogue echoed in the vaulted church foyer. "Mr. Michaels thought ye might like them as he does admire that picture of ye with the flowers."

Elisabeth blinked back tears. The same flowers in her engagement picture to Hamilton. Could this day get any worse? Heat rose in her cheeks when she replayed the mortifying conversation she had with Zane this morning, asking if their marriage could be delayed any longer. Just until they got to know one another better, and until her heart stopped aching. But with the mayor, the banker, the sheriff, and some other successful men Zane hoped to do business with in attendance, he said it couldn't be done. She took a small comfort in the fact that he agreed to wait on consummating the marriage. *"For just a while."*

She stood in a dark gray dress before Zane's pastor and willed her knees to stop shaking. Zane looked handsome in his black coat and string tie, his chest broad with pride. His face wreathed in his customary smile. But the dark red hair that curled slightly over his collar, similar in color to— She pressed her eyes shut. She would not think of Hamilton on her wedding day. Not one insipid memory. . .

At Zane's nudge, she responded to the reverend with an, "I do," but her mouth was as dry as ashes in a fire.

"Elisabeth," Zane spoke her name just before he slid a gold band etched with flowers on her finger, leaned in, and pressed his lips to hers. Soft and warm, they lingered against hers, willing her to feel the affection he did.

She did not. Could not.

A cheer around them startled her. Zane's friends, sitting in tidy rows in the pews, shouted with happiness. A few ladies shot to their feet and clapped.

Zane hugged his girls, who wrestled into his embrace. They regarded Elisabeth shyly, peeking at her from around their father's long legs.

Tears misted her eyes. Sweet girls. Could she grow to think of them as her own?

The mayor of the town came up to Zane. "Delightful wedding. Just delightful." He shook Zane's hand enthusiastically. "And thank you for giving the money to repair the town hall roof."

Zane frowned. "But I—"

"Don't be upset with Thomas." The mayor held up the envelope. "I recognized your messy handwriting on the envelope. It kind of looks like a child's scrawl."

Elisabeth's heart lurched at the tightening of Zane's jaw. The urge to defend him heated her face. Why did he have poor handwriting skills? Was he uneducated? She sighed. How little she knew of her new husband.

After the Thanksgiving dinner at Delilah's home, a small group gathered at Zane's house for a slice of wedding cake and coffee.

Elisabeth's grip on civility was faltering at best. She sat alone at Zane's kitchen table while his sister, brother-in-law, Doc Tenberger, and Thomas Worth and his wife, Clara, gathered around the wedding cake like women at a millinery shop with new hats displayed. But Elisabeth couldn't abide a bite more of food. Their sincere congratulations made her squirm. Why had she ever agreed to be a mail-order bride and move so far from home?

Her aunt's words jumbled in her mind. *"You are ruined. You have no money. No one will have you now."*

And then there was Hamilton. Whom she had loved despite the fact he wasn't a Christian. Although her own faith had faltered, she'd always hoped once they were married they would resume church-going. But Hamilton's decision to abide by his parents' wishes and become betrothed to Brigitte, a wealthy French girl, sealed Elisabeth's fate.

Had her plan to prove that she could find a place to belong come at too high of a cost? A lifetime of being married to a complete stranger?

Zane's deep laughter filled the room. His face beamed with joy. He was a fine man, and that she should have such an attractive and kindhearted husband should be of some comfort to her. But he deserved a wife who could someday grow to love him.

Right now, all she wanted to do was to crawl in bed and be left alone.

Delilah linked her arm through hers. "Shall we look out at the back of Zane's property? I think you'll find with the full moon you can just make out the view of the snow on my new house and barn."

Elisabeth bit back the ache of tiredness and accompanied her sister-in-law to the other side of the room to a large window. "You do have a lovely home."

"It's the biggest in town," Delilah crowed.

The sleeting snow hurled down in the stark moonlight. "Your husband must do very well in business."

"Reginald?" A soft laugh trickled out of Delilah's lips. "He's a clerk in a bank. Zane built that house for me."

Elisabeth surveyed Zane's gleaming wood floors, which smelled of lemon oil. The lush drapes tied back by braided cords. He must be a man of means. "I didn't know."

"I imagine there are a lot of things you don't know about my brother."

Elisabeth nodded, unsure how to respond. At least, thus far, there hadn't been anything about him that she didn't like. Except the color of his hair.

Delilah took Elisabeth's hand. "I want you to promise me, now that you're married to my brother, you'll help him handle his finances. He's not very good at keeping track of money. And he's too generous." A smile engulfed her face, but the tears in her eyes belied her false gaiety. "We don't want him to become poor again, do we?"

Elisabeth's mouth opened and closed. She could help

him with accounting, as she was good at math, but was that what Delilah was trying to imply? Obviously, Delilah assumed that Zane had told his new wife about his childhood. "I'll try to help him any way I can."

"See that you do." Delilah flounced around and headed back to the gathering.

Elisabeth touched her forehead. This had been a very long day.

As if sensing her distress, Zane paced over to her and tucked a loose curl behind her ear. "Go on to bed." He gestured with a nod of his head. "I'll see everyone out first."

Elisabeth stifled a yawn and fixed a smile in place. "Thank you, all of you, for being so welcoming and making this wedding day so. . .nice. Good night."

Before she shut the guest bedroom door, she saw Zane press an envelope into Reginald's hand. Was he giving them money? Was that what Delilah meant about him being too generous? Elisabeth's father had lost their family's fortune on speculations. Had she married a man like her father?

The chill in the room made her hands tremble as she changed into her bedclothes. Slipping under the icy layers of quilts, a heated, wrapped brick, obviously placed there by Mrs. MacIntyre, warmed up her toes. That woman had been a quiet source of kindness since she'd arrived. She must remember to thank her.

Elisabeth lay on her stomach and buried her head under her pillow. Although grateful to be sleeping alone, she wasn't afraid of being with a man. Before she died, her mother had explained the details of marriage to her thoroughly. And in many ways, it sounded comforting to be that close to someone. She shifted onto her back and stared at the light the autumn moon cast upon the far wall. But would Zane know by touching her that her heart still belonged to someone else? A fiancé who could, by now, be a married man?

The door creaked open. A candle cast a tired glow about the room.

She shut her eyes and feigned sleep. Maybe she *was* a little afraid.

Zane's steps creaked on the new floorboards. The bed shifted as he sat, and his warm hand rested on her shoulder. "Are you still awake?"

Her heart sped up. She had the irrational thought that this must be how chickens felt just before dinner. Would Zane honor their agreement to wait on consummating their marriage? She opened her eyes and rolled over. "I'm awake."

He lifted his candle higher. "I just came to say good night, and then I'm off to bed." The light flickered over his face and softened his features. His disheveled hair wasn't as red as Hamilton's. More auburn. Her gaze fell to where his string tie had been pulled loose and his top two shirt buttons undone. His firm build and broad shoulders were manlier than Hamilton's soft, banker frame.

Her face warmed as her emotions stirred with attraction.

"I agree with your suggestion that we wait a while."

She swallowed at his nearness. "You're very kind."

He gazed about the room, giving her a chance to admire the lines fanning out from his eyes. His strong jaw. The tenderness in his eyes.

"I've thought about making this room the master bedroom, but I like sleeping upstairs near the girls."

"Your daughters are—"

"*Our* daughters."

Her chest tightened. She was a mother now to two girls who needed her. Could she fill that role? "Our daughters looked beautiful today. I'm fond of them already. I'll try to be a good mother."

He smiled. "Well, it's obvious they've taken to you by the way they followed you around all day." He reached over and took one of her hands. "Before I go, I thought it would be a valuable habit for us to pray together. This morning I read the scripture, 'Two are better than one; because they have a good reward for their labour. For if they fall, the one will lift up his fellow. . . . Again, if two lie together, then they have heat: but how can one be warm alone?' I especially like this part. 'And a threefold cord is not quickly broken.' I'd like us to think of our marriage as there being three of us—God, you, and me."

Hope tinged her heart. This man had great faith. Zane surprised her at every turn.

"So what can I pray about for my lovely wife?"

She sat up and wrapped her arms around her knees. She certainly didn't feel like a wife. How could she grow to genuinely care for her new husband when her own heart hid so many hurts? The death of her parents in a fire. The rejection of her fiancé. The betrayal of her aunt. All these weights had crushed her heart and ground her emotion into mortar paste. And she had no idea how to put them back together again.

Maybe if she tried very hard to be the woman he deserved. . . "Pray that"—*Somehow, I can be a good wife and mother*—"we will be blessed."

❄

Elisabeth stumbled into the kitchen in the middle of the night and shoved her wild mane of hair behind her ears. Sweat dripped down her back; her breathing came in gasps. She'd had a horrible dream that a fire trapped her parents and Hamilton in her childhood home, and she couldn't get the front door open to save them. Their screams woke her, but by her scratchy throat, she must have been the one screaming. The name Hamilton still rested on her lips.

She grasped the water jug and poured the last of the liquid into a cup, sloshing some of it on the table.

"Elisabeth."

She gasped and whirled around. "Zane."

He stood at the bottom of the stairway, his thick, white cotton undershirt defined his chest and narrow waist.

She shivered as if she had a fever.

"Are you all right?"

If a married woman dreaming of an old love was all right. . .
"I—I. . .just a bad dream."

He came and stood beside her.

She downed all the water in her cup.

"Do you need anything?" His voice, low and caring, unfurled the tendrils of pain in her chest. An ache of tenderness trickled into its place.

Zane. She wanted to speak his name aloud, but she didn't trust her emotions. She wiped her lips with the back of her hand.

He took the cup from her hand, brushing her fingers with his.

A chill went down her spine. Her mouth had gone dry again.

"I'll take you back to bed."

Her eyes widened.

"To your room, I mean."

"Oh." Her gaze searched the room, anywhere but his penetrating eyes. Heat flushed her cheeks as she glanced down at her thin sleep attire. When she looked up, she caught his gaze flitting away from her. "I can—I'm fine." Her legs shook. "I can go back by myself."

"I was just dreaming of you when I heard you cry out." A twinkle appeared in his eyes just before he leaned in and kissed her lips.

The taste of his mouth was sweet. When he pulled away, she pressed her lips together, wishing his touch could have lasted longer.

She watched him saunter back up the stairs toward his room. If only she could dream of him. . .

Chapter 4

B ake cookies?" Elisabeth took another sip of her morning coffee and stared at the two wide-eyed girls still clad in their nightclothes, standing beside her. After being in bed for three days with a fever and the sniffles, it felt good just to sit at the kitchen table.

At the sight of their sweet, pink-cheeked faces, determination welled up inside her. She could never replace their mother, but she could try. However, would her poor housewifery skills disappoint these precious girls?

Olivia pulled out a bowl almost as big as she was from under the sink and carefully tilted it onto the counter. "We want to make Christmas sugar cookies with you."

Christmas was only three weeks away. Elisabeth set aside her pen and paper. Her letter to Caroline could wait. Besides, she wasn't sure confiding to her friend the details of her in-name-only marriage to Zane was such a good idea.

Pulling out a wooden spoon from the collection of

cooking utensils Mrs. MacIntyre kept in a pitcher on the counter, Elisabeth resolved to move forward in her new life.

Last Sunday at Zane's church when Pastor Stanton announced they would need people to help the children in the live nativity play at the Christmas Eve service, her heart leapt. She would love to do that, but would they let a newcomer volunteer?

The pastor went on to read the very scripture Zane had quoted. *"A threefold cord is not quickly broken."* She'd never thought of marriage that way or that God wanted to be a part of it. Could He help her? Did God know about her needs? The girls' needs? Either way, she must start taking care of these two girls she was growing to love. If they only knew she had no idea how to bake.

After assembling eggs, flour, butter, and vanilla in a bowl, the combined mess didn't look much like the cookie batter the cook at her aunt's house would make.

Sophia stuck her finger in and tasted it. "Eww."

A few feet away, Mrs. MacIntyre was sweeping the same spot on the floor repeatedly. She ambled over and took a taste of the batter with her finger. "Weel, it could use a wee bit of baking powder, sugar, and salt."

"Right." Elisabeth breathed a sigh of relief and smiled at the two girls. *Thank You, Lord, for Mrs. MacIntyre.* She dug around the pantry until she found the items and added them in. She had the girls spoon the mixture little by little onto a baking sheet and tucked it into the gleaming new oven. But to her disappointment, ten minutes later, when she pulled them out with the edge of her skirt, the cookies tasted like hard tack. And she'd added way too much salt.

Sophia threw her cookie down. "I like Mrs. MacIntyre's cookies better."

Elisabeth's shoulders wilted. These girls deserved someone who knew how to do such homey things.

"Not to worry. Let me see what I can do." Within minutes, Mrs. MacIntyre had another batch whipped up and baking in the oven. "Mrs. Michaels, can ye hand me an oven glove?"

Elisabeth looked around the kitchen for what she assumed looked like her leather riding gloves. "I don't know what. . . What do you mean?"

The housekeeper shook her head as she grabbed a towel and used it to pull the pan from the oven.

Mrs. MacIntyre knew her secret. Elisabeth was a complete failure in the kitchen. How long before Zane figured it out?

The aroma of hot baked cookies filled the kitchen, but all Elisabeth could do was stare out the window that overlooked the flat lands of Zane's property. If this mail-order-bride marriage was God's idea to help Zane, He'd sent the wrong girl.

Mrs. MacIntyre offered her a cookie from the plate.

"No, thank you." Elisabeth's stomach clenched.

"Yur mother didna' teach ye to cook?"

"I—I. . .well, my mother was busy, and I never learned exactly, not that I didn't want to learn. It's just when I was a child. . ." Elisabeth swallowed. She was making no sense. How could she explain that it was her aunt who had promoted her as a good cook?

Mrs. MacIntyre bit into her cookie. " 'Tis no shame in learning what ye dinna know as long as ye are willing."

Elisabeth nodded her gratitude. "You're right. Thank you."

A knock at the front door produced a sigh from Mrs. MacIntyre.

"Do you want me to answer it?" Elisabeth dusted the flour off her dark green bodice and headed for the door.

Mrs. MacIntyre undid her apron. "No, it'll be someone wanting to see Mr. Michaels."

"Who wants to see me?" Zane strolled into the room. "And who is making those delicious smelling Christmas cookies?"

The girls ran to throw their arms around him. "Poppa!" Olivia looked at her father with her intense blue eyes. "We made them with Elisabeth, but hers didn't taste so good."

Elisabeth tugged on her necklace, watching Zane's forehead furrow. Her chest burned with mortification. Should she confess her secret?

Zane hunched down by his girls. "When I married Miss Lariby on Thursday, she became Mrs. Michaels. So, I want you girls to call her momma, and from now on, no criticizing the cooking."

"Yes, Poppa," the two girls chimed together.

"Someone is at the door to see ye, Mr. Michaels. 'Tis too many hands outstretched if ye ask me." Mrs. MacIntyre gestured toward the door.

Zane leaned in, gave Elisabeth a kiss on the cheek, and snatched up a cookie. "After I speak with him, Elisabeth, I'd like to take my new bride into town and show you my store and have you meet my clerks."

Elisabeth blinked back tears. She was a failure as a bride. And how long before he figured it out?

The rays of the early December sun bounced off the frozen puddles like discarded mirrors carelessly tossed onto the well-trodden path. Zane slowed the buggy as they turned the corner on the road into town. Despite the sunshine, he was grateful for the hot bricks at their toes to keep the winter chill at bay. Especially since his jacket was a bit threadbare, but he couldn't part with it.

He sneaked a glance at Elisabeth in her fancy bonnet and dark green cloak covered by a thick blanket. Just looking at her blue eyes, the pink tinge to her cheeks, and her shiny blond hair was a pleasure. His pride had swelled at all the compliments he'd received on his beautiful new wife, and he heartily agreed. He just prayed no one would press him on how they'd met.

He sneaked another peek at her. She hadn't said much since they'd left home. Why was she was always so reserved?

He cast a glance at her gloved hands still clasped in a tight hold. Reaching over, he squeezed them. "Are you fretting over the girls' comments? I'm sure your cookies were fine."

She turned her whole body to face him. "They were awful." Her voice cracked. "I'm a terrible cook."

"A terrible cook? But in your letters—" The tears gathering in her eyes silenced his questions. Just because she couldn't bake didn't make her any less of a perfect wife. "Elisabeth Michaels, don't you fret over some cookies. I've been smitten by you since the day I saw you—"

"I'm glad you like the look of me, but"—her gaze turned cool and distant, as if she was thinking of home—"I need to be able to help you with your life here." She stared straight out ahead. "I wonder if we've made a mistake in marrying."

A mistake? His heart dropped like the frosty temperature outside. Is that what she'd been hiding? Could she tell he wasn't highly educated? That growing up poor, he didn't use fancy words or wear expensive clothes? That he wasn't the successful businessman he pretended to be? "You do help me. You being beside me warms my heart. We just need to get to know one another." He licked his dry lips. Did he have the courage to share his past with her? "We need to. . .to talk more."

Her head dipped. "I am so embarrassed. . .that I asked you to wait on. . . I just need some more time."

His insides lurched like a tree in a stiff wind. He was deeply attracted to her, but her words twisted his gut. She regretted marrying him? "I'm willing to wait a spell." He struggled with the words to tell her how he felt. "You are my gift from God."

Her gaze shifted to the barren landscape around them, and she fell silent.

This is bad. He snapped the reins and refocused his attention on the deserted road in front of him. *Lord, bring her closer to You and bind us together so that nothing can ever break our union.*

As they pulled up to a line of shops, Zane nudged Elisabeth's arm. "So what do you think of my store?"

Elisabeth admired the faded fancy lettering, Michaels' Clothing Emporium for Men, and the drapes that hung just under the sign. Two glass windows out front displayed men's hats, pants, coats, and boots. Was this how he made his money?

Twice now, an older man and a young woman with a child, all dressed in patched clothing, had come to the door to speak with him. Did he always give to everyone who asked?

Zane held the door open and greeted the two clerks who worked behind the counter. "Harry, William, I want you to meet the new Mrs. Michaels."

Both young men flushed when they shook her hand.

"Did you hire the new seamstress yet?" Harry opened a ledger and ran a finger down a page. "I think we can afford to hire someone a few hours a week."

William sorted through a pile of packages. "With business being so slow, surely the store can't afford that."

Zane's gaze swerved toward his employees. "Don't ever let me here you speak of business in front of Mrs. Michaels again."

The two clerks shared a glance then replied in unison, "Yes, sir."

Elisabeth turned away and pretended to be admiring a row of hats. If business was slow, why was Zane so generous? Was Delilah right about her brother not being able to handle money?

"I'm pleased to tell you Mrs. Michaels is deft at sewing and will start taking over the mending next week." Zane nodded with a smile.

Elisabeth stepped backward. Despite the stitches forming

in her stomach, she wasn't a seamstress. Her mouth bobbed open as she searched for the words to explain to Zane the truth, but how could she? She had already disappointed him by confessing she couldn't cook.

Harry rested his chin on his hand and sighed. "Mrs. Michaels, are you from around here? How did you meet Mr. Michaels?"

William elbowed him hard.

Zane's jaw flexed as he yanked some envelopes from his pocket. A letter slipped to the floor. He snatched it up and kissed Elisabeth's cheek before handing it to her. "A letter came for you on Friday. I'm sorry, with the wedding I forgot all about it. Why don't you sit in the office and read it while I have a word with my impolite clerks."

At the sight of Hamilton's masculine handwriting, a flame ignited inside of her. She stifled the desire to run her fingers over the thick ink letters. Had he used the pen she'd bought him for his birthday? She gripped the letter and offered Zane what she hoped was a reassuring smile. "That would be nice."

As soon as she was safely behind a closed door, she slid her shaky fingers under the lip of the envelope and eased the letter out.

Dearest Elisabeth,

My love, can you ever forgive me? Brigitte has left St. Louis. She fled to New York and will soon return to France. Seems she already had a husband. I realize with each passing day how much I still love you. Please, my darling, tell me you haven't yet married.

Her body trembled as she tore her gaze from his words. All her longing for Hamilton rushed back in a suffocating wave. She gripped the letter to her chest, crinkling the paper. These emotions were shameful. She was married to a man of great character and generosity. A man she was beginning to care for. A glance back at the envelope revealed cash tucked inside. She read on.

> *I have left my job at the bank. At twenty-five,*
> *I will no longer allow my parents to control my*
> *life. I have enclosed funds for you to come back*
> *home. We will wed as soon as we are able. Return*
> *to me.*

A hinge creaked. Zane stood in the open door. "Is everything all right?"

She gasped and squashed the letter closed. "I am. . .very missed at home."

"I'm sure you are. Here." He shoved a parcel into her hands. "This just came in. A wedding present."

She hid her letter in her reticule and took in a deep breath to calm her thudding heart. How could she have feelings for a man who deserted her? Fire raged in her chest. But didn't this correspondence prove that Hamilton still loved her? What would Zane think of her if he knew of the emotions this letter stirred? She'd never leave Zane, but that Hamilton's words could have such an effect on her rocked her to her core. God must be very angry with her.

Managing to tug the twine from the package with her shaky fingers, she pulled back the paper. "A Bible."

"Look." Zane opened the cover and flipped to the title page.

She ran her fingertips over the words, Mrs. Elisabeth Michaels, written in a fancy, swirly manner just above the date of their wedding. Her gold wedding band glimmered in her line of sight, reminding her of the commitment she had made to him. But was she a wife? She certainly didn't feel like one. She could offer no domestic duties, and then there was their agreement. . .

He bent low and searched her eyes, concern etched into every part of his face. "You look fretful."

A rush of affection eased her anguish. Not only was Zane handsome, but he was also kind and thoughtful. She hugged the Bible to her chest and stood. Maybe God wasn't so angry. Maybe there was hope for her yet. "Thank you."

"I thought we could read it jointly. Pastor Stanton says that when a husband and wife grow in their relationship with Christ, they grow together."

The earnest glow in his eyes highlighted the difference between Hamilton and Zane. Hamilton had little interest in the things of God. That one thing troubled her during her engagement. Zane talked about God as if he knew Him personally.

"I'm glad you liked my gift." Zane leaned over and kissed her forehead. Then her nose. And then her lips.

Her heart stirred, and her arm found its way around his waist. Should she show Zane the letter? What should she do? *Oh God, please forgive me for my wayward thoughts. Help me.*

Elisabeth and Zane rode home in silence. The shifting of the wagon back and forth echoed her anxious feelings.

Despite her growing feelings of attachment to Zane, she still cared for Hamilton. And it pained her to know he was now free to marry her. But she had made a commitment before God to be Zane's wife even if it hadn't been consummated. She risked a glance at her husband. By his steady gaze, he looked deep in thought. Odd that when Harry asked her how she met Mr. Michaels, Zane had quickly silenced him. Was he ashamed that she was a mail-order bride?

"Was your letter from your uncle?"

A hitch caught in her throat and she coughed. "No. A friend."

"Did you find the ink and paper I left out for you on the desk in the guest room?"

"Yes, thank you. I've written to my friend, Caroline."

"Good. Good."

When they got home, two excited little girls jumped up and down and waved papers in the air. "We drew pictures for our new momma." Olivia waved her drawing.

As soon as Elisabeth sat and took off her gloves, the girls crowded around her. "See." Sophia pressed herself against Elisabeth. "That's you and me holding hands in front of a Christmas tree."

The picture grew blurry in Elisabeth's gaze. "That's a wonderful drawing."

Olivia wedged her way in between them. "And here's mine. It's me and you dancing. See how our legs are bent?"

It was as if a hand was squeezing her heart. Elisabeth blinked back tears as her insides overflowed with gratitude. She wrapped her arms around them. "I have the two best girls."

Olivia set her face right in front of hers. "Are those happy tears again?"

Elisabeth nodded as she dabbed at her eyes. She had her answer. She needed to let Hamilton go. Then she needed to figure out how to be the perfect wife for Zane.

Mrs. MacIntyre watched her and the girls. Her approving gaze gave Elisabeth an idea. "Mrs. MacIntyre, do you think you could teach me how to cook and clean?" Elisabeth glanced over her shoulder to see Zane hanging up his coat. "I'm just not sure how Mr. Michaels likes his house. . ."

Zane came and stood beside them. "I like my house full of girls."

The two girls giggled. "Poppa."

Zane ruffled Olivia's hair. "Elisabeth, don't be intimidated by Mrs. MacIntyre's Scottish ways of running a home. I'm sure your skills are just as good."

"Weel, I might be able to teach this St. Louis lass a thing or two."

The kind glint in Mrs. MacIntyre's eyes belied her scolding tone, easing the tension gripping Elisabeth's shoulders. She would be a friend. God had heard her cry for help.

Using the excuse to put away her cloak, Elisabeth paced into her room, determined to find a minute alone to write to Hamilton and ask him never to communicate with her again. But as she strode past the window toward the desk, she stopped at the view of people skating on a frozen pond bordered by a row of fir trees on Zane's land. One couple in particular drew her attention and her mind back to a memory from her past. . .

The refreshing St. Louis winter air invigorated her body and made the sky seemed bluer than before. Her arm hooked through Hamilton's as they made their way, gliding around the frozen pond. It was her first courting, and she couldn't be prouder to be seen with such a handsome man.

At each wobble, he held her upright, his strong arm around her back. "Do you like skating?"

"I love it." Her confession gushed out before she could stop it. "I haven't done this since I was a child. But wherever did you find skates that would fit me perfectly?"

"I bought them at the store."

"For me?"

He suddenly spun around on the ice and gripped her arms as he faced her. His chiseled jaw and the cleft in his chin made her want to melt into the ice. "Nothing is too good for you, Elisabeth Lariby. I just can't believe you said yes to coming with me."

Elisabeth bit back a little cheer. She would have said yes to a walk through a cemetery in the dark just to be beside the most dashing man in all of St. Louis. Hamilton made her feel wanted, cherished, as if she belonged. Something she longed for since her parent's death. "Thank you for the skates and for a wonderful day."

He leaned over and kissed her cheek with his warm lips and whispered in her ear, "There will be many more like this."

Her heart soared. Had she found love at last?

Or a love that wasn't meant to be?

Elisabeth shivered in the cold, forcing the brittle memories away as she turned from the window. Could that have been a year ago? How much her life had changed. She sat at the desk, her pen frozen above the paper. How could she say good-bye to the only man she'd ever loved?

Dear Hamilton,

She scratched out the word *dear*, then crumbled up the paper, wincing at the waste.

Hamilton,
 I am sorry things did not work out with your fiancée, but I feel it best for us to end all correspondence. I am now a married woman and a mother to two girls. Please don't contact me again.

Yours respectfully,
Mrs. Zane Michaels

As she stuffed the money he'd sent her into the envelope, her fingers burned as if touching fiery coals. This surely was the end of Hamilton Gatesworth.

Chapter 5

A week and a half passed, and Elisabeth scurried from one end of the house to the other, with her new apron, sewn by Mrs. MacIntyre, firmly in place. She found she enjoyed putting things in order and tidying up. But cooking was still a mystery to her. How Mrs. MacIntyre ever got that stove to the right temperature was a miracle in itself. Elisabeth, so far, had burned bacon, a coffee cake, and a pot of peas.

But these small steps into her new life, joined with Zane's approving smiles, filled her with a sense of satisfaction. Often, instead of doubting God's care, she found a prayer of gratitude to Him on her lips. Encouraged by Zane's devotion to their nightly Bible reading and prayer, she could feel her own faith growing.

With Mrs. MacIntyre's help, she found her homesickness for her life in St. Louis lessening and the grip her past had on her heart easing. She was beginning to see that she could make a life for herself in Plainsville.

That was the morning. Four hours later, she stood in the freezing wind, with her unfurled hair whipping around her face as she undid the clothes and linens from the clothesline. The temperature had dropped over the last few hours, and cold nipped her fingers. There must be a storm coming in. Overhead, the gray sky looked vast and lonely.

Mrs. MacIntyre was surprised when Elisabeth insisted on taking over the laundry duties, but she felt like it made up for her poor cooking skills. But afternoons spent bending over a tub filled with hot water was exhausting work. Although to see the girls in freshly washed and ironed dresses on Sunday was at least a heartening reward.

Needing her shawl and some gloves, she lugged the laundry basket into the house and headed upstairs to put Zane's clothes away before going back to get the rest of the garments.

"Hello?" A voice called from the front of the house.

Elisabeth set the basket down and trod down the stairs. No one was home, as Zane said he needed to go make a deposit at the bank and had taken the girls with him. Mrs. MacIntyre had gone to take some medicine to a sickly neighbor.

Delilah and her husband, Reginald, were undoing their coats and hats.

"I didn't know you were coming for a visit." Elisabeth tucked her windblown hair behind her ears. "Can I get you some—" She paused. Mrs. MacIntyre wasn't here, and she still didn't make a very good a cup of coffee.

"Coffee would be great." Reginald said, stretching his lanky frame onto an overstuffed chair.

Elisabeth hung up their coats, and then whirled around

and gripped the tin coffeepot. How many scoops of coffee? How much water? Did she add the eggshells to settle the grounds now or after it boiled? She so wanted for them to approve of her, but whom could she ask for help?

It suddenly became clear that she had to make a decision about God. He either cared about her and knew the details of her life or He didn't. She could either trust Him to help her with this coffee and her new life or continue in her distrust of Him. She pressed her eyes shut. "Please, help me, Lord. In this situation and every day of my life. I give You my life, my marriage, my heartaches. I am Yours. And please help me to make a decent cup of coffee."

After a few minutes, she served a cup of the hot drink to Reginald and waited.

He took a sip. A smile touched his lips. "Perfect."

A thrill tingled through her heart. *Thank You, Lord.*

"How are you finding life in Nebraska?" Delilah took a slice of cake from the plate Elisabeth held out. "Are we Nebraskans too backward for you?"

Elisabeth forced a serene smile to her lips, unsure how to answer and anxious to earn Delilah's good opinion. "Nebraskans are very friendly and helpful."

"What about our fashion? I see you haven't given up your city way of dressing in dark colors."

Elisabeth smoothed out her damp bodice with her hands red from scrubbing the laundry. Other than the dress her aunt had made for her, it had been a long time since she'd had something new to wear. "I hope one day I can buy some new dresses. More like the lighter colored styles that you wear here."

"Well, nothing too expensive, I hope. Just because Zane got $100,000 when he sold his land in Colorado, I don't think he should be throwing it around as much as he does."

Elisabeth's pulse pounded in her neck. Zane had that much money? Was that why he handed out so much? Why hadn't he told her? "I'm sure he knows what he's doing."

Reginald leaned forward. "We were hoping he'd be here. We wanted to ask him about a—a loan of sorts. The money he gave us this month kind of ran out, and with Christmas coming. . ."

"Ran out because you wanted a new shooting gun and a new horse. Like our stable doesn't have enough already." Delilah's curls shook as she spoke. "My brother, Michael—" she slapped her hand across her mouth. "Oh dear, I hope he told you about his real name."

Elisabeth cocked her head to one side. Zane wasn't his real name?

Reginald scowled at his wife and then turned a serene gaze toward Elisabeth. "Never mind her questions. The reason we came is I wondered if you could give us some of the cash Zane keeps in that old suitcase under his bed."

Elisabeth's back and neck ached as she sat erect in her chair. Despite the cool temperature in the room, her body felt flushed with heat. She tugged on the edge of her dark purple skirt. "I—I don't know where he keeps his money, but he did go into town today to deposit some and took a large suitcase with him."

"Oh dear, he did say something to me last week about putting it all in the bank." Delilah chewed on her lower lip.

"I told you we needed to come sooner." Reginald

unfolded himself like a jackknife and stood. "Well then, we need to get going."

Delilah pulled on her cloak. "Thank you for the cake and coffee. Tell Zane I will speak to him on Sunday."

They were outdoors faster than a gust of St. Louis wind.

Elisabeth leaned her back against the closed door. What other secrets was Zane hiding? Was he ever going to tell her about the money? His name? And why did he expect her to do the mending for his store when he obviously had the funds to hire someone?

A glance at the clock told her he would be home soon, and she needed to finish the laundry. Scurrying back up the stairs, she put his shirts and pants away in his dresser and then took a moment to survey his bedroom.

Who was this man who was hiding so much? *What are you hiding from him?* floated across her thoughts. But she could never tell him about Hamilton or her lack of sewing skills or her fear of disappointing the girls or her constant worry that she would never fit in Nebraska.

She leaned over and tucked in one wayward edge of his blue and white quilt on the bed. Had it been made by his wife? Did he still love the woman? She brushed the thought away. Of course he did, as he should. But would he ever love her? For a moment, she pictured herself lying in the bed next to him. What would it be like to cuddle—

Her scalp prickled with heat, and she picked up the folded blankets from the laundry basket and lifted the lid of the painted chest at the foot of his bed where Mrs. MacIntyre stored them. She paused when she saw a woman's floral dress.

With a glance over her shoulder, she set the blankets down and lifted out the faded rose-colored dress. Zane's first wife must have been short and a full-figured woman. Elisabeth recognized her excellent dressmaking skills, as this woman's exact stitches were in a perfect row.

She held the garment up to the light and studied the differences between St. Louis and Nebraska fashion. St. Louis styles were darker in color with a few discreet embellishments. This dress was pale with no adornments. Was that how Zane wanted his wife to dress? Were her clothes too fancy? Too dark? Did he find her attractive?

She found him very handsome. Even his auburn hair was appealing to her now. An ache welled in her throat. "Please, Lord, could you help Zane to love me?"

A peek further into the chest revealed more dresses, shoes, a few hankies, and a small wooden box. Zane must have saved these items for his girls. As she picked up the box and opened it, a brooch fell out onto her lap.

Footsteps sounded behind her. Heavy boots like Zane's.

She fumbled to put the items away. The dress was folded and shoved back with the box hidden beneath it. The blankets set on top and the lid closed.

"Elisabeth?" Zane stood in the doorway.

"Oh, you scared me." Her hand was pressed against her thudding heart. She smoothed back her hair, and as she stood, the pearl brooch fell to the floor.

"What's this?"

"I'm sorry." She braced herself. "I was just putting some blankets away, and—"

"This was my wife's." A sad smile creased Zane's face as

he turned the jewelry over in his hand. "When I was a boy, my mother had to sell it for food, but with my first real job I bought it back for her." He closed his palm and looked up. "You should have seen her face when I gave it to her."

Elisabeth's heart swelled. She yearned to reach out and touch the side of his face. To smooth back the hair that hung over his furrowed brow.

"It belonged to my grandmother, and then was passed down to my mother, and then to Julia."

Julia. A beautiful name for most likely a beautiful woman. Elisabeth sighed at her own tall, thin figure with no curves. How foolish to hope a man could ever care more for his second wife.

"It's been passed down through three generations of wives." He drew his gaze away from the jewelry and fixed it on hers. "I'll just put it back."

A weight pressed against her chest. Did the brooch remind him too much of Julia?

"So, are you done with the mending I brought in from the store?"

Her mouth went dry. She hadn't even started. "I—I . . ."

He reached over and folded down the wayward collar on her dress. His warm hand brushed her cheek, and she longed to lean into it for comfort. "Don't fret. A husband and two children are a lot to take on. I'm sure you'll whip through that mending in no time."

She pressed her lips together. She had never mended anything in her life. Should she tell him? She gripped both hands behind her back. What kind of marriage would this be if they both kept their hearts so hidden? All of a sudden her secrets became too much. A tear escaped her eye.

He stepped forward and pulled her into his sturdy arms. "Why the tears?"

She laid her head on his shoulder, savoring the comfort she found in his embrace. He had a wonderful smell of outdoors and soap mixed together. Her senses began to spin as he began to leave a fiery trail of kisses across her neck. When his lips found hers, she responded to his passion, savoring the feel of his ardent lips and the taste of his mouth.

Did she love him? A lump welled in her throat. Could he ever love her? Even with all her housewifery deficiencies?

"Can you tell me what's wrong?"

She rested her chin on his shoulder, holding back her confession. She didn't belong here. If she had any hope that he would ever love her, she couldn't tell him the truth. She forced her voice to sound bright. "Everything is fine. I'm just tired."

Zane breathed in the fresh smell of Elisabeth's hair tangled about her shoulders. He pressed his eyes shut and relished the chance to hold her. He'd been hungry to take her into his arms from the first minute he saw her. But there was something in her eyes, a hesitancy that made him hold back and agree to wait on the physical side of their marriage. But sometimes, at night, when he was tossing and turning, he wondered what she thought of him. Did she regret coming to Nebraska? Was she disappointed with him as a husband?

He allowed himself a few more kisses on her soft cheek

and hauled himself away. He admired her slender figure, her lovely skin, and the tilt of her small nose. He couldn't believe she was his. What a blessed man he was. How much longer until she would be a wife in every sense?

In his eyes, despite the fact that she couldn't cook, she was still perfect. Except that he had to keep how they met a secret. It wouldn't do to be a successful businessman and have to write to an organization to find a wife. "Get to the mending when you can. But can I ask one favor? Earlier, when we visited the store, you were asked how we met. I'd like to keep that quiet. No one needs to know the details of how we came to be married."

Elisabeth swallowed the tight band in her throat as she watched Zane walk away from her and head for the stairs. Was Zane not his real name? Or was Michael his middle name? But it was his last name. . . She drifted toward the door frame and watched him hurry upstairs to his office. How could she please him when he held so many things from her?

"Momma. Momma." The girls waved striped candy sticks in her face. "Look what Poppa bought for us at the store."

"You must have been very good girls." Elisabeth hugged Sophia and Olivia.

"I brought mail back from town. Here are two letters for ye." Mrs. MacIntyre handed her the envelopes.

One from her aunt and one from Hamilton.

Elisabeth's heart sped up. She stuffed them in her apron, ashamed that even the sight of Hamilton's handwriting still affected her. "I need to bring in the rest of the laundry."

Her steps crunched on the rocky path toward the barn. She needed to be alone, and with two children about the house, this was the only spot where no one would find her. With each step, she admonished herself. *Do not open Hamilton's letter. Do not open it.* But as soon as she escaped the bitter wind and found a bench to sit on, she ripped into it.

> *Dearest Elisabeth,*
>   *Please, don't lose hope. We can still be together.*

But surely, he had gotten her letter by now.

> *My parents feel very badly about forcing me to quit our engagement and dictating whom I would marry. They have even been to visit your aunt and uncle.*

Elisabeth froze. Her aunt? Hopefully, Caroline had kept what Elisabeth had confided to her about her marriage a secret.

> *Caroline came to my house and shared, in the strictest of confidence, regarding the state of your marriage. As you know, my dearest, father is a lawyer and he says, may I speak frankly, your unconsummated union is easily annulled.*

Elisabeth's face flared hot until her scalp prickled. She glowered at the letter. Her tear-blurry gaze searched the upper loft of the barn where a battered trunk had been left open and its contents scattered about. How could Caroline betray her?

Please, my darling, I still love you. Mother and Father changed their minds after I left the bank. They are now anxious to accept you into our family. No one need know about your unfortunate alliance in Nebraska. Mother and Father have even offered to build us a home near the bank in the St. Louis city center and will provide us with servants and a cook. It is the life you were meant to lead. Write back quickly. I want you home by Christmas.

She put the letter down. The chill in the barn seeped into her bones like spilled ink. He was right. She was meant to live in a big city, married to a sophisticated man like Hamilton, entertaining, and directing servants. It was what she had known her whole life. Despite her growing attraction to Zane, she wasn't good at the things he needed from her. Tears wet her face, and she wiped them hastily away. She opened her aunt's letter.

Dear Elisabeth,

By now, I am sure that you have received Hamilton's letter. His father and I spoke for some time, and this whole mess is easily fixed. I know Hamilton has sent you money. Please use it to catch the next train back to St. Louis. We need never speak of this excursion again. Write me and let me know when you are coming home. I only want what is best for you.

Most affectionately,
Aunt Dorothy

Excursion? Her posture stiffened. As if this marriage were just some outing she'd forgotten to tell everyone about. As if being a mail-order bride was something she'd incited.

A vision of Zane came into her mind. He was a very physical man with firm muscles and broad shoulders, whereas Hamilton was more a slight, pale, city man. Zane had said she was his gift from God. Hamilton would never say that. She crushed the letter in her hand. No matter what, she had made a vow to be Zane's wife.

"Lord, I trust that You will help me to know how to respond to these letters." She wiped at her tears with her apron and sat up straighter. "And help me to have the courage to tell Zane everything."

Chapter 6

The next night, after the girls had gone to bed, Zane sat next to Elisabeth on the couch, and they took turns reading the Bible, as was their custom each evening. As he read, "The truth shall make you free," the scripture convicted him. Despite knowing and loving God, he was as trapped by his secrets as a sinner by his sins.

With the soft glow of the candles illuminating Elisabeth in her dark blue dress, a desire welled up in him to tell her about his childhood, his real name, the money. . .everything. It was only a matter of time before she figured some of things out.

Her blond curls and her prim and proper ways made his chest expand with pride. He'd already received many compliments on his new wife. He couldn't wait to give her the family brooch. It was the custom to give the ornamental pin on the first anniversary, but he didn't know if he could wait that long. He reached over and pressed her hand. "The dress you're wearing is very pretty."

She patted his hand. "Thank you." Her voice was low and quiet.

That wasn't the response he'd hoped to get from her. Was she upset about his asking her to hide the fact that she was a mail-order bride? He'd try another tactic. "I hope I didn't startle you when I came home and found you in my bedroom."

"I'm so sorry. I never intended to go through your wife's things. I just saw them there—"

"Elisabeth, you are my wife."

Her gaze fell. "Of course."

Heat seared his chest. Her unhappiness was as easy to see as one of his girls' frowns. He wanted to somehow reach this reserved woman's heart. Convey how much he felt as if God had given him a supernatural ability to love her before he even knew her very well. But could he share the truth? Thomas Worth seemed to think secrets in a marriage weren't good. "I—I wanted to let you know, of course you'll have to keep this quiet, but my name is—"

She was leaning forward, her lips parted as if she were hanging onto his every word.

"I can't sew."

He blinked. "What?"

"I can't sew or cook or clean or garden. My aunt wrote those things in her letter to Mrs. Mayberry to make me sound much better than I really am. My mother forced me to do embroidery, but I hated it. I can thread a needle, but it's been so long that's about all I can do in the way of stitchery. I'm sorry I hadn't told you this sooner."

"What did you do with your time?"

"My aunt had me accompany her to tea parties, gatherings, concerts, and when visiting and receiving guests. That was, of course, until she remarried."

Zane sat back in his seat. His desire for the perfect wife was unraveling before his eyes. Was this why she had been so reserved with him? That she felt she had to hide this secret from him? He ran his fingers through his hair. How could he explain her lack of sewing skills to Harry and William? To Thomas?

"Is there anything else I should know about you?" Even as he said the words, he felt a nudge to confess his own secrets. But what would she think of him? He and Delilah had sworn never to tell anyone how desperate their childhood was. How much they suffered under the disdain of their townsfolk. How humiliating it was to be teased and ridiculed when he'd been forced to go door to door to beg for food. And now, because he hadn't had much schooling and was poor with figures, his clothing store was failing. He didn't give the store the attention it needed. Truth was his heart wasn't in it.

Just as she opened her mouth to reply, a knock at the door sounded.

Zane sighed. He wanted to hear what she had to say. He strode over and opened the door, surprised to make out a small figure amongst the steady fall of snow.

"Hullo." A little boy with a shock of blond hair held his cap in his hands. A layer of frosty white covered his shoulders.

"Hello." Zane stuck his head out to see if a mother was nearby. His face stung with the cold. When he didn't see anyone, he pulled the boy indoors and shut the door. As he blew on his hands to warm them back up, he looked closer at the boy. This was him. This was exactly what he had done when his family had no food. Sweat gathered on Zane's forehead. "Is anyone with you?"

"Someone told me a rich man lived here." The boy shivered.

Elisabeth stood beside Zane. "He needs to be by the fire." She reached out to take the boy's hand, but he pulled away.

"I need money to buy bread for my brother and sister." The boy's blue lips quivered.

Tension tightened Zane's neck. He slanted a glance at Elisabeth. What would she think if she knew this boy represented his childhood? "Where are your parents?"

The boy wrinkled up his nose and shoved his hands to his waist. "Listen, mister, I gots to get back. Are you gonna give me money?"

Suddenly, amazement replaced Zane's tension. He resisted the urge to pat the lad on his head. All this boy needed was dark red hair and he would look just like him. "Where are you going to buy bread this late at night? Are you an orphan?"

Elisabeth touched Zane's shoulder. "We can't let him go back out in this."

Zane nodded, surprised by the firm tone in her voice. "You'll have to spend the night here. How old are you?"

"Nine, and I'm not staying." The boy brushed the snow off the top of his thin and dirty shirt and set his oversized worn cap in place. "If you won't help me, I'm leaving."

Zane's heart lurched. He remembered what it was like to wear a hard exterior. To shroud himself in distrust. To feel shame, buried by a mound of desperation to prove he was a better man than his father.

Elisabeth knelt down to the boy's level. "Why don't you show us where your siblings are? If you have no parents, then I can bring everyone here to sleep for tonight where it's warm."

"I ain't got no parents, so either you give me money or I walk." The boy folded his arms against his chest, but his shivering undid his tough chap performance.

"Listen, son." Zane pointed a finger at him.

Elisabeth touched Zane's arm. "Hold on."

In a few minutes, Elisabeth returned holding a cumbersome blanket. "I've wrapped up some bread, oatmeal, cookies, and a couple of apples. Share this with your siblings."

The boy snatched the coverlet out of her hands, wrenched open the door, and, without a look back, ran off dragging the blanket behind him. Soon, all that could be seen was a line drawn in snow, disappearing into the darkness.

Despite the tip of her nose burning with cold, she blinked back tears. "That poor boy."

Zane closed the door. "Did you see that? Not even a thank you. At least I—I think you should say thank you."

"He was just a little boy. I wonder if he does have parents."

"Well, maybe. I do admire the way you handled him." Zane rubbed his face with his hand.

"You do?" Hope rose inside of her. Would he share some of his childhood with her?

He stood up straighter. "I mean. . .there were some poor kids in the town that I grew up in. They were hungry and callous like that."

She rubbed the cold from her arms. "I felt so bad for him. Are there many children like him in Plainsville?"

"Not that I know of. I'll ask my friend Thomas if he's heard about them. He seems to know everyone—" Zane studied her. "Of course you knew what to do. You were an orphan."

Sadness squeezed her chest. It was as if someone had put a name to the wound that had silently lingered within her. She nodded, as a hidden hurt welled up inside her. "Yes, I guess you're right. I never thought—yes, I guess with no parents. . ."

He took her in his arms and pressed her to him. "I am so sorry your parents are gone."

A sob shook her whole frame.

"I'm so sorry you had to live with your aunt."

She pressed her face into his chest and suppressed a moan.

He pulled her back and held her by both arms. "But you're not alone anymore. You have a family. With the girls and me."

She bit her lips to silence her crying. It was as if a final piece to a puzzle fell into place. "God has brought me here to be your wife and a mother to your girls." A well of joy rose up from the ashes inside of her. God loved her. She had a place to belong.

"And you're a good wife and a good mother."

Her shoulders wilted. "I'm not. I'm not what you need."
And that's why I'll never wear the family brooch.

"You're exactly what I need. I—I—Elisabeth, my store is failing. I made a lot of money when I sold some land in Colorado. I made $100,000, but I've given lots of it away, and I'm not so good at keeping track of what I've passed out. I'm not the success you think I am."

She pressed her lips together. She admired him so much. He was a good man. A man of integrity. A man who cared for others. "I think you're wonderful."

"Thank you, but only you and my sister know the truth."

"Oh, I forgot to tell you," she blurted out. "Your sister and her husband came by when you were in town and asked for money."

"I always help my sister." He rubbed the back of his neck. "We grew up very poor, so we spent a good portion of our childhood hungry. I can't say no to her. I just wish I could manage things better."

A spark of hope lit up like a candle inside of Elisabeth. "Zane, I may not be good at cooking or sewing, but I've always had a head for figures. Let me help you with managing your finances. I could manage the store and your giving."

"No." He pulled away. "A successful businessman doesn't have his wife helping him like that. I can manage this on my own."

"But—but—" Her mouth opened and closed. "Then maybe I'm not the wife you need."

He paced away from her and then paced back. "I'm seen

as a very successful man in this town. I have a reputation to protect. I can't have you tarnishing that."

A piercing realization burned inside of her. This marriage would never work. "Then maybe God sent you the wrong bride." She scurried into her room and slammed the door.

❄

Two days later Elisabeth got up extra early and made coffee, hoping she'd get a chance to talk to Zane before he headed out for his store. Yesterday, he'd left early and hadn't come home until after bedtime.

The coffee tasted a little strong, and the porridge was a little watery, but she had made it. She peered outside in the fading darkness, glad to see no hoof prints in the snow, which was already starting to melt.

Zane strolled into the room, trying to button his shirt. "Mrs. MacIntyre, the way you sewed the—"

Elisabeth whirled around. A couple of days ago, she had sewn on those buttons. "I'm sorry. That was my—"

"Oh no, it's fine."

But when she reached for his shirt, her fingers brushed against his chest.

He stepped back. "I'll just ask Mrs. MacIntyre."

Her spirits fell off a cliff. She was no more what he needed than a riverboat in his backyard. "Of course."

"I'm sorry." He reached up and cupped her cheek. "I'm sorry for getting upset with you the other night. I just had an image in my mind—"

"An image of a wife that I don't live up to."

A smile spread across his face, as if he found something

about this conversation amusing. "No, actually you exceed it."

She shook her head. She didn't even feel like his bride. "I have failed you at every turn, except my appearance. That is not being a wife."

"You have not failed. You are my—"

"Poppa. Momma." The girls ran down the stairs from their bedroom and gave them both hugs.

Mrs. MacIntyre drew the curtains, flooding the room with light. "Good morning to ye."

He leaned over the girls' heads. "Elisabeth, I want to take you on a ride later today. I want to show you something."

About a quarter of a mile out of town, Elisabeth shifted in her seat when Zane pulled on the heavy reins to stop the carriage. In front of them stood a vast field. She took in the small cottage, a large barn, the acres of fenced property, and the other outbuildings scattered across the property.

When she looked over at Zane, he just stared at his gloved hands, as if struggling with something. "I think God is telling me to buy these 120 acres, but I don't know why." His blue eyes shone wide with sincerity.

Elisabeth nodded in amazement. This man surprised her at every turn. "Well, do you want to live here?"

"No, and I haven't bought it yet. It belonged to Doc Tenberger's parents before they died. Doc's willing to give me a fair price, but I'm just not sure. It's not for my use, I know that much. It's just. . .Elisabeth, I don't know what you think of me, but my father was a drunkard. My mother struggled to put food on the table. We were very poor. So I guess over the years I've developed a need to rely on God and to provide for others."

Overcome by admiration for his openness, she touched his arm. "I admire the way you take care of your sister. The giving I see you do. Your faith has been an inspiration to me."

He placed his hand on hers. "I needed to hear that."

"I'm glad." A small door of hope opened in her heart. Maybe God had sent her here to help him in ways neither of them ever imagined.

"Ever since I committed my life to God, He has blessed me in many things, including with you. But I don't know that I've handled the financial gift the Lord has given me in the right way. I want to please God. I'm just not sure who to help or how."

She liked the way Zane talked about God in his everyday life. "Then you will be like Noah and trust Him to tell you what to do"—she looked over the land and then back at him—"what to build and who it's for."

"You are absolutely right." He squinted at her as if seeing her for the first time. He leaned in and kissed her, nuzzling her ear.

Heat warmed her despite the intense cold. Zane Michaels was a handsome man. "I'm glad I could help."

"And now for a surprise." He reached behind him and pulled out a picnic basket. "I've brought wood and a blanket, and we are going to have an indoor picnic."

Inside the cottage were a table and two chairs, a braided rug, a large black hearth, and little else. He added the wood and kindling he'd brought. She admired how he took time to carefully arrange each piece of wood and tuck in the kindling. He was good at starting fires.

Feeling suddenly warm, she took off her coat and smoothed back her hair. But she couldn't help noticing his broad shoulders and the way his hair curled over his collar.

Once the fire chased the chill from the room, she emptied out the basket, full of Mrs. MacIntyre's cooking—fried chicken, biscuits and jam, green beans, and mashed potatoes. The food tasted delicious.

When they were done eating at the table, Zane spread out the blanket in front of the fire and threw on a few more logs. He sat down next to her.

Her face burned with the roaring fire and with what burned in her heart. Zane was an amazing man. A man she'd grown to trust with everything except her love. Was she falling in love with him?

He flashed a grin that lit up her insides like a candle in a lonely room until he reached over and touched her necklace. "Is that from someone back home?"

Her pulse raced. She'd always worn it hidden beneath her neckline. Here was her chance… "There was someone"—her gaze skittered toward him to measure his response—"whom I once loved. But he is in my past." She couldn't tell him about the letters and money Hamilton had sent.

"Did he give you that?"

"Yes." Tension eased from her shoulders as the burden of carrying secrets left.

"You should wear it more often. It's very pretty on you. And I don't want you to forget your life in St. Louis."

Her shoulders sagged. Zane meant well, but if he only knew her biggest struggle had been to forget another man.

His brow furrowed. "Did he mean that much to you?"

A "yes" rested on her lips, but how could she crush Zane? "Not anymore."

He leaned in and pressed his lips to hers. She responded to his gentle touch and the sweet smell of his breath. Zane Michaels was a good man. And he deserved a wife who loved him completely.

He enveloped her in his arms and smothered her face in kisses, but she went as stiff as a flat iron. How could she explain how deeply she cherished him but that she still hadn't confessed everything to him? And then there was this nagging feeling that she didn't somehow feel like his wife. Somehow, she couldn't give all of herself to him. Not yet.

"What? Don't you care for me, Elisabeth?"

"I do. Very much. But, I just need more time."

Chapter 7

The next Sunday, as Elisabeth, Zane, and the girls made their way to their seats at church, Elisabeth saw the little boy who had come to their home at night for food. "Zane, the boy."

Zane stepped out of the way so she and the girls could slide across the pew. "So he does have a family."

Elisabeth looked but saw no parents. Just the boy, a smaller version of him, and a little girl. "I've never seen them at church before. I wonder if they came here just to get out of the cold?"

After the hymn singing, Pastor Stanton stood in the pulpit and asked again for volunteers to work with the children's live nativity play.

Elisabeth's insides soared. She loved being a mother, and she'd yearned to work with the church children. Her gaze slid to the orphans. She smiled as she saw the orphan boy nudge his sister when she talked in church. Maybe if she helped with the nativity program, she could convince them to be a part of the production. She leaned over and whispered into Zane's ear. "I'd like to help out with the play, if you don't mind."

His gaze twinkled with pleasure. "Good, good. I'm so glad you're going to be a part of that, and it's a great way to serve God."

Serve God? She hadn't thought of taking care of children as serving God. She eased back further in her seat and admired her two girls, dressed in their Sunday best, their hair neatly braided, cheeks pink with health. And even more were the happy mornings they shared lately as she taught the girls how to make pancakes, grits, and eggs over-easy. The bedtime stories and the walks when little hands slipped into hers, sending a contented warmth through her heart. A smile spread across her lips. She was a good momma.

After the service, Elisabeth went to find Pastor Stanton to offer her services, but he was already talking with Delilah.

"Mrs. Roberson, we could use your help with the nativity."

Delilah shook her pretty curls. "Oh no, I don't know anything about children."

"All that's needed is a gentle hand and firm directions." The pastor grinned broadly.

Reginald chuckled. "She's good at the directions part."

Delilah shot her husband a withering stare.

Elisabeth stepped forward. "I'd like to help." She nodded toward the orphans, who were chasing each other through the pews. "And I'd like to see if I could get those children involved."

Pastor Stanton nodded. "Mrs. Michaels, if you would

be in charge of the nativity, that would be a blessing to our whole church."

"Oh, pastor"—Delilah wiggled her way in front of Elisabeth—"I will take charge." She offered a pasted-on smile toward Elisabeth. "And she and Mrs. MacIntyre can be my assistants."

The next Sunday after church, Elisabeth, Delilah, and Mrs. MacIntyre gathered up the children who wanted to be a part of the production. They had quite a large group, as Mrs. MacIntyre had told the boys and girls she'd be bringing her fruitcake and gingerbread men.

Elisabeth found a trunk with the costumes that the church had used over the years. Delilah immediately handed her nieces angel costumes.

Elisabeth noticed the boy who had come to their home and his younger brother and sister eating their third gingerbread man. Was that all they'd had to eat today? "Would you two boys like to be the wise men?" She turned toward the girl. "And you could be Mary." She held up the different costumes with bits of shimmery fabric and imitation jewels sewn on.

The littlest girl reached out to touch the cloth, when her brother slapped her hand. "Don't touch that. Them's for rich people. We're poor, so I think we'd better be the shepherds."

Elisabeth's heart ached to take them into her arms and hug them. "Well, I think you would all make excellent shepherds. I'm Mrs. Michaels. Can you tell me your names?"

A smile covered the little girl's face, and she hugged

Elisabeth's leg. "I'm Kellie Walker."

The oldest boy folded his arms. "I'm Luke Walker, and this is my brother, Seth."

"Nice to meet you. Why don't you try these costumes on and see if they fit?"

Delilah went over the lines with the children and was surprisingly good at keeping them in order without being too firm. So there was a soft side to her sister-in-law.

As the practice was ending, Mrs. MacIntyre came alongside Elisabeth to help her spread the fresh straw on the floor of the stable. "It'll be a fine nativity."

"With Christmas Eve only three days away, I'm so glad you are handy with a needle and thread. I didn't know where we were going to come up with additional costumes for all the kids who wanted to participate. And I'm surprised to find so many of them are orphans."

" 'Tis a shame they have no one to care for them. But ye are very gentle." Mrs. MacIntyre tucked the straw into the manger. "They're not the only ones who need yer loving care."

Elisabeth paused. Did Mrs. MacIntyre think she wasn't a good mother? "I try very hard to care for the girls—"

"I'm not talking about the girls." She nodded toward the men who were heaving the two front pews aside for the Christmas Eve service. "I'm talking about yer man."

Elisabeth watched Zane, on the other side of the church with his jacket off and his sleeves rolled up, helping another man move the pews against a wall. Her heart melted to hear the deep rumble of his laugh. Her eyes misted as delight filled her chest.

She loved him.

❄

Pulling open the door to the church, Zane reached into his pocket and touched his Christmas present for Elisabeth—the family brooch. He'd decided he couldn't wait until their first anniversary to show her how much he loved her. He would give it to her tonight. But before he could, Elisabeth gave him a quick kiss to his cheek and hurried off with Mrs. MacIntyre to get the children dressed and assembled.

He loved his wife with every bone in his body. She had such a tender heart and had even begun to crack Delilah's hard exterior by complimenting her directing of the nativity play. As he watched Elisabeth dress the children, he stifled a laugh at the new characters she'd created for the extra orphans, presumably friends of the Walker children, who wanted to take part. So now, the revised manger scene included four angels, five wise men, six shepherds, and two farmers. A tide of desire to help these parentless children nearly overwhelmed him.

Make a home for them.

He pondered this impression in his heart. Make a home? But there wasn't enough room at his house.

Make a home for them.

He watched Luke as he stood proudly holding his staff made from a tree branch. That boy needed a. . . Zane stiffened. That was what he was supposed to do with the land! It was for the town's orphans. Then another realization came. He and Elisabeth could oversee the home. He pounded his fist into his hand to hold back a shout. He had to tell her now, but as he paced over to her, someone touched his sleeve.

"Do you have a minute to talk with me?" Pastor Stanton's brow was deeply furrowed. "It's important."

Zane pulled his gaze away from Elisabeth. "Sure."

Pastor Stanton's face looked ashen as he closed the door to the manse located just off the foyer and sat behind a desk. "I have something very weighty to tell you, son."

Zane's stomach tightened. "Is there a problem? Is it the check I gave the church? I know I have the funds—"

"Zane, I don't know of any way to soften this, so I'm going to shoot straight with you. You and Elisabeth are not officially married."

Elisabeth scurried from the front of the church to the spacious foyer to find her satchel with the extra clothing she'd brought. One of the five wise men had thrown up on his costume.

As she dashed passed all the townsfolk coming in for the service, a tall gentleman blocked her way. *Someone in fancy city attire,* rang in her mind as she caught a glimpse of a dark, well-cut coat. In a hurry, she dismissed the thought, grabbed her satchel from behind the large church Christmas tree, and turned.

"Elisabeth."

The familiar voice sent a bolt through her. "Hamilton?"

A large gathering of people walking through the foyer blocked her view. Suddenly, he was beside her. She stepped back from him. "Hamilton, what are you doing here?" She glanced around, relieved to see the decorated tree partially hid them. "How did you find me?"

"I had to see you. I found out the truth—"

She held up her hand. "Hamilton, it's over between us. I'm married—"

He leaned in and pressed his fingers to her lips.

She jumped back. His brazen touch was as shocking as the burn of a hot coal. She cast another furtive glance around the foyer. "I have nothing to say to you. I need to get back to—"

"I still love you."

She looked over her shoulder again, grateful no one was close enough to hear his words. The attraction she'd once held for him was long gone. She blinked at the realization. It was gone because she loved Zane. She almost laughed out loud. Leaning forward, she planted her face an inch from Hamilton's. "I am a married woman and I don't want to see or hear from you again."

Hamilton eased out a smile. "First of all, this"—he glanced around the simple church, wrinkling his nose—"is not where you belong. You're a St. Louis gal. You're my gal."

There had been a time when she would have been tempted by his words, but no longer. "I belong here. I made a vow before God to be faithful to my husband, and I intend to keep it."

"You aren't married."

She folded her arms. This man didn't have the morals and character that Zane had and was obviously lying to her. She turned to leave. "I'm not going to listen to this nonsense."

He grabbed her upper arm. "You're not married, which means you're free to come with me, and I can prove it."

❄

Sweat broke out on Zane's forehead as he stared back at

265

Pastor Stanton. "How can I not be married?"

"According to this letter, you changed your name when you moved to town."

Zane nodded. "So, people do it all the time."

"Well, Nebraska law says you have to use your legal name to get married or the marriage is invalid."

Zane fell back in the chair. How could he tell Elisabeth? He ran his fingers through his hair. How could this have happened? "Are you sure?"

The pastor came around the desk and clamped Zane on the shoulder. "A lawyer from St. Louis, a Mr. Gatesworth, wrote to me concerning Miss Lariby. Somehow he figured out your real name. Probably a relative of some busybody in the church. Nevertheless, you must take care of this."

As Zane stood, his legs trembled as if he'd ridden a million miles. "I—I can't believe this."

"I suggest you go find Mrs. Mich—er, Miss Lariby and let her know."

Zane nodded and strode through the foyer back into the church in a daze to find her. How could she not be his wife? He loved her. The tinkling sound of "Joy to the World" mocked his weighted heart. He rushed to the church stage.

"Are ye looking for Mrs. Michaels?" Mrs. MacIntyre held a baby doll in one hand and swaddling clothes in another.

He nodded.

"She's in the foyer."

He hurried back down the church aisle. Worries crowded his thoughts. What if she didn't want to stay with him? She'd never told him that she loved him. Dread clawed at his throat as he strode into the entrance hall and froze.

Elisabeth stood close to a tall man with red hair. A man who was gripping her upper arm.

"Let go of my woman." Zane enunciated each word.

Elisabeth's gaze swept toward Zane. What must he be thinking? Why hadn't she told Zane about Hamilton? She immediately pulled away from him and came to stand by Zane's side. But when she touched his arm, she found it rigid. Did he think she was doing something inappropriate? "I can explain—"

"Why didn't you call her your wife?" Hamilton tugged on his satin waistcoat. "Is it because you two aren't married, Michael Lane?"

She looked up at Zane, who remained silent. *Say something.* But his expression was as hard as ice. "Is this true. You're—you're not Zane Michaels?"

He hung his head for the briefest of seconds. "My real name is Michael Lane." He turned toward her, his eyes full of desperation. "I changed my name when me and the girls moved to Plainsville. I think you know enough about my past to know why I wanted to escape the Lane last name." Zane directed his gaze briefly toward Hamilton. "Who is this man?"

Hamilton stepped forward. "I'm Hamilton Gatesworth from—"

"He's the man who gave me the pendant." Her voice softened. "Is what he's saying true?"

Zane slowly removed his stare from Hamilton. "It's true. Pastor Stanton just informed me our marriage isn't valid. So it looks like you've got a decision to make."

Her mouth opened, but before she could speak, a group of men, the elders of the church, gathered around them.

Mrs. MacIntyre came bursting through the horde. "We've no time for idle chatter. I've got the wee ones lined up and ready for the show. Come on. Time's a wasting." She grabbed Elisabeth's hand and pulled her back into the church. "Come along."

Elisabeth's gaze swerved back toward Zane. "But, but—"

With a quick glance over her shoulder, the housekeeper drew her into a pew. "I got wind of what was happening, and I knew ye'd need a moment alone to think."

Tears filled Elisabeth's eyes. "I don't know what to think. Zane never told me about his name change. Are you certain Zane wanted to marry me? Maybe he was forced into it, as I was. I'm not sure I belong here." Her hands covered her face. "I'm not sure I'm good for Zane. I don't even feel like his wife."

"Weel, obviously ye aren't, but I know what would settle that." Mrs. Macintyre gripped Elisabeth's hand. "There is no predicament too big for God. When I am unsure what to do, I always go back to the last thing the Lord told me."

Elisabeth looked up. What was the last thing God had told her about her marriage to Zane? She thought back. . .

"A threefold cord is not quickly broken."

That's it. A surge of strength rushed through her. She shot to her feet. "I know what to do."

"Ye do?"

"I do." A smile broke out on her face. "I do." She wrapped her arms around Mrs. MacIntyre. "I do." Elisabeth dug into her reticule and pulled out her gold pendant. "I was going to give this to you on Christmas Day, but I want you to have it now."

Mrs. Macintyre shook her head. "This is too bonnie—I canna' take—"

Elisabeth squeezed her hand. "Please, it will help me more than you know." She lifted her skirts and dashed back into the foyer to find Zane, but it was empty. She peeked outside. No Zane. Had he gone home? A few late church members passed her by on their way in, wishing her a Merry Christmas, but all she could think about was finding Zane.

"Elisabeth." Zane stood in the doorway of the pastor's manse.

She ran to him and threw her arms around him. "I love you, Zane Michaels, no matter what your name is."

Zane leaned down and kissed her. "Good. Good."

"Is that all you can say?"

"Let's get married. Right now."

"On Christmas Eve?"

Zane looked over his shoulder at the smiling pastor and elders. "I've told them everything. They know my real name, why I changed it, and they know you're a mail-order bride."

At their approving nods, tears welled up in Elisabeth's eyes. "Then I will gladly be your Christmas bride."

Zane took her hands in his. "And I've told them I want to open an orphanage, on the land I showed you. I thought once we were married, we could run it together. As long as you keep the books."

"Really?" A wave of happiness flowed into her heart.

"Shall we get started?" The pastor gestured toward the sanctuary.

"Just a minute, Pastor." Zane pulled the box from his pocket and opened it. He pulled out the pearl brooch. "I want you to wear this."

She wiped at the tears flowing down her face as he pinned it in place. Her chest filled with joy to know that her and Zane's hearts were no longer hidden from one another.

Mrs. MacIntyre poked her head in the door. "I just pulled two shepherds apart who got in a shoving match, one of the wise men dumped his gold coins on an angel's head, and the goat we borrowed from Mr. Worth is eating all of baby Jesus' hay. By all that's Scottish, what is going on here?"

"A wedding." Elisabeth clasped Zane's hand.

"Weel, hurry it up then. We've got a nativity program to get started."

With Sophia and Olivia dressed in their angel costumes by their sides, with the entire congregation watching from the pews, Elisabeth Lariby married Michael Lane in front of the crèche.

As they sealed their union with a kiss, a chill tingled up Elisabeth's spine. "Now I feel like your true wife."

He twined his fingers with hers and kissed her. "I love you, Elisabeth."

"And I love you, whatever your name is."

Obsessed with all things British, Therese Stenzel's first book was *A Bride By Christmas*, and her second is *Christmas Mail-Order Brides*. She has also coauthored *God's Little Devotional Book for Grandparents*. Her writing has appeared in *Women's Day*, *Family Fun*, and *Time* magazines. In addition to being active in American Christian Fiction Writers, Writers of Inspirational Novels (WIN), she is the creator of His Writers, a group for those who write European-based historicals. She is also the founder of *British Missives*, an e-mail newsletter for those who love to read or write British novels.

In love with English history, English tea, and reading historical novels, she is currently working on her fifth historical manuscript. She and her husband, Neal, keep busy raising their three kids. Her Web site is www.theresestenzel.com.

MRS. MAYBERRY
MEETS HER MATCH

by Susan Page Davis

Dedication

To my fellow authors, Vickie, Carrie, and Therese.
Thanks for making this journey with me!

I have been young, and now am old; yet have I not seen the righteous forsaken, nor his seed begging bread.
Psalm 37:25

Chapter 1

Gentlemen: Christian ladies with impeccable references and domestic skills seek matrimony with conscientious and responsible men. Contact Mrs. Mayberry's Matrimonial Society for Christians of Moral Character, in care of this newspaper. Only gentlemen who are reverent, ethical, reliable, and solvent need apply.

December, 1886

I'm ruined." Amelia Mayberry picked up her bone china cup and sipped her tea. "In this business, all it takes is one jilted groom. One stubborn woman who refuses to marry a fine man."

Her neighbor and dearest friend, Deborah Fulton, frowned. "Really, Amelia. I'd hardly say your name has been sullied. For one thing, few people know about the jilting. And for another, look at all the successful matches you've made."

"I know you're right, but this one fiasco has bothered me for the last two years. It makes me feel like an utter failure. I want to resolve the situation if I can." Amelia set her teacup down and patted her knee. Her cream-colored cat, Fluffy, jumped into the lap of her light gray woolen skirt and purred industriously as she settled down. Amelia stroked the cat absently. "If I can only persuade him to let me try again."

"And where does this gentleman live?" Deborah took one of the small lemon cookies off the serving plate.

"Sacramento."

"You're traveling to Sacramento? Amelia Mayberry, you surprise me."

Amelia smiled at her. "I know. I'm the homebody who never travels. But I shan't be able to retire and feel at ease unless I at least try to fix this. So you will look after Fluffy for me while I'm gone?"

"Of course." Deborah bit into the cookie. When she'd swallowed the first bite, she said, "Delicious. This gentleman you're so concerned about is your husband's old friend, isn't he?"

"Yes, Lennox Bailey. He was Micah's sergeant when he served at Fort Laramie thirty years ago. Micah was promoted to corporal, and he told me they were practically inseparable, on duty and off. They remained close friends until the day Micah died, though they only saw each other a few times after Micah left the army."

"Personally, I think you should forget about it."

"Why? I thought you'd support me in this."

"You know how fond I am of you, Amelia, but this seems unnecessary. You've worked hard for fifteen years, and you've finally bought the house you want and can afford to stop working and enjoy yourself. Why fret over something from the past?"

Amelia scratched between Fluffy's ears. "You know me. I can't leave a job unfinished. Mr. Bailey asked me to find him a wife, and I haven't completed the task."

"But I thought he released you of your obligation." Deborah reached for the teapot and refilled her cup.

"Yes, and he refused my offer of a refund for the fee he'd paid me. I never felt right about it."

"But if he no longer wishes to marry. . ."

"I'm not convinced of that. If I can just bring the right woman to him. . . Last time, I thought I'd found the ideal bride for him, but somehow I overlooked something, and the plan went awry. I still don't know what passed between them, or why she gave him the mitten after traveling all the way to Sacramento with the intention of marrying him. If I knew what went wrong, I could avoid making the same mistake again. I know I could."

Deborah's eyes narrowed. "My dear, I say this in love. Please take it as such. I think there is but one thing prompting you to make this arduous journey."

"That's right. My failure."

"No, Amelia. Your stubborn pride."

❄

"Going all the way to the end of the line?" George Dutton, the stationmaster, opened his ticket book.

"Yes. Sacramento. I'm not sure how many days I'll need there to conduct my business. I'd like to be back by Christmas, but I'll have to see how things go out there."

"You can purchase your return ticket when you're ready to come home."

"Perfect." Amelia opened her purse and took out enough money to cover the cost.

"I thought you were about to retire from business," Dutton said.

"I am, but there's one thing I must settle first."

"I sort of hate to see you retire. Think of all the people you've helped—and all those who could still use your services."

She smiled at that. "It has been an adventure, but I think it's time for me to close shop. After I do this one last job."

"What's special about this one?" Dutton's brow furrowed. "Mrs. Mayberry, you must have matched dozens of couples."

"One hundred ninety-three over the last fifteen years," she admitted.

He whistled softly. "So after this one, it will be one hundred ninety-four?"

"Precisely." She let out her breath in a huff. It wouldn't matter so much if the client in question were anyone but Lennox Bailey. She wanted very much to find him a bride so that he could spend his sunset years in congenial company.

Over the years, she'd had a couple of cases where the bride ended up marrying a different groom than was first intended, but all parties had been satisfied with the outcome. In a few other cases, the first match hadn't suited the clients, but she'd persisted and helped find the right mates for them in time. Not so with Mr. Bailey.

Dutton handed over her change and her train ticket. "To

what do you attribute your high rate of success?"

"Prayer. That, and I made sure all my clients had good character and impeccable references before I agreed to represent them." Amelia straightened her shoulders. She *had* done good work. She had no reason to be ashamed of one failure. And yet, it would be so much nicer if she could bring this one matter to a satisfactory conclusion.

"All I know is you found the perfect bride for me," Dutton said. "Parthy and I have been happily wed for eight years now, and I couldn't be more pleased with the service we received."

Amelia smiled at that. George and Parthinia Dutton were one of several couples living in Kansas City whom she had helped to the altar. She loved to see her clients happy in their marriages. Most of those she had matched lived farther west, and she rarely saw them once they'd tied the knot. In fact, quite a percentage of them had never met Mrs. Mayberry face to face. But most of the brides dropped her a line at Christmastime, and dozens had stopped to see her as they traveled through the city on their way to their new homes.

But Lennox Bailey was the cloud on her horizon. The fox in her henhouse, the flea on her newly bathed hound. In short, he was the one person who made her feel like a disgrace to the matchmaking profession.

"I shall see you tomorrow, when I come to board the train," Amelia told George. She went home and packed a valise and watered her plants. Next she unpacked her valise and repacked it with different clothes. Suppertime had arrived. She went to the pantry and set out all the leftovers that might spoil during her absence and determined to make her supper and breakfast from the assortment. Then she went back to her bedchamber and repacked the valise again.

At last she sat down in the rocker near her bed. "I've got to stop this. One serviceable traveling outfit, two day dresses, and one evening dress should be sufficient." Why was she so nervous about her wardrobe? Anything she pulled from her closet would pass the most critical eye for style, modesty, and good taste. She closed her eyes for a moment. "Lord, You'll have to calm me down. I don't know why this trip has me so flummoxed. It's just a train ride to Sacramento and a visit with an old friend."

But she knew it was more than that. She told herself she hoped to save her reputation as the most successful match-maker in the business. But really, Deborah was right, and her reputation hadn't suffered so far as she knew. Then why did it grate on her so badly? With a start, she realized that perhaps Deborah was also right about her other conclusion. Amelia's pride had taken over her actions.

"Lord, forgive me. My reputation is not what matters in the eternal scheme. Your will be done. Whatever the outcome, please let Lennox be content, and let me accept whatever You bring from this."

She rose and repacked her clothing for the last time. Setting the valise near the front door, she determined not to open it again.

The little house on the edge of Kansas City embodied the comfortable home she'd wished for all her life. Her minister husband hadn't been able to provide that before his untimely death. Her years of hard work since then had paid off, and she'd earned enough to finally buy the house this spring. Not only did it suit her needs perfectly, but it also sat next door to her friend Deborah's home.

Amelia wished Micah had lived to share its coziness with her. Even so, she felt blessed to have a snug place to spend her later years. At fifty-one, she hoped to have many more happy years, but without the need to earn an income. If she lived sensibly, she should be set for life. Time to relax and enjoy her new home and her friends. If this trip to Sacramento went well, she might even consider further travel to visit some of the couples she'd matched. She received dozens of invitations every year.

She took out the telegram she'd received yesterday from Lennox Bailey, in answer to the letter she'd sent last month.

Delighted. Send arrival time and will meet. L. Bailey.

She smiled at his terseness. Of course, telegrams did cost so much per word. Her inquiry had run:

Dear Mr. Bailey,
    I shall be traveling to Sacramento in December, and I wondered if I might call upon you while I'm in town. It would be wonderful to see you again after all these years. If it is not convenient for you, I shall understand.
                    Sincerely,
                    Amelia Mayberry

And of course, being the gentleman that he was, he'd offered to meet her train—exactly as she had hoped.

So far, so good.

❄

"I don't understand why that woman is coming here."

Lennox Bailey frowned as he knotted his cravat just below his collar. "She's an old friend, Helen." His daughter was not happy. He didn't need the reflection of her sour face to tell him that. You'd have thought she'd just drunk some lemonade and forgot to put the sugar in.

"But she's coming halfway across the continent to see you."

"Not me. She has business in Sacramento, and she asked if she could see me while she's here."

"And so you're meeting her at the depot and driving her to her hotel."

"Yes. I thought it was the polite thing to do. It will save her having to hire a hackney when she's tired from the journey." In the mirror, Lennox saw that his daughter watched him closely. "What?"

"I didn't realize she was a businesswoman."

Lennox wished he'd bitten his tongue. He'd never told Helen about his transaction with Amelia Mayberry two years ago or her role in the arrival of that misguided woman, Renata Enderly—and he didn't want to now. It was bad enough that Helen had met the Enderly woman and been insulted by her. He hoped his face wouldn't betray him. "Well, she's had to support herself for the last fifteen years or so, since Micah passed away."

"Of course."

"What are you worried about?"

"Nothing." Her downcast eyes said otherwise.

At last the cravat passed muster. Lennox turned and

reached for his jacket. "Anyway, I shall deliver her to her hotel, and if she's not too tired, I plan to invite her to have dinner with me. If she's available, I expect we'll have a pleasant time catching up on old acquaintances, and that will be the end of it."

"She'll probably be exhausted when she arrives."

"Perhaps. In which case, I shall take my leave of her and wish her well." He took out his watch and looked at it. "And now, I should head over to the depot."

"And I should get home. Good-bye, Papa. I hope you have a nice visit." Helen rose on her toes to kiss his cheek.

Lennox stooped just a bit to meet her. It still amazed him that his little raven-haired daughter had turned into such a poised, beautiful woman. "Tell Samuel I'll come around tomorrow to see him."

"I will." She smiled and shook her head, and he could tell she thought him silly for sending messages to a six-month-old baby.

They left the house together and parted before the carriage house, where Lennox's hired man had his surrey and team ready. Helen walked toward her home three blocks to the north, and Lennox turned south, toward the depot.

He did hope Mrs. Mayberry wouldn't bring up the fiasco that had resulted from his unfortunate request for her to find him a bride. That disaster was best forgotten.

Chapter 2

After four days of dusty, sooty travel during which her feet always seemed cold, Amelia stepped down from the train on the platform at Sacramento. Weary to the bone, she kept her chin up with an effort.

People bustled around her on the platform. She turned her head, looking for Lennox while trying to avoid the appearance of anxiety. Those little lines crept into one's skin so easily if one frowned overmuch.

She hadn't seen Lennox since a year before Micah died. She recalled him as a tall, handsome, dark-haired gentleman with a military bearing and a deep adoration of his wife, Susie. The Bailey family had passed through Kansas on their way to California, where they had settled. During the break in their journey, they had spent a delightful weekend with the Mayberrys. Lennox and Micah had talked about their army days and agriculture and theology. Amelia and Susie talked about knitting and preserving and their husbands. Helen, the Baileys' six-year-old daughter, had joined them in the kitchen and on an excursion to visit the wives of some of the men Micah ministered to.

Amelia had enjoyed Mrs. Bailey's company tremendously and found the dark-haired little girl enchanting. She and Susie found an instant empathy for each other through their energetic, idealistic husbands. The two men had picked up their friendship as though they hadn't been separated for thirteen years. They'd survived a horrible war after their service together at Fort Laramie, but that hadn't changed their camaraderie.

The news of Susie's death a few years later had deeply saddened Amelia. She'd wished she could do something to comfort Lennox and Helen, and had sent her heartfelt condolences. She hadn't seen either of them since but had maintained contact with brief letters around the holidays each year. But it had been so long! She probably wouldn't recognize Helen now, but she ought to know Lennox when she saw him.

She spotted a man walking slowly along the platform. He was tall enough for Lennox Bailey, and his impeccable clothing made her check her own appearance and brush some dust off her skirt. He came closer, searching along the cars as he walked. When he turned his head, she was certain.

Her gaze caught his, and he hesitated then smiled. Hurrying toward her, he doffed his hat and extended a hand. "Mrs. Mayberry!"

"Sergeant Bailey." She smiled up into his creased face. Of course he looked older. His dark hair had swaths of pure white at his temples, but it suited him and made him look more distinguished. He'd kept his lithe form, and if anything he'd grown more handsome with age.

"Oh, please. It's been more than twenty years since I wore the uniform. Besides, we're old friends. You must call me Lennox, as you did in your home in Kansas City."

They walked along the platform toward the baggage car.

"I'd be happy to take you to your hotel," Lennox said. "Where are you staying?"

"The Royal."

"That's a very nice place. I hope you're free this evening."

Surprised, she looked up into his eyes. He did indeed seem pleased to see her. "Why, yes, I am."

"I thought we might have supper together. Your hotel is renowned for its excellent cuisine, if you care to dine there."

"Why thank you." Amelia smiled at him. This was better than she'd hoped. Having dinner with Lennox would surely give her the opportunity to discuss his unmarried state. "I'd like that very much."

"Wonderful. I'll drop you at the Royal now and give you a couple of hours to rest. If I come back at six, would that suit you?"

"Perfectly."

They stopped where the baggage car was being unloaded and retrieved her valise. She hadn't known what to expect for a conveyance, but his smart bay horse was harnessed to a surrey with wheels and thills made of dark, polished wood and fringe fluttering in the breeze. It had room for her luggage behind the seat. Lennox stowed the bag and offered his hand to help her into the vehicle. A black canvas cover partially enclosed them and kept the intense sun off her complexion.

"Perhaps I should have brought the carriage," Lennox said, "but it's warm today, and I felt like driving myself."

Amelia enjoyed the ride to the Royal Hotel. For twenty minutes they trotted in and out of traffic, first between large warehouses and then in the business district.

"How is Helen doing?" Amelia asked as they rolled past stores that promised hours of good shopping.

"She's well. I did tell you about my grandson?"

She smiled at his eagerness. "You mentioned the little fellow's arrival in the note you wrote last summer. How's the boy doing?"

"Oh, he's wonderful. He's got Helen's eyes, and that shock of black hair. But he's placid like his father. Very tranquil baby—not at all like Helen was."

Amelia chuckled. "I hope I'll get to see him before I leave."

A shadow crossed Lennox's face. "Perhaps. I'll have to see if we can arrange it. They live only a few blocks from me, but Helen and Daniel keep a busy social calendar. He's a lawyer." His tone said that should explain everything.

Amelia said, "Ah," and turned her attention back to the stores. They were passing a large mercantile, and she made note of its location in case she wanted to purchase some stationery or other sundries during her visit.

Finally they turned off onto a quieter street with large elms shading them. The imposing hotel looked quite elegant. Amelia wondered if she should have chosen someplace more modest, but she'd determined to enjoy this trip and pamper herself a bit. She would have a pleasant excursion, no matter whether she completed her goal or not.

A boy ran over to the surrey as they pulled up, and Lennox gave him a coin to hold the horse. He jumped down and took Amelia's valise from the back then came to help her to the ground.

A man met them halfway to the front door. "Help you, sir?"

Lennox handed over the valise and another coin.

Amelia felt her face flush. She hadn't meant for Lennox to spend money on her, though his fine suit and spirited horse indicated he could well afford it. "Thank you," she said as they approached the front desk.

"Think nothing of it." Lennox nodded to the desk clerk. "Mrs. Mayberry has arrived."

"Good afternoon, ma'am. Sir." The clerk flipped a page of the ledger before him. "Ah, Mrs. Micah Mayberry."

"That's correct," Amelia said.

The clerk reached for a key. "We've put you in room twenty-six, ma'am."

"Thank you." She took the key and turned to Lennox. "I appreciate all you've done."

"You're welcome." He said to the desk clerk, "I'd like to reserve a table for two for dinner in your restaurant."

"Certainly, sir. In the name of Mayberry?" He picked up his pen.

"No, Bailey."

"Ah, Mr. Bailey." The clerk's eyebrows shot up in apprehension, as though he had made an error in not recognizing one of the hotel's preferred customers. "Of course, sir. I'll be sure you have a good table at. . ."

"Six o'clock."

The clerk scribbled on a piece of paper.

Lennox turned to the man still holding Amelia's valise. "You take good care of Mrs. Mayberry."

"Yes, sir."

He smiled at Amelia. "I shall call for you at six."

Amelia followed the bellboy to her room, where he deposited her valise and retreated in silence. As much as she craved a nap, Amelia couldn't stop her mind from racing. Her well-appointed hotel room looked down on a quiet garden behind the building. She was glad it didn't front on the street. Even so, she could still hear the distant noise of trains, carriages and wagons, dogs barking, and shouts.

She took off her shoes and lay down on the coverlet, but her mind kept revisiting her reunion with Lennox Bailey. Had he changed over the years? He looked almost noble, yet his handsome face held the same honest lines it always had. She felt he'd grown more reserved, or maybe it was just because they'd not had Micah and Susie there with them today, as they always had when they'd met other times. Still, he'd cordially invited her to dinner. That was promising.

Had he thought her dowdy and travel-worn? She jumped from her bed to check over the dress she planned to wear to supper. Not her best, but a very nice silk and woolen blend, which she'd had made a month ago. A good, proper dress for the widow of a minister with modest means. Perhaps she could sponge the wrinkles with a damp handkerchief, and they would smooth out. And the pearl gray hat that so nearly matched the material would set off her hair—still a rich brunette.

Oh dear, she thought. *I'm as vain as an actress.*

She walked to the dressing table and studied her face in the mirror. Young she was not. She'd heard people say she was a handsome woman, and she supposed that was better than prettiness, which could fail miserably when one hit the sixth decade of one's life.

Her skin was smooth and unwrinkled, and her eyes were still a vibrant brown. Micah used to tease her and say they looked like mud puddles. But that was usually before he kissed her soundly, so she hadn't minded.

Now. . .how would she approach the topic she'd come to discuss? She had let Lennox think she had other business in town. It seemed easier that way—not to let him realize her main purpose for the trip was to try to undo her misstep with him. He wouldn't like the idea that she'd undertaken the trip largely out of concern for him.

After the first attempt had gone bad, he'd sent her a letter politely declining her offer to try to find another match for him. At the time, Amelia had thought it best not to push the matter. For a year or so, she'd had a vague, nagging feeling that something wasn't quite right. But after she'd achieved her financial goal—saving enough of a nest egg so she could buy her own home and retire—her failure to find him a compatible wife niggled at her. Then it became a solid, full-formed thought that nagged at her. She ought to have done better by Micah's old friend.

As she'd wound up her last few matches, she'd kept Lennox in the back of her mind. Every time a woman over forty contacted her, Amelia measured her against Lennox's specifications for a wife. And over the last six months, she'd collected three she thought might suit him. Any one of them would be delighted to become the supportive mate of a fine man like Lennox. Of course, she hadn't mentioned him to any of the ladies. In fact, she'd informed them that she was retiring and would probably not be able to search out husbands for them. However, she'd said to each that if she ran across a Christian man of good character who seemed to meet their requirements, she would keep her in mind.

But now she had to get Lennox to change his mind.

Amelia sat down on the edge of the four-poster bed. It would be best if he thought it was his idea.

Lennox drove to his place of business to spend the two hours allotted him before returning to the hotel. The fruit-packing plant thrived these days. California's finest peaches, oranges, lemons, and grapefruit came to Bailey and Co., for tender packing and refrigeration. They shipped several boxcars full of local produce east every week, and the company's profits soared.

He spoke to his foreman and walked toward his office. The packing house would close for the day soon, but the loading crew would work into the evening, putting the crates on the train cars. His desk sat beside a large window that afforded him a good view of the loading platform.

As he stood looking down on the bustling crews, his thoughts returned to Amelia Mayberry. She had aged well. He'd always agreed with Micah that she was a lovely woman. She'd kept her figure and, if anything, looked more beautiful as a mature woman than she had as a young bride. He'd told Micah several times in jest that Amelia was too good for him.

How he missed his old friend! He and Micah hadn't seen each other much after they'd finished serving together at Fort Laramie thirty years ago, but they'd kept in touch. They'd met up once during the war, when he'd stayed on active duty and Micah served as a chaplain.

Knowing that his dependable corporal-turned-preacher was reachable if he really needed a friend had been a comfort to Lennox. At the end of the war, they'd met again before returning to their homes. Then he and Susie had managed a visit of several days with the Mayberrys in Kansas City on their way to California. After he started the fruit-packing business, he'd not had time to travel, and they hadn't met in person again.

News of Micah's death had staggered him, and for a while he'd felt the keen edge of mortality. But Susie and Helen had filled his life with joy. His business success brought a measure of satisfaction. If the truth were told, he'd seldom thought about Micah's widow except when her card came every Christmas. Susie always wrote back. When his wife had died, Amelia had sent him a tender, thoughtful letter.

An errand boy knocked on his door and came in with a message.

"Say, how would you like to earn an extra two bits today?" Lennox asked.

"I'd like it very much, sir." The boy waited eagerly.

Lennox sat down and scrawled a note saying he wouldn't be home until late evening on a sheet of paper and folded it in half. He stood and reached into his pocket for a coin. As he placed the note in the boy's hand with a quarter, he said, "Run to my house and give this to my housekeeper, Mrs.

Santos. You know the place, don't you?"

"Yes, sir. Shall I wait for an answer?"

"No need."

The boy scurried off, and Lennox turned once more to the window, thinking back over his past connection with Amelia. Three years ago, on a trip to San Francisco, he'd seen an ad in the newspaper there. An ad for Mrs. Mayberry's Matrimonial Society for Christians of Moral Character. At first he couldn't believe the proprietor was his friend's widow, even though the Kansas City address made it possible. For a rather steep fee, gentlemen could engage her services to find them wives.

The idea had startled him and even offended him at first. He'd had no idea Amelia had been making her living by matchmaking. He'd torn out the ad and tucked it away in his wallet.

To his surprise, a few days later he met a man who had made use of Mrs. Mayberry's aid in finding a bride. His new acquaintance said Mrs. Mayberry had done what he'd failed to do, and he was ecstatic with the result. He admired his new wife and quickly developed affection for her. His praise for the matchmaker embarrassed Lennox. The man claimed he didn't have the time or the patience to go and look for a wife, but he had the money with which to hire someone to do it. And Mrs. Mayberry's choice for him had exceeded his expectations.

Lennox thought of that man often, after he returned to Sacramento. His house was empty now, but for himself and his hired help. Helen was grown and married, and there were days when he ached with loneliness. Perhaps the San

Francisco businessman had made an astute move.

The more he thought about it, the less the idea offended him. Amelia even knew him slightly—surely she would be able to find a woman who could adapt to the life of an old soldier who'd gone into commerce.

Why had he ever thought such a harebrained scheme would work? In the first place, he didn't need a new wife. Susie had been his true love, and he missed her terribly, but he'd had no thoughts of replacing her until he saw that ad.

He supposed he felt sorry for Amelia, being alone so long and having to make a living. If she'd have been a seamstress, he'd have ordered a dozen shirts from her. But she wasn't a seamstress. She was a matchmaker. And that fellow he'd met in San Francisco had given a glowing testimonial. So he'd written a tentative letter, feeling almost shy. What would Amelia think of him?

As soon as he'd sent that letter, he'd regretted it. Knowing he'd done it appalled him. He couldn't bring himself to tell Helen and Daniel. He had wanted to telegraph Amelia and rescind the inquiry.

Then he'd begun to think once again that perhaps it could work. He was lonely—he admitted that. Since Helen married and moved out of the house, he rattled around by himself. The couple he'd hired were good people. Anna cooked and cleaned for him, and Richard kept up the garden and the horses. And he did have lots of friends in town. But it wasn't the same as a family—a life's companion. He'd always imagined himself and Susie sharing these golden years.

And so he'd kept quiet and waited. What a mistake!

A glance at his pocket watch told him that the time had come for him to go back to the hotel and fetch Amelia for dinner. He must be careful not to mention the botched bit of matchmaking. He found himself looking forward to seeing her again, in spite of the sticky topic neither of them had yet mentioned.

When he arrived in the hotel lobby, she was just coming down the stairs. She wore a simply cut but stylish dress in a becoming bluish-gray, and her hat framed her face adorably. Amelia would make a pleasant dinner companion, he was sure, and every man in the room over thirty years of age would be jealous of him. He met her at the bottom of the staircase and offered his arm.

She took it with a smile. "Good evening, Lennox. So good of you to invite me."

"My pleasure." He led her into the dining room, where the waiter ushered them to a table near a window.

"What a lovely view of the mountains," Amelia said as she unfolded her napkin.

Her reaction pleased Lennox. His forethought to reserve a good table had paid off. "I eat here often with business acquaintances."

"It's a pleasant room, and a certain gentleman told me the food is excellent." She gave a little wink, and he chuckled. Amelia gazed about the large room, taking in the holiday greenery and ornaments. "I love the Christmas season. They've made it seem very homelike, though it's much warmer outside than it would be in Kansas City right now."

"I don't usually feel festive at Christmastime anymore, but when Helen and Daniel bring their little boy over, I'm sure I'll brim over with seasonal goodwill."

"Children do make the holidays more joyful."

"Yes. I look forward to picking out some interesting gifts for Samuel when he's a wee bit older." He picked up the menu. "The fish is very good here."

"Would you order for me, since you know this place?"

"Certainly, if you wish."

"It would save me a great deal of anxiety."

Her sheepish smile warmed him. Surely she wasn't ill at ease. She seemed perfectly poised, though she continued to look around at the elegant dining room with a discreet appreciation. Some of the society women he knew felt it was their duty to act bored wherever they went. Some acted as though nothing could shake them from their ennui, short of a major earthquake.

When the waiter reappeared, Lennox placed the order for the two of them.

"Would you like some wine this evening?" the waiter asked.

"No thank y—" He broke off and looked to Amelia for confirmation. He was 90 percent certain she didn't imbibe, and yet he hadn't seen her in seventeen years. "Unless you. . ." He raised his eyebrows.

"Oh no, thank you."

He sent the waiter away, feeling they'd slipped more solidly into their old friendship. "Shall we return thanks now?"

"Yes, that would be lovely."

She bowed her head, and Lennox added another mental chalk mark to his invisible tally. So far, Amelia had passed every small test he'd thrown in her path.

"Dear Lord, we thank You for Amelia's safe journey. We

ask that You would bless this meal and our fellowship, and give her success in her business here."

"Amen," she said softly but adamantly.

"Will your business keep you occupied during your entire stay?" he asked.

She hesitated only an instant. "I think not. I've allowed some extra time for sightseeing and such."

"Would you have time for a drive out into the country? I'd love to show you some of the farms and orchards in the valley."

"I should like that very much."

They arranged a time for the next afternoon, and Lennox sat back in contentment. They talked of the old days, when he and Micah had served at Fort Laramie, and Lennox recalled when Micah had fulfilled his enlistment and left for seminary. "The next time I saw him, during the war, the two of you were married. Micah was looking forward to getting back to you and starting his ministry."

She nodded with glistening eyes. "He felt God called him to go back into the army to serve the men during the war. It was a difficult time for me, but I knew it was something Micah had to do. Praise God, he came home safe, and we spent five years together there in Kansas City at our missionary church."

"Micah's letters were full of the cattlemen and war veterans he ministered to."

"Yes. He had such a burden for them. God blessed him, and we saw a lot of souls saved. And then Micah..." Her face went sober and she let out a little sigh. "Then he died."

Lennox reached across the table and patted her hand.

"I'm so sorry. It was sudden and unexpected."

"Yes. He caught influenza while tending to the sick. But he's with the Lord now. I have that assurance."

"I've missed Micah all these years," Lennox said. "Just knowing he was no longer there, but also knowing you were left alone. You've kept us informed with your letters, but tell me, Amelia, how have you really been?"

Her gentle smile eased his anxiety. "It was very difficult at first. You understand."

"Indeed I do. When I lost Susie. . .well, I think I know exactly how it was for you."

"Yes. But over time. . ." She brightened and looked up at him. "The Lord does heal, doesn't He? The pain is less now, and I know I'll see Micah again in heaven."

"I tell myself the same thing about Susie. We shall meet again."

She nodded. "For a while I wasn't sure what I could do to support myself. I thought of returning to New England and throwing myself on the mercy of my cousins, but I didn't want to burden them."

"Oh? They were unsympathetic?"

"No, quite the opposite. And they'd have taken me in without a murmur, but I knew their circumstances were strained as it was. By then we had a small but faithful church in Kansas City. The people were very supportive. One dear friend and her husband offered me a place to stay until I decided what to do, and then a businessman in the congregation offered me a position as a clerk. The pay was low, but it allowed me to give my friends a little toward my board and keep my dignity."

"How long did you pursue that?"

"For about a year. It was hard work, but it kept me busy. I began to feel some satisfaction at being able to earn my own way."

The waiter returned and set their dishes before them. The broiled flounder, rice, and carrots steamed, sending off an enticing fragrance.

"This looks and smells delicious," Amelia said. "I just realized how famished I am."

"By all means, let's eat." Lennox picked up his fork and took a bite of the fish. The chef had prepared it perfectly.

After a few bites, she said, "You know, I fell into the matchmaking business by accident."

"Really?" Lennox reached for his water glass. He'd hoped they could avoid this topic, but he'd have to be rude to change the subject now. "Er. . .how did it come about?"

"A man in our church told me how miserable he'd been since his wife died. He longed for a new partner, a wife who could help him on his farm. He had two children who desperately needed a mother. He would take care of her if she would help raise his children, keep house, and be his life's companion."

"Why didn't you marry him?" Lennox asked.

She chuckled. "Oh no, he was not for me. For one thing, I was thirty-seven, and he was only twenty-eight. But I knew of a young woman back in Connecticut who had been bitterly disappointed a few years earlier. Her fiancé had betrayed her and jilted her only a week before their wedding day. I had corresponded with her for some time, and I felt she was ready to move into a new relationship, perhaps to fit into a family that needed a loving mother and wife."

"Your first match?"

"Yes." Her smile warmed him and eased the negative feelings that had badgered him. "It gave me the utmost satisfaction. I talked to Andrew first—he was the widower. He said that if I could find him a woman who would willingly come to his farm and step into the role of wife and mother—a woman devoted to Christ and yet practical and clever about the house and tender with children—then he would reward me well."

"Ah." Lennox had finished his fish and vegetables. He sat back and waited while the waiter poured coffee for them both. "And this match was successful, I take it?"

"Very. Andrew and Mary have thanked me many times for working on their behalf. I had told Andrew I didn't need any payment for my service, but he insisted. The amount he placed in my account staggered me, but he assured me that any serious man who wanted the right kind of wife but was too tied down by his family and business commitments to go looking for one would pay well for a go-between who could introduce him to the right woman."

"And so. . ."

"And so Mrs. Mayberry's Matrimonial Society for Christians of Good Moral Character was born."

"Just like that?"

"Oh no, it took time. But I realized that I knew quite a few spinsters and widows who could fill the empty places in homes if only they could be introduced to the potential husbands. I continued in my place of employment for another two years, until I was certain I could make enough through the society to keep me solvent. By then I had built up a solid collection of satisfied clients who were willing to give testimonials on my behalf."

Lennox smiled. "I can easily believe it. My dear Amelia, you could charm the world if only someone would introduce you properly."

"Why thank you." She sat opposite him, her eyes twinkling. Her expression brought to mind someone who perpetually waited for something good to happen.

Lennox found himself regretting that his own transaction with her had failed. She made it sound so attractive, so promising, so fulfilling.

She leaned toward him across the table and arched her shapely eyebrows. "So, Lennox, will you let me try again to find the right match for you?"

Chapter 3

Lennox didn't answer her question immediately. He waited until after the waiter brought their dessert—chocolate sponge pie with a drizzle of raspberry sauce.

Amelia watched him. He fidgeted a little in his chair. Was he waiting for her to lift her fork? Or was he trying to think of a way to dodge the question?

She leaned back and fluttered a hand through the air. "Forgive me. I didn't mean to make you uncomfortable. I only wanted to rectify my mistake if I could."

He shrugged slightly. "No offense taken. But I've decided I'm not ready for a new marriage. Susie and I. . .we had something rare. I'm not sure it's possible to recapture that."

"Perhaps not, but one can find a different happiness in one's later life." She picked up her fork and cut into the tempting dessert. "We're different people than we were thirty years ago, Lennox. We face different problems. We're no longer struggling to get established in life or facing military issues. Look at you—head of a prosperous company, grandfather to an adorable little boy. The life you would share with a new bride is much different from that you had with Susie."

"True."

They ate in silence for a minute.

"How long do you expect to be in Sacramento?" he asked.

"I'm not exactly sure. A few days, I think. However long it takes me to complete my errands. If things aren't well in hand by Friday, I shall stay over the weekend."

"Tell you what," he said at last. "I'll give your suggestion my consideration."

Amelia hummed as she dressed the next morning in her green dress. She ate breakfast in a smaller dining room than the one where they'd dined the evening before and asked the desk clerk to summon a cab for her. She took the hired carriage to the shopping district and spent the morning exploring the shops and buying a few trifles to take back with her to Kansas City.

She could hardly wait for her outing with Lennox that afternoon. The hotel maid had taken away her sensible shoes for polishing and her other dresses for pressing. It seemed an extravagance at first, but Amelia reasoned that this was a once-in-a-lifetime trip, and making a favorable impression on Lennox was vital. He had not yet agreed to let her try to find him another bride, but she felt he was weakening.

If only she could find the right woman for him this time. She prayed off and on all morning as she went about her shopping and purchased a light luncheon at a café in the city. For several months she had subtly gathered information about the three women she thought might suit Lennox. One was quite a bit younger than he was—only thirty-nine, in fact, but Nancy was a mature, self-possessed woman who had taught in a women's college for fifteen years. Secretly she longed for a home and a family, though she no longer expected the Lord to give her children of her own. She would jump at the chance to marry a widower with youngsters. Amelia thought Lennox's grandchild might do.

The second candidate, Ethel, was a personal friend. At forty-five, she was closer to Lennox's age, but she'd only been widowed eighteen months, and Amelia wasn't sure she was ready to put her first marriage behind her. Ethel had come to call one day and rather sheepishly inquired about Amelia's methods of helping people find each other. She was a lovely woman with a nest egg, thanks to her hardworking husband. She'd given birth to four children, but only two had survived to adulthood. She hated living alone but hated worse the idea of asking one of her daughters to take her in. Surely there was a gentleman out there who would trade the security of his name for her housekeeping skills and dowry.

Mildred, the third possibility, had passed her fiftieth birthday but would not divulge by how much. Amelia had included her because of her sunny personality and practical way of looking at life. She, too, had grown children. In fact, she was currently living with her eldest son and his wife—and she longed to escape. Though she loved her children and grandchildren, she found that Grandma was thrust into a role of cook/nursemaid in their home. She wished for freedom. She wished to remarry and move into a childless home where she could keep house without overtaxing herself.

Any one of the three would be happy to marry a fine man like Lennox, Amelia was certain. In fact, any woman in her right mind would be proud to be Mrs. Lennox Bailey. If only she could introduce Lennox to all three and let him see which one best suited his temperament. But that was impossible, as the three women lived in scattered corners of the nation.

The one who had refused to become his wife two years ago still baffled Amelia. What had gone wrong? How could that woman—Renata was her name—how could she have backed out of the agreement? What had she seen when she arrived in Sacramento that turned her opinion against Lennox? Amelia had spent only a few hours with him, but she was charmed. He was a fine, handsome, responsible man whose faith was evident. The woman must have been insane to reject him.

Or maybe. . . She crumpled her brow and sank down on her bed. Maybe Lennox was the one who'd found a flaw in Renata. But no, both had communicated to her that Renata had backed out, not Lennox. His letter had sounded sorrowful and brimmed with regret. He'd had hopes that the two of them would spend the rest of their lives together. Until she broke his heart.

Unless they'd agreed to say so in order to let Renata save face. Would Lennox back out of the relationship but tell Amelia he was the one jilted? She didn't think so. His discriminating honesty wouldn't allow that.

Well, however the break came about, she was here, not to heal it, but to substitute something just as good. And she would do that before Christmas, which was only a week away. That way she could return home by year's end and begin her retirement.

She nodded firmly. "That's what I'll do. A little more conversation with Lennox and I'll be able to see which of the ladies would be the best fit—Nancy, Ethel, or Mildred. Then I shall ask his permission to write to her on his behalf."

Lennox had agreed to pick her up at half past one, and Amelia made sure she got back to the hotel in time to freshen up. He again met her in the lobby and whisked her into his conveyance, this time a carriage driven by a young man he called Richard.

Their drive up the Sacramento Valley enthralled her, and Lennox gave her his full attention. The lush farms and orchards, the color of the fields and hills delighted her. Even in December, the countryside was green, so unlike the bleak landscape she'd left behind in Kansas.

"This is a wonderful place," she declared when Richard pulled the carriage to the side of the road at a spot that gave her a scenic view of the farmlands with the city in the distance.

"I love it here," Lennox said, looking out over the vista.

"Does it ever get cold?"

"Not for very long." He smiled over at her. "Amelia, I've so enjoyed the time I've spent with you yesterday and today. I confess I was a little hesitant at first." He laughed. "I was afraid you'd spend the entire time telling me about prospective wives you have lined up for me."

She gulped and managed a smile. "I can see that you're content in your business pursuits and your family. . ."

"Speaking of which, I'd like to re-introduce you to

Helen. I'm...not sure if I can manage it, though."

"I'd love to see your daughter again."

"I'll have to go round to her house and see if she and Daniel could dine with us. That is—if you are free tomorrow."

"Why, yes."

"I don't want to monopolize your time. I know you have other concerns to attend to."

"Oh, I...I did take care of some of my business this morning, and I expect I can whittle away at the rest tomorrow."

"Good. Then I shall leave you alone tomorrow. Except, I'll send an errand boy around to the Royal with a message to let you know if I've been able to arrange something for the evening."

His smile set Amelia's heart aflutter. Lennox had the same energy and charm as when she'd known him almost two decades ago. But now his attention was focused on her.

Be careful, she told herself. *You're not here to draw his interest. You're here to undo your mistake, and that means directing his affections toward another woman.*

Lennox drove Amelia back to town and insisted on stopping at a tea room before he delivered her to the hotel. She didn't bring up the matter of finding him a bride, and neither did he. If she would just forget about the whole thing, he'd be content. But he couldn't forget about her. Amelia's enthusiasm for the valley and her eager participation in the outing he'd planned had puffed him up inside, making him feel like a twenty-year-old out to impress a girl. It was silly, he supposed, since both of them had passed into their fifties, but he hadn't felt so carefree and so anxious to spend time with a woman since before Susie's passing.

He left Amelia at the Royal and walked back to the carriage. With a sudden determination, he told Richard to drive him to his daughter's house, or rather to Daniel Frye's house, for Daniel had owned it for several years before he married Helen. The two-story home lay on a quiet street in one of the city's older residential neighborhoods. It would have been right at home in a suburb of Boston or Philadelphia, bespeaking elegance and comfort. Daniel was young to own such a substantial home, but his success as an attorney brought in a more than adequate income. When he'd courted Helen, Lennox had questioned him about his finances, and Daniel had supplied him with assurance that Helen would lack for nothing.

As he walked toward their front door, Lennox wondered if that was such a good thing. The early days with Susie, when they'd lived in one room at the army post and later in a tiny cabin on the plains, were some of the best times in their marriage. They'd faced hardships that forced them to work together to overcome poverty. Their long separation during the war had only strengthened their love. But Helen and Daniel hadn't had any real trials to test and strengthen their marriage. He prayed that when they came, Helen would find herself as strong as her mother had been.

A housemaid opened the door and showed him into the parlor, where Helen was rocking her six-month-old son.

"Hello, Papa." She smiled up at him. "Samuel's just drifted off to sleep."

"Don't disturb him. Just let me get a look." Lennox bent down and peered over Helen's shoulder at the cherubic little face. "That's my boy. Soon he'll be running about the orchards with me and visiting Grandpa at the packing plant." He took a seat in an overstuffed chair near her. "I wondered if you and Daniel are busy tomorrow evening?"

"As a matter of fact, we have tickets to the Christmas theatrical at the Strand. I meant to tell you yesterday, but I forgot. We're hoping you'll join us."

"Oh." Lennox frowned.

"What is it, Papa?"

"I had hoped you would dine with me and Mrs. Mayberry."

"What? Mrs. Mayberry? I supposed she'd be gone by tomorrow. You're seeing her again?"

He sat back in the chair and watched her face cautiously. "As a matter of fact, I spent the afternoon with her. We drove up the valley and looked at the groves."

Helen's face contracted as though a pain had struck her. "You're not. . . ?"

"What?"

She shrugged. "Forget it."

"I'd prefer not to. Helen, why are you against my spending a few hours with the widow of the dearest friend of my youth?"

"I don't know."

"I think I do." He gazed steadily at her until she lifted her eyes to meet his. "I think you're afraid I'll become entangled with another woman."

"I didn't say that." She looked away and sighed, patting the baby's back.

"You don't like the idea of my setting my affections on someone new—someone you're not completely comfortable with."

"All right, I admit that I was appalled when that one woman showed up here wanting to marry you."

"She came at my invitation. I've told you already how sorry I am that I undertook that venture. If I'd had any idea what the woman would think of—"

"No, Papa, please. Let's not discuss it. You know it was humiliating for both of us. It's true I don't want to go through that again. But I don't wish it on you either."

"So you wouldn't object to my making a liaison with a lady if she were truly a lady? Or would you be angry with me no matter how genteel she was?"

"What are you saying?"

"I'm saying you don't want to see another woman in your mother's place."

There. It was out in the open.

Helen's dark eyes snapped, and her lips twitched. "I'm hurt that you would say such a thing."

He leaned toward her. "Helen, my dear, you know I loved your mother to distraction, and she'll always be precious in my heart. I'm not looking to replace her. But I'll tell you something. There are days when I think I'll go crazy in that house by myself."

"But—"

"I know. I have you and Daniel and Samuel, and I love you all. But you have your own lives. I have Anna and Richard, who take very good care of me and my home, and I have friends and business associates. But sometimes

I'd just like to have someone congenial to talk to. To do things with. To work in the flower beds beside, or to dote on my grandson with. Mrs. Mayberry is only staying here a few more days. But I'm not ashamed to tell you that if I could find a woman half as amiable as she is here in Sacramento, I'd be calling on her regularly."

Helen blinked at him and swallowed hard. "I'm sorry, Papa. I didn't mean to imply that you shouldn't have companionship. I just don't want to see you hurt again."

"Apology accepted. Now, would you and Daniel consider dining out with us before you go to the theater?"

The baby stirred and let out a minuscule wail. Helen rocked him and patted his back again. "I'll do better than that, Papa. Bring Mrs. Mayberry here for dinner at six o'clock tomorrow. I'm sure Daniel can get another ticket for the performance."

"You mean, you would allow me to invite her to attend with the three of us?"

"Yes, if you'd like that."

He stood and walked over to her chair. Stooping, he kissed the top of her head, then the baby's. "Thank you, my dear. And I promise. . .Mrs. Mayberry will give you no cause for embarrassment."

Lennox smiled more during Friday's dinner than he could remember doing for a long time. Helen had learned to be a gracious hostess, even if she wasn't sure she entirely approved of the guest. Amelia seemed genuinely delighted to be reunited with his daughter and meet her family. Helen's husband, Daniel, spoke attentively to Amelia from behind his precisely groomed mustache, and she asked all the questions he loved to answer about his law practice. But the infant Samuel effortlessly won Amelia's heart.

Helen brought the baby out before they ate, and Amelia declared him to be the stoutest little fellow she had ever seen. Lennox proudly took the baby in his arms and coddled him while they chatted, and Amelia made faces of delight at the child and tried to get him to return her smiles.

After about ten minutes of this, Lennox asked if she would like to hold Samuel. Instead of reaching out for the baby, Amelia turned and asked Helen if she minded. Lennox beamed at his guest. Her fine manners earned Helen's grudging approval.

When they went in to dinner, Helen had the maid take Samuel away to his bed. Daniel questioned Amelia politely about her home in Kansas City. Lennox held his breath. What if Daniel or Helen inquired into Mrs. Mayberry's business?

He asked Helen what their plans were for Christmas Eve, and the turn of the subject succeeded in drawing attention away from Amelia. After Helen had explained that they planned to spend Christmas Eve with Lennox and Christmas Day with the Frye family, Amelia inquired about Helen's lovely china pattern. That set his daughter off for a good ten minutes telling how she'd hunted for just the right design and finally found it in an import warehouse.

Before the meal was properly finished—Lennox hadn't gotten his second cup of coffee—Daniel declared it was time to leave for the theater. They left the baby in the care of the housekeeper and drove together in Lennox's carriage.

Amelia and Helen both fell into the holiday spirit as they entered the abundantly decorated theater. While the men discussed the fine Rococo architecture, the two ladies chattered about the greenery swags and brass lanterns strewn throughout the auditorium. Things went so well that during the program Lennox found himself humming along with some of the carols.

After a string quartet played several numbers, a group of local amateur actors performed a sentimental one-act play. Lennox was surprised when he looked over during *Mama's Christmas Gift* and saw Amelia dash away a tear. She smiled and shrugged a little as though she knew the melodramatic piece was rather silly, but women were entitled to cry a little at such nonsense. Lennox quite liked that in her—she didn't try to hide her emotions.

Not until the intermission did his pleasant evening threaten to crumble.

The gentlemen excused themselves during the intermission and promised to bring the ladies a glass of punch. Amelia noticed that Helen fidgeted in her chair.

"Thinking about the little fellow?" she asked.

"Yes. I rarely leave Samuel in the evening. Of course, he usually sleeps through until early morning now, but I should hate for him to wake up and cry because I wasn't there."

"I'm sure he's fast asleep."

Helen let out a little sigh. "You're probably right. Forgive me if this is too personal, Mrs. Mayberry, but were you blessed with children? I don't recall any little ones when we visited you at your home, but I was so young then myself that I might have forgotten."

"No. Micah and I hoped for a family, but it didn't come about. We were wed twelve years, but the Lord didn't see fit to give us children."

"I'm sorry." Helen leaned toward her and spoke earnestly. "Papa told me that you are in business, and that since Mr. Mayberry died, you've earned your own living. What is it that you do?"

Amelia chuckled. "He didn't tell you? I'm surprised at him. I stumbled into a very rewarding career."

Helen's dark eyes sparked with interest. Amelia noted how well her mulberry-colored dress, with ecru lace trim, suited her. She had inherited her mother's somewhat exotic beauty. "Now I'm intrigued," Helen said. "Tell me more."

"Why, my dear, I bring happiness to those who are lonely. At least. . .most of the time. Your father was the one client I couldn't help. It's grieved me for the last two years."

"Papa? Your. . .client?" Helen stared at her, and her eyes looked larger than ever in her finely chiseled face.

Amelia hesitated. Helen was serious. Lennox hadn't told his daughter about her attempt to find him a bride. "Oh, dear. I fear I've said too much."

"No, no. Tell me." Helen laid an eager hand on her sleeve. "What business did you undertake for Papa?"

Amelia's mouth went dry. How could she betray his trust? "I'm sorry. I thought your father had told you at the time. My dear, if I'd had any idea how Mrs. Enderly would—"

"Mrs. *Enderly*?" Helen's jaw dropped.

"I. . .well, yes. I assure you that I corresponded with her and with all her references. She seemed the ideal answer to your father's needs. I don't doubt her faith, but still. . .it never occurred to me that things would run so badly amok when the two met each other. And I never did learn—"

By this time, Helen had recovered her ability to speak, and she did so, quite loudly. "You sent her here!"

All around them, theater patrons quit talking and stared at them.

Helen leaped to her feet.

Amelia stood, too, unsure of how to proceed. "I never intended—"

"How could you?"

Amelia's heart sank. Her chest constricted as she stared at Helen's blotchy face. She grabbed the back of the chair in the next row to steady herself.

Behind her, Lennox's voice came sharply, as it had when he barked at the new recruits of Fort Laramie. "Helen! What is the problem here?"

Chapter 4

Lennox glared at his daughter, wishing he wasn't holding two dainty punch cups.

Helen scowled back. "I just learned that Mrs. Mayberry was responsible for *that woman* coming here." Helen's rigid stance dared either of them to deny it.

Amelia murmured, "Oh dear," and shot him a sorrowful glance.

Daniel stopped in the aisle next to Lennox and looked from him to Helen and back again. "What seems to be the matter, sir?"

"I'll tell you," Helen replied, ignoring her father. "Mrs. Mayberry sent that despicable—"

"Helen." Lennox kept his voice low but put his years of practiced authority into it. "Darling, I submit to you that this is not the best place to discuss the matter."

Daniel looked to his wife again, but Helen still smoldered, her lashes lowered.

"Yes. Helen, let's sit down. We brought you ladies some

punch. The program will begin again soon, but you can tell me all about this later. I'm sure it's nothing serious." His troubled eyes shot a question at Lennox.

"That's right, Daniel. I believe I know what Helen is referring to, and we can put it all to rest after the program. Let's stay calm and enjoy the rest of the evening." Lennox took his seat beside Amelia and held out her cup of punch. "Here you go."

"I. . .thank you." Amelia took it and sipped the sweet liquid, saying no more. When an usher walked by, they handed over their empty cups.

To Lennox's consternation, Helen had a whispered conversation with her husband, the result of which was that she changed seats with Daniel, so that she no longer sat beside Amelia. Instead, she sat on the aisle, with Amelia between the two men.

Lennox leaned forward and glared daggers at his daughter, but Helen refused to let him catch her eye, so his histrionics were wasted. When he realized Amelia eyed him cautiously, he sat back, giving himself a mental kick. If he wanted Helen to behave like an adult, he'd better set the example. "I did enjoy the string music earlier," he said.

Amelia nodded. "Oh, yes. Very nice."

His stomach hurt. He ought to have told Helen about Amelia's connection to Renata Enderly, but he hadn't thought it necessary, and he hadn't wanted Helen to have bad thoughts about Amelia. He'd never foreseen this happening—that Amelia would actually come to Sacramento. He should have confessed all to Helen as soon as he learned of her impending visit. Ah, hindsight.

"Are you all right?" Amelia whispered over the strains of "Silent Night."

He realized he must have let out a heavy sigh. "Yes, I'll be fine. I just wish Helen was still young enough for me to paddle her."

Amelia did not seem amused, and he decided to keep quiet.

❄

The second half of the program dragged on. Amelia shivered as the singers slid the tiniest bit off-key. The youngsters who gave recitations forgot their lines, and the pianist dropped her music. At last the blessed finish arrived, and the foursome shuffled to the cloakroom with the rest of the crowd.

As they stepped out into the cool evening air, Lennox took Amelia's arm and steered her toward where his carriage awaited them, with Richard sitting on the box.

Amelia leaned close and murmured, "Lennox, I never. . ."

"I know, my dear. I know. Don't worry about this. I shall set Helen straight on the matter."

Richard opened the carriage door, and Lennox helped her climb up. He stood back and let Daniel assist Helen, and then the two men entered the carriage.

As Lennox settled on the seat next to Amelia, he said, "Helen, I shall be around tomorrow morning before I go to the plant, and we shall discuss this matter in full. But right now, I shall get you home to your little son, and then I shall take Mrs. Mayberry to her hotel."

"Yes, Papa."

Amelia's throat felt as tight as a new corset. An uneasy

quiet accompanied them as they rode along.

Finally Daniel cleared his throat. "Have you been shipping lots of fruit this month, Mr. Bailey?"

"Yes, the farmers got a good crop. We've shipped a record amount of citrus."

They fell silent again. Amelia cast about for something to say, but Helen's stillness disheartened her. She should have stayed home. If her visit caused a rift in the Bailey family, she would count it a worse blot than her failure to find a wife for Lennox.

They turned in at the Fryes' gravel driveway, and Richard guided the horses to the front entrance. Daniel hopped out and reached to help Helen down.

"Thank you for a pleasant evening, sir," he said to Lennox. "Mrs. Mayberry, it was a pleasure to make your acquaintance."

Amelia almost cringed at the seeming insincerity of his words. Daniel, as a proper young husband, must be livid at her for his wife's sake. She managed a squeaky, "Thank you, and thank you again for your hospitality."

"Good night," Helen said and turned away.

Daniel shut the door.

Lennox grunted. "I've never seen her so rude in my life. I feel like calling her back here and—"

"Please don't," Amelia said. "Lennox, I'm so sorry. She inquired about my line of business. I never intended to make things uncomfortable for you. Or for Helen, when it comes down to it."

"Of course you didn't." He lapsed into silence. The horses' hooves clopped on the packed gravel street.

Richard turned the carriage toward the Royal Hotel

once more. Amelia hated to end the evening on this bleak note, but Lennox seemed inclined to avoid the subject.

As they turned onto the cobbled street that led to the hotel, she gathered her courage. "Lennox, I fear I shan't sleep unless we talk this over a bit more. Is there any way I can turn things around with Helen?"

He reached for her hand. The warmth of his touch, even through her gloves, heartened her. "I believe there are withdrawing areas in the lobby at the Royal," he said. "Perhaps we can find a quiet spot to talk for a few minutes."

She squeezed his fingers lightly and allowed him to keep hold of her hand until they reached the hotel.

When the carriage drew up, he got out and helped her down. "Richard, I shall be perhaps twenty minutes," he said to the driver.

Richard touched his hand to his cap to signal he understood and would wait while Lennox escorted her inside.

As they entered the lobby, he removed his hat and pointed toward an archway that led into a quiet lounge. "Over there, I think."

Amelia let him lead her into the room, where comfortable chairs and settees were arranged in small groupings. Only two other people were present, engaged in quiet conversation near a fireplace. Lennox guided her to the opposite end of the room, where a velvet-covered Empire sofa waited.

She took her seat and looked up at him. Why had she never noticed how attractive his blue eyes were? So different from Helen's deep brown ones. The unmistakable flurry in her chest told her that she was beginning to care deeply about Lennox.

"I know it's late," she said, "but I simply can't go on wondering what happened between you and Renata Enderly. I shall stay awake all night fretting about it if I don't know."

"I suppose you have a right to know, though there's no excuse for Helen's rudeness."

"Perhaps she had some cause," Amelia suggested.

He sighed and set his hat on the cushion beside him. "When Mrs. Enderly and I corresponded, I thought you were right—you'd found me a woman of like spirit and mind. I was eager to meet her. I offered to travel east to visit her, but she said she would come to California if my mind was made up. And it was, or so I thought."

"Did you tell Helen?"

"Yes. I informed her that I had exchanged several letters with a lady and that I was prepared to marry her on her arrival in Sacramento. Helen didn't like it, but she told me I knew my own mind. When I assured her that this woman's references had been checked and that she was an upstanding member of her community, Helen kept her peace."

Amelia eyed him, waiting for more, but he sat frowning down at his interlaced fingers. After a minute, she prompted gently, "Until. . ."

He sighed. "I suppose I might as well tell you all."

"If it's not too painful for you."

"I hope it won't be too painful for you to hear, dear friend. . ."

Amelia's heart tripped, and she inhaled deeply. "I'm flattered that you consider me such, especially after I caused what seems to have been a tragic event in your life."

The other couple rose and headed for the door to the

lounge, chatting amiably. When they had left the room, Lennox nodded. "I shall tell you, since you are so curious, and since I wouldn't like to know you'd lost sleep over it. You remember my wife, Susie."

"Of course. I considered her a close friend, though I only saw her a few times face to face."

"Yes. She thought highly of you as well. I assume you remember her heritage."

"You mean. . ."

"That's right," he said. "She was of the Sioux tribe. I met her during my days at Laramie and lost my heart to her. We were married back in '56—while Micah was still at Fort Laramie."

Amelia nodded. "He told me about the wedding many times."

"Yes. I thank God for Susie. We were very happy together."

"I know you were, and it was never my intention to make light of that."

He raised one hand in protest. "I never thought you did. I admit that after I learned you were in the matchmaking business, I pondered the situation long and hard. Yes, and I prayed about it, too. I never once considered during our transaction that you implied I should forget about Susie. I thought this might be a way for me to end my loneliness and to help you at the same time."

"I considered it a high compliment that you trusted me to find someone for you. That was why I felt so disappointed when I learned that Renata Enderly had turned you down. I'd spent months seeking just the right woman." She'd tried twice afterward to get him to accept a refund of her fee, but

Lennox had refused outright. Amelia shook her head. "I gave her all the information you passed on to me, and I told her my personal high opinion of you."

"Ah, but did you tell her about Susie?"

"Of course. I told her you'd been widowed three or four years and that you felt you were ready for a new marriage. And naturally I told her what a wonderful woman Susie was."

Lennox studied her face. "My dear Amelia, you are an intelligent woman, but I can't help feeling you're also a bit naive." Before she could protest, he took her hand once more. "Did you tell Mrs. Enderly that my wife was a full-blooded Indian?"

Amelia started to speak but froze as enlightenment swashed over her brain like a sea wave sweeping the beach. "I. . .I don't know. Do you mean to tell me *that* is why she rejected you? Why, that's unconscionable!"

Lennox sighed and pursed his lips. "For some—especially those in the East, it seems—marrying a person of another race is unthinkable. And marrying a savage—"

Amelia's whole body tightened, and she scowled at him. "Susie Bailey was most certainly *not* a savage."

"I agree, but Mrs. Enderly thought otherwise."

"I don't know what to say." Amelia shook her head slowly. "I'm embarrassed for her. I truly didn't expect that kind of reaction from her, or I certainly wouldn't have sent her your way. It simply never occurred to me."

"It's all right, my dear. Don't let it trouble you. I've put it behind me."

"But Helen hasn't."

"You're right. She's obviously held it against the woman

for the last two years. I fear it's partly on my account—Helen feels I was humiliated. But it's also for her mother's sake, and her own when it comes right down to it. Mrs. Enderly is severely prejudiced, and she is not afraid to voice her opinions. Her remarks when she learned about Susie hurt Helen deeply."

"I'm so sorry."

He drew in a deep breath. "Don't worry. I shall speak with Helen in the morning and explain to her that the incident did not scar me too badly, and it shouldn't do so for her either. If she'll see it in a different perspective, she may even come to see it as a blessing."

"How is that?" Amelia asked.

"I shall tell her that I decided months ago that this was God's way of telling me He didn't want me to remarry."

Amelia tossed and turned that night, going over the conversation in her mind. She could hardly believe Mrs. Enderly—whom she had investigated rigorously—had held such firm prejudice against Indians. When she came west with Micah, how had she felt about the native people? All Amelia could recall was the tremendous burden God had placed in her heart for them.

Though Micah's outreach had focused on the cowboys and Civil War veterans in the Kansas City area, they had also had some contact with Indians and ministered to one Kansa village in particular, a few miles from the town. Some of the women had become Amelia's friends, and two had been guests in her home when they came into town. Only a few years after Micah's death, the people of the local villages had been removed to the Indian Territory, and Amelia had grieved to see them forced to leave their homes, but was powerless to help them, beyond giving her friends gifts of clothing before they left.

Given her own experience and love for the native women, Amelia didn't think she could ever snub a man who had married a woman of Indian heritage.

And yet, much as she hated to admit it, she could picture her proper aunts doing just that. Interracial marriage was considered a scandal where she'd grown up. She'd been glad that Renata Enderly seemed to have high standards, but she hadn't known how straight-laced the potential bride could be. Odd, she'd never made such a mistake before. Had she focused too intently on finding someone for Lennox?

Many times she'd imagined how happy he would be once he found a new love. And his new bride would be happy as well. How could she be otherwise? After all, Lennox was a fine man, and he'd always treated Susie like a queen. Renata Enderly's attitude was out of line with scripture, though perhaps typical of her upbringing. Amelia scolded herself again for not seeing this potential pitfall when she recommended a match.

Yet now that she'd spent more time with him, she realized she hadn't known Lennox very well at all.

She intended to change that. She had a few more days in Sacramento, and she planned to learn as much about him as she could. He'd invited her to tour the fruit-packing plant on Saturday, and then to go around with him to visit the Crocker House, recently donated to the city along with the

Crocker family's art collection.

She rolled over on her feather pillow, away from the window and the moonlight spilling in, and spoke her prayer aloud. "Lord, thank You for allowing Lennox to forgive my poor judgment. I find it hard to believe he still wants to spend time with me. Dare I ask that he would give me another chance? And please give me wisdom in dealing with Helen. If possible, I'd like to see her again and ask her to forgive me."

Amelia sighed and closed her eyes, pushing away the certainty that Helen did *not* want to see her.

Chapter 5

I can show myself in." Lennox handed the housemaid his hat and strode down the hall to the breakfast room.

Daniel and Helen sat at the table. Daniel was dressed in a black suit for the office, and Helen looked charming in her cream-colored morning dress. Though it was early, little Samuel was awake and jabbering as he sat on his mother's lap.

Lennox stood in the doorway and watched as the baby flailed his arms and swiped at his mother's spoon. He'd prayed all the way over that he wouldn't let his anger rise, and his little grandson's antics were just what he needed to soften his mood.

Daniel glanced up and noticed him. "Good morning, sir." He rose and nodded toward the empty chair to his right. "Won't you join us?"

"Don't mind if I do, but I've eaten. Just a cup of coffee, please."

The housemaid had followed him in and set a cup and saucer at his place before he'd finished speaking.

Instead of taking his seat immediately, Lennox walked to Helen's chair and stooped to look Samuel in the eye. "Good morning, young man. You're looking chipper today."

Helen eyed him cautiously. "Would you like to hold him, Papa?"

"I surely would." He took the baby and jostled him up and down a few times, looking into Samuel's wide, dark eyes. "Hey, fella. Say good morning to Grandpa."

Samuel burbled and reached for his grandfather's nose.

Lennox bussed the baby noisily and bent to kiss Helen's cheek. He rounded the table and sat down, taking care to move his coffee cup out of Samuel's reach.

Daniel resumed his seat. "How are you this morning, sir?"

"I'm fine. I wondered how Helen is doing."

His daughter patted her lips with her linen napkin. "I confess I spent a troubled night. Why did you not tell me that entire machination of a mail-order bride was initiated by Mrs. Mayberry?"

"Because it wasn't. She happened to be in the business many years before I knew about it. I approached her as a client. She found a woman she felt would suit me. But when Mrs. Enderly came here, we found that we had insurmountable differences, and so nothing came of it. Nothing except your deep-seated hurt and bitterness, it seems."

Helen looked down at her plate of half-finished sausage and eggs. "You know she was inexcusably rude. She insulted Mama—and you and me. The entire family."

"Yes, and she left, and that was the end of it. Helen, look at me."

Slowly she raised her chin.

328

Lennox bounced Samuel gently on his knee. "The things she said when she met you and saw the photograph of your mother and me cut deep. I don't deny it. I was appalled that she would hold such sentiments. But it wasn't the first time I'd heard them."

Helen's lip trembled. "I suppose not."

"Do you think your mother and I were always accepted, wherever we went? She was shunned and rejected and insulted many, many times. I was ridiculed for marrying a Sioux woman. I've received more set-downs because of it than I can remember."

A tear rolled down Helen's cheek. "People don't understand."

"Some people." Lennox sighed and shifted Samuel to his other arm. "Sweetheart, I can tell you this: Anyone who ever got to know your mother loved her. She was accepted here by everyone with whom I did business. If not, then I no longer did business with those people. My colleagues and their wives took your mother into their hearts. She held a position in society here in Sacramento. No one looked on her as a savage or as an inferior. Susie Bailey was a lady, through and through."

Helen gulped hard. "I took my share of teasing at school."

"I know you did. Children can be cruel. But you also had some very good friends. Look at Mary Jonassen. She never ridiculed you. She's been your friend since grammar school. And Ida Pilcher, and—"

"You're right, of course. I suppose it's the few bad times that stick out in my memory."

"I tried to protect you, but I knew you'd do best if you

went to the public school and learned to grow a thick skin. Some days you came home crying, and that nearly killed me. Especially after your mother died and you didn't have her to comfort you. I hated to send you back. But I felt that if I didn't, you'd hide from the world for the rest of your life and feel like a misfit." He shot a glance at his son-in-law.

Daniel cleared his throat. "Helen, darling, your father is right. No one in this town would belittle you now."

"Because I'm your wife and Papa's daughter."

"No, because you are a lady. As your father says, it's your character they look at. And though I never knew your mother, I'm told she was a lovely woman, inside and out. I've never heard anyone speak ill of her or smear her because of her heritage."

Helen sat in silence.

Lennox turned his attention to Samuel, who had grabbed his cravat and pulled for all he was worth. "There, little man. Take it easy, or you'll choke me." Lennox pried the baby's hands away and joggled him back and forth. "You have to take good care of your old grandpa, so I'll be around to take you fishing in a couple of years."

Helen took a sip of her cooling tea and set the cup down carefully. "Well, Papa, I still think Mrs. Mayberry is a meddler."

"How can you say that? She didn't approach me. I asked her to find me a bride."

"Why?" Helen's brow furrowed. "Are you really that lonesome?"

"Some days. Not all the time. But look at yourself, Helen. I walked in here this morning and I found this loving little family at breakfast. It made me glad to see how well your marriage has turned out and how pleasant your home is." He didn't mention her grumpiness from the encounter with Amelia—best let that alone. "My dear, it made me think, how wonderful it would be if I had the same harmony in my home. Someone to love, someone to be with and to share things with."

She sniffed. "So. . .even though it's been two years, you still feel that way?"

"I do. I know I told you the other day that I didn't feel God would have me remarry, but those were hasty words. Things change with time, and perhaps. . .well, perhaps it's time now for me to reconsider. I've tried to ignore my feelings of loneliness, but seeing Amelia again brought back all the hope I felt two years ago, when I thought I could enter a new stage of life and live in happiness with a woman again. It's unfortunate that you discovered the details of that ill-fated transaction the way you did, and I apologize. But it doesn't mean I shall remain single for the rest of my life."

"Mrs. Mayberry. . .took your money to dredge up that woman?"

Lennox sighed. He must choose his words more cautiously. "She offered to refund the fee after the plan fell apart. I refused. She'd done the work she promised."

Helen opened her mouth, and he raised his hand to halt her. "Before you get started, let me say that she did a fine job of it. She investigated this woman, as we both thought, thoroughly. She didn't think to ask one question. One question, Helen. If she had asked it, and if Mrs. Enderly had told her that she couldn't abide the idea of marrying a widower whose first wife was of Indian heritage, why then, Amelia would have dismissed her as a possibility for me immediately. But it never occurred to her to ask that particular question."

"Why ever not?"

"Because Amelia is, to a degree, innocent. She loved Susie. She couldn't imagine another woman, respectable on all accounts, would feel otherwise."

Helen turned her dark eyes toward Daniel.

"I must leave for the office," he said, "but, my dear, I feel you should listen to your father. He speaks wisdom. And if he still wants to look for companionship, then a new wife would be the respectable solution."

Helen whipped around to stare at her father. "You wouldn't. . ."

"What?" Lennox asked, though he thought he knew what was on her mind.

"You're not going to ask her to try again, are you? Papa, there are nice ladies in the church. You could pay court to one of them."

He arched his eyebrows. "Oh? Which one? Mrs. Snead? She'll be eighty in a few months. And please don't say Mrs. Rich."

"Well, no. I daresay she outweighs you a good bit, and she's a gossip."

Lennox laughed. "There. You see? I trust Amelia Mayberry's judgment. If I decide to go this route again—and I don't say I will—then, yes, I might very well ask for her assistance in the matter." He rose and walked around the table. "Now I must be going, too."

Helen rose and took the baby from him. "I'm sorry, Papa."

He smiled and touched her cheek. "All is forgiven. Now, Daniel, my carriage waits outside. Can I drop you at your office?"

"Thank you, sir."

"Papa—"

He turned back. "Yes, Helen?"

"Are you going to see Mrs. Mayberry again before she leaves?"

"Yes, I am. Why?"

"I thought. . .well, if she's staying over Sunday, perhaps she might attend church with us all."

Lennox smiled. "I'll convey your invitation to her. I'm going to see her later today and take her around to the Crocker House."

He and Daniel walked out to the carriage together.

Once inside and on their way, Daniel turned to him, his expression grave. "Sir, I can't thank you enough for coming by this morning."

"Oh, Helen gave you a bad time last night, did she?"

Daniel flushed and looked out the window. "A bit. She was certain this Mrs. Mayberry—whom I found to be charming, by the way—was out to land you for herself. You and your bankbook."

Lennox frowned. "Amelia is not a moneygrubber. If she were, she'd have asked me for help years ago. No, when her husband died, she didn't look around to her friends for handouts. Instead, she went to work."

"I can see you admire her greatly."

"I suppose I do. Can't help it really."

Daniel nodded. "And she is quite pretty."

"Very well preserved." Lennox eyed his son-in-law sharply and almost laughed aloud. "What are you saying, Daniel?"

"Nothing, sir. Not a thing. Except that if you *are* thinking of looking for a second Mrs. Bailey, perhaps you should look no further than the Royal Hotel."

Daniel had never spoken to him in such a manner before. It was highly irregular. Still, the idea had some merit. Lennox grunted and folded his arms across his chest. "I shall not tell Helen you've been impertinent."

❄

Amelia spent Saturday morning window shopping and sent off a few postcards. She returned to the hotel, planning to eat luncheon in the dining room before Lennox came to get her.

As she approached the curved staircase in the lobby, the desk clerk approached her. "Mrs. Mayberry, I'm glad I caught you."

She halted, her heart hammering. Had Lennox sent a message to cancel their engagement for this afternoon?

"We received a telephone call for you from Kansas City," the clerk said.

"For me?"

"Yes, just a few minutes ago. I asked the party if she wanted to hold while we went to see if you were in your room, but she asked if we would have you return her call instead. That's if you've a mind to, ma'am. If not, we can let it go, and if she calls again I will tell her—"

"I shall make the call. Where is your telephone?"

"The instrument is through here, ma'am." The clerk led her behind the desk and into an office hardly bigger than the massive oak desk in the center. He indicated the telephone box on the wall. "Are you familiar with telephones?"

"Yes."

"Very good, ma'am. If you'll ask the operator to tell you the charges afterward, we can add it to your hotel bill. Here is the party's name and number." He put a slip of paper in her hand and left her alone in the office.

Amelia opened the paper and stared down at the precise writing. Mrs. Fulton—Deborah. Why would her neighbor go to the expense of placing a long-distance call to her? She studied the number. It was the exchange at the emporium on Burlington Street. People who didn't have telephones in their homes could go there and place calls.

She wondered if Deborah was waiting in the store for her to call back. Quickly she lifted the instrument's receiver to her ear and spoke to the operator.

In a surprisingly short time, she heard Deborah's breathless voice. "Amelia! I'm so glad they could get hold of you. My dear, it's terrible."

"What's terrible?" Amelia's pulse raced at hearing her friend's agitation.

"Your sweet little house that you've saved so long to buy. It's. . .my dear Amelia, it's gone!"

"Gone?" Amelia grabbed the edge of the desk beside her. "What's happened?"

"It burned last night. My husband said lightning struck it. We had a terrible storm. Oh, Amelia, I'm so sorry. By the time we saw the smoke, there wasn't much we could do."

Amelia sucked in a breath. "Fluffy?"

"James saved her. He opened the kitchen door, and she tore out and ran under our porch. I couldn't get her out until this morning, but I finally coaxed her with a bowl of milk and a piece of fish. She's in our house now, poor thing."

"Bless you."

"The fire department came, but the building was so far gone by then that nothing could be salvaged. What do you want us to do?"

"Let me think." Possibilities whizzed through Amelia's mind. Should she leave for Kansas City today? "I was going to stay here until Monday, but perhaps. . ."

"There's nothing to be gained by cutting short your visit. You did have insurance, didn't you?"

"Yes. That's one thing I made sure of when I purchased the property."

"Well, then, a couple of days won't make that big a difference."

Amelia wasn't so sure. This news was distracting enough to keep her from concentrating fully on her mission to find Lennox a bride. Perhaps she should go upstairs and pack. Her appetite had fled anyway. When he came to take her to tour the fruit-packing plant, she could ask him to take her to the train station instead.

"Deborah, I'm not sure what I shall do. I'll need some time to think it over. But I shall send you a telegram when I know my plans and let you know my time of arrival."

"All right. And James will make sure no one pokes about your place until you get home. Amelia, I'm so, so sorry."

"Thank you." Amelia replaced the earpiece and sat down

heavily in the chair behind the desk. She drew in a deep breath and bowed her head. *Heavenly Father, calm my heart. Please show me what to do.*

She sat there another ten minutes until a discreet knock on the door pulled her attention back to Sacramento.

"Mrs. Mayberry?"

"Yes." She stood and headed for the door.

"Is everything all right, ma'am?" the desk clerk asked.

"Yes, thank you. I received some bad news, and I took a few minutes to compose myself. But I shall be fine."

"If you're sure. . ."

She walked past him and toward the staircase. "Yes. Thank you very much." She would have to remember to leave a tip for him, as well as the chambermaid. A sudden thought caused her to turn back. "I'm sorry, but I forgot to inquire about the charges."

"We'll attend to it, ma'am."

An hour later, a bellboy knocked on the door of her room. "You have a caller in the lobby, ma'am. A gentleman to see you."

"Thank you." She handed the boy a nickel and made her way downstairs, taking pains not to hurry.

Lennox waited to one side of the stairs, his hat in his hand. Relief swept over her. He would surely give her sound advice in this matter.

His face lit in a smile when he saw her, but the smile drooped after a moment. He stepped forward and offered his arm. "My dear, is everything all right? I spoke with Helen and Daniel this morning. Please don't let what happened last evening trouble you."

"It's not that," Amelia said. "About an hour ago, I received word from my closest neighbor that a fire destroyed my home last night."

He caught his breath. "How awful. What will you do?"

"I'm undecided as to whether I ought to keep my planned schedule and leave Monday or head home immediately."

"I should hate to see you go so soon, but that is merely selfishness. Have you checked the schedule? There is a train later this afternoon, but it's a local. I think you might do as well to sleep here and take the morning express. That is, if you feel you must go as quickly as possible."

"I confess I'm at a loss. The neighbors rescued my cat, for which I'm thankful, but they tell me the house and its contents are destroyed. I only bought the house a month ago, but I did buy insurance on it. . ." She looked up into his concerned face. "Please advise me, Lennox. What should I do?"

"Perhaps you could send a telegram to your insurance company. Are they located in Kansas City?"

"Yes. That sounds sensible."

He nodded. "You could tell them your planned itinerary and ask their advice."

"Would you help me word the telegram? I'm afraid my wits are not to be trusted just now."

"I'd be happy to, but perhaps you should sit down."

"I'd like to do this right away. The hotel has a booth right over there." She pointed across the lobby to where a young woman sat behind a barred window in a small room with the telegraph key.

"In that case, let's take care of it."

After they sent off a rather businesslike telegram, Lennox

took her hand. "And now, dear lady, you look like a woman who could use a cup of tea. Why don't we ask for a pot to be sent into the lounge while we await a reply to your telegram?"

Amelia smiled wearily. "That sounds delightful."

Lennox stepped to the front desk and asked the clerk to speak for refreshment for them, and then he led Amelia into the side room, which was empty.

As they sat down near the fireplace, he did not release her hand. "I cannot tell you how vexed I am to hear about your house. If there is anything I can do at all, please don't hesitate to ask. Even when you return to Kansas City."

"I can't imagine what you might do from here."

"Well, I can imagine several things. For instance, if the insurance company is slow in dealing with your claim, I could wire them or telephone them and urge them to settle your case quickly."

"Oh, I hope it won't come to that."

"So do I, but we both know that some businessmen are not as quick to tend to things for a woman as they are for a man. It's unfortunate, but I've seen it happen. I'm offering my services if you need them."

"Thank you," she murmured. She had no doubt that Lennox could scare an insurance agent into prompt action.

"I wish your property weren't so far away, or I could tend to it for you."

"Please don't worry about it, Lennox. I've been praying, and I'm sure the Lord will work things out."

"But you've lost all your belongings, excepting the things you brought here with you."

She frowned. "That does trouble me a little, but you know,

all those things were wood, hay, and stubble, not riches that will last for eternity."

"That is true, but there must be things you will need."

"I am traveling with the photograph of Micah and me. I admit I shall miss my business records—but, after all, I was about to retire from business. It's not like I have open transactions." *Other than yours,* she thought. "As to my furnishings and decorations, they are replaceable."

"I admire your spirit." Lennox looked up as a maid entered carrying a tray.

"Here's your tea, sir. Madam." She set the tray down and curtsied. "The cook put on a plate of sandwiches and some digestive biscuits." She placed the dishes on a low table before them.

"That looks lovely." Amelia reached for a cup, realizing her stomach wanted lunch, even if her mind had rejected it.

"I had lunch an hour ago, but I must say those sandwiches look attractive."

"I agree." Amelia placed a quarter-sandwich on the edge of her saucer.

"Mrs. Mayberry?" The telegraph operator entered the lounge, still wearing her eyeshade. "We have a reply from Kansas City."

"Well now, that was fast," Lennox said.

"I'll get back to my station," the operator said. "If you want to send a reply, simply bring me the message."

"Thank you." Amelia opened the paper. " 'Our man will inspect property. Contact us on your return.'" She looked at Lennox.

"There, now. No need to rush. Do you feel at ease staying

340

over until Monday morning?"

"Why, yes, I think I shall. Thank you so much—just having you here to discuss this with has made it less daunting."

He smiled gently, and the fine lines at the corners of his eyes deepened. "Then perhaps you'll feel up to inspecting the plant when we've finished our tea. Or, if you prefer, we can skip that and go straight to the Crocker House. The gallery there is worth seeing."

Amelia sipped her tea, feeling its warmth comfort her.

"Oh, and I've a message from Helen," Lennox said, reaching for a sandwich.

Amelia froze. "From Helen?"

He smiled. "Don't look so apprehensive. She realizes she was less than cordial last evening, and she said she hopes that if you're still in town tomorrow, you'll attend church with our family."

"Helen said that?"

"She most certainly did. Amelia, she didn't set out to hurt you. I fear she's carried the sting of Mrs. Enderly's words for the last two years, and other wounds I didn't know of since childhood. Apparently she suffered more than I realized from teasing and ridicule because of her Sioux ancestry. I'd hoped she would toughen up and learn to ignore it, but perhaps I expected too much."

"You mustn't blame yourself." Amelia sent up a swift prayer of thanks for Helen's change of heart. "And I should be delighted to sit with your family in church tomorrow."

She insisted on seeing his place of business, and the vastness of it impressed her.

"In the harvest season, this place would be humming,

even on a Saturday," Lennox said. But because fruits were not ripening in the orchards, only a few people worked that day. He showed Amelia his office, the sorting and packing areas, and the loading platform. "Agriculture has replaced mining and cattle raising as the number one source of income in the Sacramento Valley."

"It's easy to see why. You have such good soil, and such a beautiful climate."

They took his carriage to the Crocker House and toured it, admiring both the architecture and the collection of paintings. By the time they'd seen all the exhibits, Amelia was ready to retire to her hotel room and rest.

"I'll leave you alone for a quiet evening," Lennox said as he helped her out of the carriage in front of the Royal. "In the morning, I'll call for you at ten o'clock, if that suits you."

"It suits me very well," Amelia said. She hadn't brought up her offer to find him another match yet. She'd hoped Lennox would mention it that afternoon, but he hadn't. Tomorrow would be her last chance. She determined to open the subject on Sunday if he didn't, yet the idea saddened her. She had come to care more deeply for Lennox than she'd expected. It seemed somehow disloyal to steer him toward another woman. Would she always feel a pang of regret for doing so?

Buck up, she told herself. She'd come all this way to do the job, and she'd be going home to a pile of ashes. All her possessions were gone. She sensed that would distress her more when she stood before the ruins, but for now she would concentrate on her purpose. For all she knew, the insurance company might find some reason not to pay her, in which case she would have to go back to work.

She resolved *not* to leave California without at least trying to fulfill her mission. If she had to reopen the Society, it would be with a spotless reputation.

Chapter 6

Helen and Daniel met them in the vestibule of the church the next morning. Lennox's apprehension was put to rest when Helen greeted Amelia warmly, taking both hands in hers. "I was terribly rude the other night. Can you forgive me? What happened was not your fault."

"Of course, my dear," Amelia said. "Thank you for being so understanding. The matter has troubled me as well."

Daniel held the baby during this exchange. "We hope you and Mr. Bailey will join us for dinner after the service."

Amelia looked to Lennox.

He smiled. "We shall be delighted."

They spent two pleasant hours with his daughter and her family after church, but Lennox began to fidget. This was Amelia's last day in town, and he wanted to have some private time with her as well.

At last he deemed enough time had passed for him and Amelia to leave without offending Helen. She had conversed amiably with the guest and seemed to have truly put away her ill feelings toward Amelia.

"I do hope we'll see you again, Mrs. Mayberry," Helen said, as she walked them to the door. "I can see that you're good for Papa."

Amelia smiled and kissed her cheek. "Thank you so much. I cherished your mother's regard, and it would grieve me if we couldn't be friends."

"Do let us know your situation after you get home. We all wonder whether you'll rebuild your house or find another place to live."

"I shall drop you a line soon. But to set your mind at ease, I plan to stay with my friend, Deborah, and her husband, at least for a short time."

They drove at a leisurely pace back toward her hotel. Sunday was Richard's and Anna's day off, and Lennox held the reins himself today.

"Lennox," Amelia said a bit tentatively.

He turned to look down at her. She made a charming picture in her forest green hat and merino wool dress. "What is it? You look worried."

"It's only that I've wanted to discuss finding a potential bride for you. I did hope you would come to a decision before I left."

"You said you were ready to retire and stop matchmaking."

"Yes, but I'd like to do this one bit of business as my last case. I have three ladies, any of which would make a charming wife, housekeeper, and hostess for you. I'd be happy to send a letter of introduction for you to any of them. May I tell you a little about them?"

Lennox's heart sank. He'd become fond of Amelia over the last week, and he'd hoped she had forgotten about trying to marry him off. Apparently not.

"Oh, I don't know. It's so difficult, trying to get to know someone who is so far away. You can't truly see what she's like until you meet her, and I'd hate to ask another lady to make the journey. No, Amelia, I think we'd best let well enough alone."

She let out a little sigh. "Tomorrow is Christmas Eve, and I shall be leaving. I so hoped to give you this gift—that is, to start the introductory process—before I left Sacramento."

"But these three women—are they expecting something from me?"

"Oh no. I've promised them nothing."

"Good. Where do they live?"

"One lives in Baltimore, one in Cincinnati, and the third in Hartford, Connecticut."

"Hmm. Well, let's leave them there. What do you say?"

Her eyes flickered, and he was sure she struggled to keep disappointment from marring her features. "Whatever you wish, Lennox."

"Would you like to take a detour and drive a little way along the river? It's such a beautiful day, and I'd hate to take you back to your hotel so early."

"All right," she said.

He headed the horses away from town, toward the farmland that grew the best fruit.

"Lennox," she said after they'd gone a good mile.

"Yes?"

"What if I knew another woman who was not very far

346

from here? Now, wait." She laid a hand on his sleeve before he could protest. "Hear me out, you dear man. This lady is within a day's journey, and I'm positive she would accept and respect your family and make you a good wife."

He shook his head, amazed that she was still trying. Tenacity, that's what she had. "Sorry. I'm not interested."

"Oh." Her features slid into a frown. "I didn't mean to badger you about it. I care too much for you to bother you with a frivolous pursuit."

"You see it as necessary, then, to find me a wife?"

"Well, not necessary exactly. But I did think you'd like to have a companion." She shook her head. "Forgive me. I've been selfish. I hate to go back a failure, and my friend, Deborah, tells me that is my stubborn pride. Perhaps she is right. But if you won't accept this effort as a Christmas gift from me..."

Lennox looked down into her brown eyes. His pulse accelerated as he gazed once more on her sweet face. "I do hope I haven't disappointed you too badly. The first attempt did leave me a little gun-shy, it's true. I'm not going to start over with someone I don't know. I've decided there is only one woman I would ever consider proposing to."

Amelia blinked, and her eyes looked suspiciously moist, as though tears had pooled in them. Almost inaudibly, she said, "Oh."

He nodded firmly. "Yes. I've thought it over, as you asked me to. But this one woman kept coming to mind. My dear, I shall forego your services, and if she turns me down, I'll live out the rest of my life a bachelor."

"Really! You never told me you had your eye on someone.

I wouldn't have pressed the issue if I'd known. Please forgive me. I've overstepped—"

"Nonsense!" He reined in the horses and turned to face her. "Amelia, I didn't have anyone in mind—that is, not until this week. Not until you came and reminded me how delightful it is to spend time with a lady of character and grace. It's you I want to marry, Amelia. No other. Will you consider becoming my wife?"

She stared at him for a full ten seconds, and then she said again, "Oh." Slowly, a smile spread over her face. "I find the prospect intriguing."

Lennox smiled back. He wrapped the reins around the dashboard and slid his arm around her. "Amelia, my dear, I think we should suit very well."

"I totally agree."

"Then allow me to give you my Christmas gift now. I picked it out yesterday, hoping you would say yes." He brought a small wooden box from his pocket and opened it.

Amelia looked down at the ring nestled in the velvet lining and sighed. "That is the loveliest Yule gift I've ever received. Thank you."

He kissed her thoroughly, until the horses began to stamp. He sat back with a laugh.

Amelia blushed prettily, her eyes dancing.

The next Friday, Amelia and Lennox sat opposite Helen and Daniel in the carriage, as Richard drove them from the church to the train depot. Helen held little Samuel facing his grandfather so that he could coo at him while they rode.

"The wedding was lovely," Helen said with genuine approval.

"Thank you." Amelia looked over at her new husband. "For such a hastily planned affair, I thought so, too."

Lennox patted her hand where it rested in the crook of his arm. "And I appreciate your changing your plans on my account. We'll go to Kansas City together, settle your affairs, and retrieve Fluffy from your friend's house."

Amelia chuckled. "It still hasn't fully hit me that Fluffy is all I have left in Missouri."

"I expect it will when you see what is left of your home," Helen said gently.

"You're probably right. And this will make packing much simpler." Amelia threw Lennox a sidelong glance.

He smiled. "My dear, whatever has been lost, we shall replace for you when we return."

"I'm counting on Helen to help me." Amelia arched her eyebrows at her daughter-in-law.

Helen smiled in return. "Oh yes. There are several shops we didn't have time to visit this week."

"Careful now, sir," Daniel said. "It seems you're giving our wives permission to shop as much as they want."

"I know these two ladies fairly well," Lennox assured him. "They both have good taste, but they're also practical. They won't bankrupt us."

"No fear of that," Amelia said.

They arrived at the station, and Richard transferred the luggage to the platform while the Baileys bid the Fryes a warm good-bye. At last Amelia and Lennox settled in their seats on the train. The whistle blew, and they began to move.

Lennox glanced around then leaned over to give her a quick kiss. "You see, my dear? You did find me a new bride."

Amelia sat back smiling. "Yes, one I'm certain will love you for the rest of her life."

Susan Page Davis is the author of more than two dozen books. She is the mother of six and grandmother of six, and is the wife of Jim, a retired news editor. She loves history, animals, puzzles, and people. Visit her Web site at: www.susanpagedavis.com.

A Letter to Our Readers

Dear Readers:

In order that we might better contribute to your reading enjoyment, we would appreciate you taking a few minutes to respond to the following questions. When completed, please return to the following: Fiction Editor, Barbour Publishing, Inc., P.O. Box 719, Uhrichsville, OH 44683.

1. Did you enjoy reading *Christmas Mail-Order Brides*?
   - ❏ Very much. I would like to see more books like this.
   - ❏ Moderately—I would have enjoyed it more if _____
   _____
   _____

2. What influenced your decision to purchase this book?
   (Check those that apply.)
   - ❏ Cover   ❏ Back cover copy   ❏ Title   ❏ Price
   - ❏ Friends   ❏ Publicity   ❏ Other

3. Which story was your favorite?
   - ❏ *A Trusting Heart*   ❏ *Hidden Hearts*
   - ❏ *The Prodigal Groom*   ❏ *Mrs. Mayberry Meets Her Match*

4. Please check your age range:
   - ❏ Under 18   ❏ 18–24   ❏ 25–34
   - ❏ 35–45   ❏ 46–55   ❏ Over 55

5. How many hours per week do you read? _____

Name _____

Occupation _____

Address _____

City _____ State _____ Zip _____

E-mail _____